Sara Paretsky

Killing Orders

PENGUIN BOOKS

PENGUIN BOOKS

Published by the Penguin Group
Penguin Books Ltd, 27 Wrights Lane, London W8 5TZ, England
Penguin Books USA Inc., 375 Hudson Street, New York, New York 10014, USA
Penguin Books Australia Ltd, Ringwood, Victoria, Australia
Penguin Books Canada Ltd, 10 Alcorn Avenue, Toronto, Ontario, Canada M4V 3B2
Penguin Books (NZ) Ltd, 182–190 Wairau Road, Auckland 10, New Zealand

Penguin Books Ltd, Registered Offices: Harmondsworth, Middlesex, England

First published in the USA by William Morrow & Company, Inc., New York 1985
First published in Great Britain by Victor Gollancz 1986
Published in Penguin Books 1987
9 10 8

Printed in England by Clays Ltd, St Ives plc

For Courtenay

All other things to their destruction draw

ACKNOWLEDGEMENTS

Thanks to Bill Tiritilli, director of research for the brokerage firm Rodman and Renshaw, for advice on law and practice in takeovers of publicly held companies.

Marilyn Martin, J.D., is a public defender. Unlike V. I. Warshawski, she has not allowed the discouragements of the job to stop her from practicing it. She supplied me with information about the Illinois criminal code, probable grounds for arrest, and about Chicago's Women's Court. Any mistakes are due to my ignorance, not her information.

Kimball Wright, enraged by repeated errors regarding the Smith & Wesson in V.I.'s previous adventures, provided me with better information about the weapon.

The Reverend Albertus Magnus, O.P., has often allowed me the great pleasure of visiting him and his brother Dominicans at the House of Studies in Washington. Because I know this order better than any other, I chose it as part of the setting for this story. The Priory of Albertus Magnus in Chicago is totally fictitious, as are the friars who reside there.

And many thanks, too, to James H. Lorie.

CONTENTS

I

Old Wounds

MY STOMACH MUSCLES contracted as I locked the car door. I hadn't been to Melrose Park for ten years, but, as I walked up the narrow pavement to the house's side entrance, I felt a decade of maturity slipping from me, felt the familiar sickening, my heart thudding.

The January wind scattered dead leaves around my feet. Little snow had fallen this winter, but the air blew cold. After ringing the bell I jammed my hands deep into the pockets of my navy car coat to keep them warm. I tried to argue my nervousness away. After all, they had called me . . . begged me for help . . . The words meant nothing. I had lost an important battle by responding to the plea.

I stamped my feet to loosen the toes frozen inside thin-soled loafers and heard, at last, a rattling behind the painted blue door. It swung inward into a dimly lit vestibule. Through the screen I could just make out my cousin Albert, much heavier than he'd been ten years ago. The screen and the dark behind him softened his pout.

"Come in, Victoria. Mother is waiting for you."

I bit back an excuse for being a quarter hour late and turned it into a neutral comment on the weather. Albert was almost bald, I noted with pleasure. He took my coat ungraciously and draped it over the banister at the foot of the narrow, uncarpeted stairs.

A deep, harsh voice called to us. "Albert! Is that Victoria?"

"Yes, Mama," Albert muttered.

The only light in the entryway came from a tiny round window facing the stairs. The dimness obscured the pattern in the wallpaper, but as I followed Albert down the close corridor I could see it hadn't changed: gray paper with white loops, ugly, cold. As a child, I thought the paper oozed hate. Behind Albert's wobbling thighs the old chill stuck out tendrils at me and I shivered.

I used to beg my mother, Gabriella, not to bring me to this house. Why should we go? Rosa hated her, hated me, and

Gabriella always cried after the long L ride home. But she would only set her lips in a tight smile and say, "I am obligated, *cara*. I must go."

Albert led me into the formal parlor at the back of the house. The horsehair furniture was as familiar to me as my own apartment. In my nightmares I dreamed of being trapped in this room with its stiff furniture, the ice-blue drapes, the sad picture of Uncle Carl over the fake fireplace, and Rosa, thin, hawk-nosed, frowning, seated poker-backed in a spindle-legged chair.

Her black hair was iron-colored now, but the severe, disapproving stare was unaltered. I tried taking diaphragm breaths to calm the churning in my stomach. You're here because *she* begged *you*, I reminded myself.

She didn't stand up, didn't smile—I couldn't remember ever seeing her smile. "It was good of you to come, Victoria." Her tone implied it would have been better if I'd come on time. "When one is old, one doesn't travel easily. And the last few days have made me old indeed."

I sat down in what I hoped was the least uncomfortable chair. "Yes," I said noncommittally. Rosa was about seventy-five. When they performed her autopsy, they would find her bones were made of cast iron. She did not look old to me: She hadn't begun to rust yet.

"Albert. Pour some coffee for Victoria."

Rosa's single virtue was her cooking. I took a cup of the rich Italian coffee gratefully, but ignored the tray of pastries Albert proffered—I'd get pastry cream on my black wool skirt and feel foolish as well as tense.

Albert sat uneasily on the narrow settee, eating a piece of *torta del re*, glancing surreptitiously at the floor when a crumb dropped, then at Rosa to see if she'd noticed.

"You are well, Victoria? You are happy?"

"Yes," I said firmly. "Both well and happy."

"But you have not remarried?"

The last time I'd been here was with my brief husband for a strained bridal visit. "It is possible to be happy and not married, as Albert doubtless can tell you, or as you know yourself." The last was a cruel remark: Uncle Carl had killed himself shortly after Albert was born. I felt vindictively pleased, then guilty. Surely I was mature enough not to need that kind of satisfaction. Somehow Rosa always made me feel eight years old.

Rosa shrugged her thin shoulders disdainfully. "No doubt you are right. Yet for me—I am to die without the joy of grandchildren."

Albert shifted uncomfortably on the settee. It was clearly not a new complaint.

"A pity," I said. "I know grandchildren would be the crowning joy of a happy and virtuous life."

Albert choked but recovered. Rosa narrowed her eyes angrily. "You, of all people, should know why my life has not been happy."

Despite my efforts at control, anger spilled over. "Rosa, for some reason you think Gabriella destroyed your happiness. What mysterious grievance a girl of eighteen could have caused you I don't know. But you threw her out into the city on her own. She didn't speak English. She might have been killed. Whatever she did to you, it couldn't have been as bad as what you did to her.

"You know the only reason I'm here: Gabriella made me promise that I would help you if you needed it. It stuck in my gut and it still does. But I promised her, and here I am. So let's leave the past in peace: I won't be sarcastic if you'll stop throwing around insults about my mother. Why not just tell me what the problem is."

Rosa tightened her lips until they almost disappeared. "The most difficult thing I ever did in my life was to call you. And now I see I should not have done it." She rose in one movement, like a steel crane, and left the room. I could hear the angry clip of her shoes on the uncarpeted hall and up the bare stairs. In the distance a door slammed.

I put down my coffee and looked at Albert. He had turned red with discomfort, but he seemed less amorphous with Rosa out of the room.

"How bad is her trouble?"

He wiped his fingers on a napkin and folded it tidily. "Pretty bad," he muttered. "Why'd you have to make her mad?"

"It makes her mad to see me here instead of at the bottom of Lake Michigan. Every time I've talked to her since Gabriella

11

died she's been hostile to me. If she needs help, all I want is the facts. She can save the rest for her psychiatrist. I don't get paid enough to deal with it." I picked up my shoulder bag and stood up. At the doorway I stopped and looked at him.

"I'm not coming back to Melrose Park for another round, Albert. If you want to tell me the story I'll listen. But if I leave now, that's it; I won't respond to any more pleas for family unity from Rosa. And by the way, if you do want to hire me, I'm not working out of love for your mother."

He stared at the ceiling, listening perhaps for guidance from above. Not heaven—just the back bedroom. We couldn't hear anything. Rosa was probably jabbing pins into a piece of clay with a lock of my hair stuck to it. I rubbed my arms involuntarily, searching for damage.

Albert shifted uneasily and stood up. "Uh, look, uh, maybe I'd better tell you."

"Fine. Can we go to a more comfortable room?"

"Sure. Sure." He gave a half smile, the first I'd seen that afternoon. I followed him back down the hall to a room on the left. It was tiny, but clearly his private spot. A giant set of stereo speakers loomed from one wall; below them were some built-in shelves holding an amplifier and a large collection of tapes and records. No books except a few accounting texts. His high-school trophies. A tiny cache of bottles.

He sat in the one chair, a large leather desk chair with a hassock next to it. He slid the hassock over to me and I perched on that.

In his own place, Albert relaxed and his face took on a more decisive look. He was a CPA with his own business, I remembered. When you saw him with Rosa, you couldn't imagine him managing anything on his own, but in here it didn't seem so improbable.

He took a pipe from the desk top next to him and began the pipe smoker's interminable ritual with it. With luck I'd be gone before he actually lit it. All smoke makes me ill, and pipe smoke on top of an empty stomach—I'd been too tense for lunch—would be disastrous.

"How long have you been a detective, Victoria?"

"About ten years." I swallowed my annoyance at being

12

called Victoria. Not that it isn't my name. Just that if I liked using it I wouldn't go by my initials.

"And you're good at it?"

"Yes. Depending on your problem, I'm about the best you can get . . . I have a list of references if you want to call someone."

"Yeah, I'd like a name or two before you go." He had finished drilling out the pipe bowl. He knocked it methodically against the side of an ashtray and began packing it with tobacco. "Mother's gotten herself involved with some counterfeit securities."

Wild dreams of Rosa as the brains behind Chicago's Mob ran through my head. I could see six-point screamer headlines in the *Herald-Star*.

"Involved how?"

"They found some in the St. Albert Priory safe."

I sighed to myself. Albert was deliberately going to drag this out. "She plant them there? What's she got to do with this priory?"

The moment of truth had come: Albert struck a match and began sucking on the pipestem. Sweet blue smoke curled up around his head and wafted toward me. I felt my stomach turn over.

"Mother's been their treasurer for the last twenty years. I thought you knew." He paused a minute to let me feel guilty about not keeping up with the family. "Of course they had to ask her to leave when they found the securities."

"Does she know anything about them?"

He shrugged. He was sure she didn't. He didn't know how many there were, what companies they were drawn on, how long since they'd last been examined, or who had access to them. The only thing he knew was the new prior wanted to sell them in order to make repairs on the building. Yes, they'd been in a safe.

"Her heart's broken because of the suspicion." He saw my derisive look and said defensively, "Just because you only see her when she's upset or angry you can't imagine she has real feelings. She's seventy-five, you know, and that job meant a lot to her. She wants her name cleared so she can go back."

"Surely the FBI is investigating, and the SEC."

13

"Yes, but they'd be just as happy to hang it on her if it made things easier for them. After all, who wants to take a priest to court? And they know she's old, she'd get off with a suspended sentence."

I blinked a few times. "Albert. No. You're out of touch. If she were some poor West Side black, they might railroad her. But not Rosa. She'd scare 'em too much for one thing. And the FBI—they'll want to get to the bottom of this. They're never going to believe an old woman masterminded a counterfeiting scheme." Unless, of course, she had. I wished I could believe it, but Rosa was malicious, not dishonest.

"But that church is the only thing she really loves," he blurted, turning crimson. "They might believe she got carried away. People do."

We talked about it some more, but it ended as I suppose I'd known it had to, with me pulling out two copies of my standard contract for Albert to sign. I gave him a family rate on the fee—sixteen dollars an hour instead of twenty.

He told me the new prior would be expecting my call. Boniface Carroll his name was. Albert wrote that on a piece of paper along with a rough map of how to find the priory. I frowned as I stuck it in my bag. They were taking an awful lot for granted. Then I laughed sourly at myself. Once I'd agreed to make the trek to Melrose Park they could take a lot for granted.

Back at my car I stood rubbing my head for a few minutes, hoping the cold clean air would blow the pipe fumes from my throbbing brain. I glanced back at the house. A curtain fell quickly at an upstairs window. I climbed into the car somewhat cheered. To see Rosa spy furtively on me—like a small child or a thief—made me feel somehow that more of the power lay in my hands.

II

Remembrance of Things Past

I WOKE UP sweating. The bedroom was dark and for a moment I couldn't remember where I was. Gabriella had been staring at me, her eyes huge in her wasted face, the skin

14

translucent as it had been those last painful months of her life, pleading with me to help her. The dream had been in Italian. It took time to reorient myself to English, to adulthood, to my apartment.

The digital clock glowed faintly orange. Five-thirty. My sweat turned to a chill. I pulled the comforter up around my neck and clenched my teeth to keep them from chattering.

My mother died of cancer when I was fifteen. As the disease ate the vitality from her beautiful face, she made me promise to help Rosa if her aunt ever needed me. I had tried to argue with Gabriella: Rosa hated her, hated me—we had no obligation. But my mother insisted and I could not refuse.

My father had told me more than once how he met my mother. He was a policeman. Rosa had thrown Gabriella out on the street, an immigrant with minimal English. My mother, who always had more courage than common sense, was trying to earn a living doing the only thing she knew: singing. Unfortunately, none of the Milwaukee Avenue bars where she auditioned liked Puccini or Verdi and my father rescued her one day from a group of men who were trying to force her to strip. Neither he nor I could understand why she ever saw Rosa again. But I made her the promise she wanted.

My pulse had calmed down but I knew more sleep was out of the question. Shivering in the cold room, I padded naked to the window and pulled back the heavy curtain. The winter morning was black. Snow falling like a fine mist glowed in the streetlamp at the corner of the alley. I kept shivering, but the still morning held me entranced, the thick black air pressing at me comfortingly.

At last I let the curtain drop. I had a ten o'clock meeting in Melrose Park with the new prior of St Albert's. I might as well get going.

Even in the winter I try to run five miles a day. Although financial crime, my specialty, doesn't often lead to violence, I grew up in a rough South Side neighborhood where girls as well as boys had to be able to defend themselves. Old habits die hard, so I work out and run to stay in shape. Anyway, running is the best way I know to ward off the effects of pasta. I don't enjoy exercise, but it beats dieting.

In the winter I wear a light sweatshirt, loose pants, and a

15

down vest. Once warmed up I donned these and ran quickly down the hall and three flights of stairs to keep my muscles loose.

Outside, I wanted to abandon the project. The cold and damp were miserable. Even though the streets were already filling with early commuters, it was hours before my usual waking time, and the sky had barely begun to lighten by the time I got back to Halsted and Belmont. I walked carefully up the stairs to my apartment. The steps were shiny with age and very slippery when wet. I had a vision of myself sliding backward on wet running shoes, cracking my skull on old marble.

A long hallway divides my apartment in half and makes it seem bigger than its four rooms. The dining room and kitchen are to the left; bedroom and living room to the right. For some reason the kitchen connects to the bathroom. I turned on water for a shower and went next door to start coffee.

Armed with coffee, I took my running clothes off and sniffed them. Smelly, but not too bad for one more morning. I dropped them over a chair back and gave myself up to a long hot shower. The stream of water drumming on my skull soothed me. I relaxed, and without realizing it, I started to sing a bit under my breath. After a while the tune drifted into my consciousness, a sad Italian folksong Gabriella used to sing. Rosa was really lying heavy on my mind—the nightmare, visions of my skull breaking, now mournful songs. I was not going to let her control me this way—that would be the ultimate defeat. I shampooed my hair vigorously and forced myself to sing Brahms. I don't like his *Lieder*, but some, like "Meine Liebe Ist Grün'" are almost painfully cheerful.

Coming out of the shower I switched to the dwarfs' song from *Snow White*. Off to work we go. My navy walking suit, I decided, to make me mature and dignified. It had a three-quarter-length double-breasted jacket and a skirt with two side pleats. A knit silk top of pale gold, almost the colour of my skin, and a long scarf bright with red and navy and brushed again with the same gold. Perfect. I edged the corners of my eyes with a faint trace of blue pencil to make their gray color bluer, added a little light rouge and lipstick to match the red in the scarf. Open-toed red-leather pumps, Italian. Gabriella

16

brought me up to believe that my feet would fall off if I wore shoes made anyplace else. Even now that a pair of Magli pumps go for a hundred forty dollars, I can't bring myself to wear Comfort-Stride.

I left the breakfast dishes in the sink with last night's supper plates and those from a few other meals. And the bed unmade. And the clothes strewn around. Perhaps I should save the money I spend on clothes and shoes and invest in a house-keeper. Or even a hypnosis program to teach me to be neat and tidy. But what the hell. Who besides me was going to see it?

III

The Order of Preachers

THE EISENHOWER EXPRESSWAY is the main escape route from Chicago to the western suburbs. Even on warm sunny days, it looks like a prison exercise yard for most of its length. Run-down houses and faceless projects line the tops of the canyons on either side of its eight lanes. L stations are planted along the median. The Eisenhower is always choked with traffic, even at three in the morning. At nine on a wet workday it was impossible.

I could feel tension tightening the cords in the back of my neck as I oozed forward. I was on an errand I did not wish to make to talk to a person I had no desire to see about the troubles of an aunt I loathed. To do so I had to spend hours stalled in traffic. And my feet were cold inside their open-toed pumps. I turned up the heat further but the little Omega didn't respond. I curled and uncurled my toes to get the blood moving but they remained obstinately frozen.

At First Avenue the traffic eased up as the offices there sucked up most of the outbound drivers. I exited north at Mannheim and meandered through the streets, trying to follow Albert's roughly sketched directions. It was five after ten when I finally found the priory entrance. Being late did nothing to improve my humor.

The Priory of St. Albertus Magnus included a large block of neo-Gothic buildings set to one side of a beautiful park. The architect apparently believed he had to compensate for the beauties of nature: In the misty snow the gray stone buildings loomed as ungainly shapes.

A small lettered sign identified the nearest concrete block as the House of Studies. As I drove past, a few men in long white robes were scuttling into it, hoods pulled over their faces so that they looked like medieval monks. They paid no attention to me.

As I crept slowly up the circular drive I saw a number of cars parked to one side. I left the Omega there and quickly ran to the nearest entrance. This was labelled simply ST. ALBERT'S PRIORY.

Inside, the building had the half-eerie, half-tired atmosphere you often find in religious institutions. You can tell people spend a lot of time praying there, but perhaps they also spend too much time feeling depressed or bored. The entryway had a vaulted concrete ceiling that disappeared in the gloomy light several stores up. Marble flagstones added to the coldness.

A corridor ran at right angles to the entrance. I crossed to it, my heels echoing in the vaulted chamber, and looked doubtfully around. A scarred wooden desk had been stuck in a corner formed by the entry hall and a stairwell. A thin young man in civvies sat behind it reading *The Greater Trumps* by Charles Williams. He put it down reluctantly after I'd spoken several times. His face was extremely thin; he seemed to burn with a nervous asceticism, but perhaps he was merely hyperthyroid. At any rate, he directed me to the prior's office in a hurried whisper, not waiting to see if I followed his directions before returning to the book.

At least I was in the right building, a relief since I was now fifteen minutes late. I turned left down the corridor, passing icons and shut doors. A couple of men in white robes passed me, arguing vigorously but in subdued voices. At the end of the hall I turned right. On one side of me was a chapel and across from it, as the youth had promised, the prior's office.

The Reverend Boniface Carroll was on the phone when I came in. He smiled when he saw me and motioned me to a chair in front of his desk, but continued his conversation in a series of grunts. He was a frail man of perhaps fifty. His white

18

woolen robe had turned faintly yellow with age. He looked very tired; as he listened to his caller he kept rubbing his eyes.

The office itself was sparsely furnished. A crucifix over one wall was the only decoration, and the wide desk was scuffed with age. The floor was covered with institutional linoleum, only partly hidden by a threadbare carpet.

"Well, actually she's here right now, Mr. Hatfield . . . No, no, I think I should talk to her."

I raised my eyebrows at that. The only Hatfield I knew worked on fraud for the FBI. He was a competent young man, but his sense of humor left something to be desired. When our paths crossed, it was usually to our mutual irritation, since he tried to overcome my flippancy with threats of the might of the FBI.

Carroll terminated the conversation and turned to me. "You are Miss Warshawski, aren't you?" He had a light, pleasant voice with a trace of an eastern accent.

"Yes." I handed him one of my cards. "Was that Derek Hatfield?"

"The FBI man. Yes, he's been out here with Ted Dartmouth from the Securities Exchange Commission. I don't know how he learned we were going to meet, but he was asking me not to talk to you."

"Did he say why?"

"He thinks this is a matter for the FBI and the SEC. He told me an amateur such as yourself might muddy the waters, make the investigation more difficult."

I rubbed my upper lip thoughtfully. I'd forgotten the lipstick until I saw the smear on my forefinger. Cool, Vic. If I were being logical, I'd smile politely at Father Carroll and leave; after all, I'd been cursing him, Rosa, and my mission all the way from Chicago. However, there's nothing like a little opposition to make me change my mind, especially when the opposition comes from Derek Hatfield.

"That's sort of what I said to my aunt when I talked to her yesterday. The FBI and the SEC are trained to handle this kind of investigation. But she's old and she's scared and she wants someone from the family in her corner.

"I've been a private investigator for almost ten years. I've done a lot of financial crime and I've got a good reputation—I could give you the names of some people in the city to call so you don't have to take just my word for it."

Carroll smiled. "Relax, Miss Warshawski. You don't have to sell me. I told your aunt I would talk to you and I feel we owe her something here, if only a conversation with you. She's worked for St. Albert's very faithfully for a long time. It really hurt her when we asked her to take a leave of absence. I hated doing it, but I've made the same request to everyone with access to the safe. As soon as we get this business cleared up, she knows we want her back. She's extremely competent."

I nodded. I could see Rosa as a competent treasurer. It flashed through my mind that she might have been less angry if she had channeled her energy into a career: She would have made a good corporate financial officer.

"I don't really know what happened," I said to Carroll. "Why don't you tell me the story—where the safe is, how you came to find the fakes, how much money is involved, who could have gotten at them, who knew about them—and I'll butt in when I don't understand."

He smiled again, a shy sweet smile, and got up to show me the safe. It was in a storeroom behind his office, one of those old cast-iron models with a combination lock. It was stuck in a corner amid stacks of paper, an ancient mimeo machine, and piles of extra prayer books.

I knelt to look at it. Of course, the priory had used the same combination for years, which meant anyone who'd been there a while could have found out what it was. Neither the FBI nor the Melrose Park police had discovered any signs that the lock had been forced.

"How many people do you have here at the priory?"

"There are twenty-one students at the House of Studies and eleven priests on the teaching faculty. But then there are people like your aunt who come in and work during the day. We have a kitchen crew, for example; the brothers do all the washing up and waiting at table, but we have three women who come in to do the cooking. We have two receptionists— the young man who probably directed you to my office and a woman who handles the afternoon shift. And of course there are a lot of neighborhood people who worship with us in the chapel." He smiled again. "We Dominicans are preachers and scholars. We don't usually run parish churches, but a lot of people do treat this as their parish."

I shook my head. "You've got too many people around here to make sorting this out easy. Who actually had official access to the safe?"

"Well, Mrs. Vignelli, of course." That was Rosa. "I do. The procurator—he handles the financial affairs. The student master. We have an audit once a year, and our accountants always examine the stocks, along with the other assets, but I don't think they know the combination to the safe."

"Why'd you keep the things here instead of in a bank vault?"

He shrugged. "I wondered the same thing. I was just elected last May." The smile crept back into his eyes. "Not a post I wanted—I'm like John Roncalli—the safe candidate who doesn't belong to any of the factions here. Anyway, I'd never been at all involved in running this—or any other—priory. I didn't know anything about it. I didn't know we kept five million dollars' worth of stock certificates on the premises. To tell you the truth, I didn't even know we owned them."

I shuddered. Five million dollars sitting around for any casual passerby to take. The wonder was that they hadn't simply been stolen years before.

Father Carroll was explaining the history of the stocks in his gentle, efficient voice. They were all blue-chip shares—AT&T, IBM, and Standard of Indiana primarily. They had been left to the priory ten years ago by a wealthy man in Melrose Park.

The priory buildings were close to eighty years old and needed a lot of repairs. He pointed to some cracks in the plaster on the wall and I followed the line of damage to a wide brown stain on the ceiling.

"The most urgent problems are the roof and the furnace. It seemed reasonable to sell some shares and use the money to repair the plant, which is, after all, our main asset. Even though it's ugly and uncomfortable we couldn't begin to replace it today. So I brought up the matter at chapter meeting and got an agreement. The next Monday I went into the Loop and met with a broker. He agreed to sell eighty thousand dollars' worth of shares. He took them from us then."

That had been the last of the matter for a week. Then the

broker had called back. The Fort Dearborn Trust, the company's stock-transfer agent, had examined the shares and found they were counterfeits.

"Is there a possibility the broker or the banker made an exchange?"

He shook his head unhappily. "That's the first thing we thought of. But we had all the remaining certificates looked at. They're all fakes."

We sat silently for a bit. What a dispiriting prospect.

"When was the last time the shares were authenticated?" I asked at last.

"I don't know. I called the accountants, but all they do is verify that the shares are there. According to the FBI man, these certificates are extremely good forgeries. They were found out only because the serial numbers had not been used by the issuing companies. They'd fool any ordinary observer."

I sighed. I probably should talk to the former prior, and to the student master and procurator. I asked Carroll about them. His predecessor was in Pakistan for a year, running a Dominican school there. But the student master and procurator were both in the building and would be at lunch.

"You're welcome to join us if you like. Ordinarily the refectory in a convent is cloistered—that means only friars can use the room," he explained in answer to my puzzled look. "And yes. We friars call this a convent. Or a friary. Anyway, we've lifted the cloister here at the school so that the young men can eat with their families when they come to visit . . . The food isn't very interesting, but it's an easier way to meet Pelly and Jablonski than trying to track them down afterward." He pulled back a yellowed sleeve to reveal a thin wrist with a heavy leather watchband on it. "It's almost noon. People will be gathering outside the refectory now."

I looked at my own watch. It was almost twenty of twelve. Duty had driven me to worse things than undistinguished cuisine. I accepted. The prior locked the storeroom carefully behind him. "Another example of locking the barn door," he said. "There was no lock on that storeroom until we discovered the fake securities."

We joined a throng of white-robed men walking down the corridor past Carroll's office. Most of them said hello to him, eyeing me covertly. At the end of the hall were two swinging doors. Through their glass top halves I could see the refectory, looking like a high-school gym converted to a lunch room: long deal tables, metal folding chairs, no linens, hospital-green walls.

Carroll took me by the arm and led me through the huddle to a pudgy middle-aged man whose head emerged from a fringe of gray hair, like a soft-boiled egg from an egg cup. "Stephen, I'd like you to meet Miss Warshawski. She's Rosa Vignelli's niece, but she's also a private investigator. She's looking into our crime as an *amica familiae*." He turned to me. "This is Father Jablonski, who's been the student master for seven years . . . Stephen, why don't you dig up Augustine and introduce him to Miss Warshawski. She needs to talk to him, too."

I was about to murmur a social inanity when Carroll turned to the crowd and said something in Latin. They answered and he rattled off what I assumed was a blessing; everyone crossed himself.

Lunch was definitely uninteresting: bowls of Campbell's tomato soup, which I loathe, and toasted cheese sandwiches. I put pickles and onions inside my sandwich and accepted coffee from an eager young Dominican.

Jablonski introduced me to Augustine Pelly, the procurator, and to some half dozen other men at our table. These were all "brothers," not "fathers." Since they tended to look alike in their fresh white robes I promptly forgot their names.

"Miss Warshawski thinks she can succeed where the FBI and the SEC are baffled," Jablonski said jovially, his nasal midwestern accent blaring above the dining room cacophony.

Pelly gave me a measuring look, then smiled. He was almost as thin as Father Carroll, and very tanned, which surprised me—where did a monk go sunbathing in mid-winter? His blue eyes were sharp and alert in his dark face. "I'm sorry, Miss Warshawski—I know Stephen well enough to tell he's joking, but I'm afraid I don't get the joke."

"I'm a private investigator," I explained.

Pelly raised his eyebrows. "And you're going to look into our missing securities?"

I shook my head. "I don't really have the resources to match

23

the FBI on that type of thing. But I'm also Rosa Vignelli's niece; she wants someone from the family on her side in the investigation. A lot of people have had access to that safe over the years; I'm here to remind Derek Hatfield of that if he starts breathing down Rosa's neck too hard."

Pelly smiled again. "Mrs. Vignelli doesn't strike one as the type of woman to need protection."

I grinned back at him. "She certainly doesn't, Father Pelly. But I keep reminding myself that Rosa's been aging just like any other human being. At any rate, she seems a little frightened, especially that she won't be able to work here anymore." I ate some of my sandwich. Kraft American. Next to Stilton and Brie my favorite cheese.

Jablonski said, "I hope she knows that Augustine and I are also forbidden access to the priory's finances until this matter is cleared up. She's not being singled out in any way that we aren't."

"Maybe one of you could call her," I suggested. "That might make her feel better . . . I'm sure you know her well enough to realize she's not a woman with a lot of friends. She's centered a good part of her life around this church."

"Yes," Pelly agreed. "I didn't realize she had any family besides her son. She's never mentioned you, Miss Warshawski. Nor that she had any Polish relatives."

"Her brother's daughter was my mother, who married a Chicago policeman named Warshawski. I've never understood the laws of kinship too well. Does that mean that she has Polish relatives because I'm half Polish? You don't think I'm posing as Rosa's niece just to get inside the priory, do you?"

Jablonski gave his sardonic smile. "Now that the securities are gone, there's nothing worth worming your way into the priory for. Unless you have some secret fetish for friars."

I laughed, but Pelly said seriously, "I assume the prior looked into your credentials."

"There wasn't any reason for him to; he wasn't hiring me. I do have a copy of my P.I. license on me, but I don't carry any identification that proves I'm Rosa Vignelli's niece. You could call her, of course."

Pelly held up a hand. "I'm not doubting you. I'm just concerned for the priory. We're getting some publicity which

24

none of us relishes and which is really detrimental to the studies of these young men." He indicated the intently eavesdropping young brothers at our table. One of them blushed in embarrassment. "I really don't want anyone, even if she's the pope's niece, stirring things up here further."

"I can understand that. But I can also see Rosa's point—it's just too convenient to have her on the outside of the priory taking the fall. She doesn't have a big organization with lots of political connections behind her. You do."

Pelly gave me a freezing stare, "I won't attempt to untangle that one, Miss Warshawski. You obviously are referring to the popular myth about the political power of the Catholic Church, the direct line from the Vatican that was going to control John Kennedy, that sort of thing. It's beneath discussion."

"I think we could have a pretty lively discussion about it," I objected. "We could talk about the politics of abortion, for example. How local pastors try to influence their congregations to vote for anti-choice candidates regardless of how terrible their qualifications may be otherwise. Or maybe you'd like to discuss the relations between Archbishop Farber and Police Superintendent Bellamy. Or even between him and the mayor."

Jablonski turned to me. "I think pastors would be gravely lax in their moral duty if they didn't try to oppose abortion in any way possible, even urging their parishioners to vote for pro-life candidates."

I felt the blood rush to my head, but smiled. "We're never going to agree on whether abortion is a moral issue or a private matter between a woman and her physician. But one thing is clear—it is a highly political issue. There are a lot of people scrutinizing the Catholic Church's involvement in this area.

"Now the tax code spells out pretty specifically how clear of politics you have to stay to keep your tax-exempt status. So when bishops and priests are using their offices to push political candidates, they're walking a pretty thin line on tax-exempt status. So far, no tax-court judge has been willing to take on the Catholic Church—which in itself argues some hefty clout."

Pelly turned an angry crimson under his tan. "I don't think you have the least idea what you're talking about, Miss

Warshawski. Maybe you could keep your remarks to the specific points that the prior asked you to discuss."

"Fine," I said. "Let's concentrate on the priory here. Is there anyone who would have reason to take close to five million dollars?"

"No one," Pelly said shortly. "We take vows of poverty."

One of the brothers offered me more coffee. It was so thin as to be almost undrinkable, but I accepted it absently. "You got the shares ten years ago. Since then, almost anyone with access to the priory could have taken the money. Discounting random strangers walking in off the street, that means someone connected with this place. What kind of turnover do you have among your monks?"

"They're actually called friars," Jablonski interjected. "Monks stay in one place; friars roam around. What do you mean by turnover? Every year students leave—some have been ordained, others find the conventual life doesn't suit them for some reason. And there's a lot of movement among the priests, too. People who taught at other Dominican institutions come here, or vice versa. Father Pelly here just returned from six months in Ciudad Isabella. He was a student in Panama and likes to spend a certain amount of time down there."

That explained his suntan, then. "We can probably eliminate people who move on to other Dominican seats. But what about any young men who've left the order in the last decade? Could you find out if any of them claimed coming into an inheritance?"

Pelly shrugged disdainfully. "I suppose so, but I would be most reluctant to do so. When Stephen said young men find the monastic life doesn't suit them, it's not usually because of lack of luxury. We do a careful screening of our applicants before we allow them to become novices. I think we'd turn up the type who would steal."

Father Carroll joined us at that point. The refectory was clearing. Knots of men stood talking in the doorway, some staring at me. The prior turned to the brothers lingering at our table. "Don't you have exams next week? Perhaps you should be studying."

They got up a little shamefacedly and Carroll sat in one of the empty seats. "Are you making any progress?"

26

Pelly frowned. "We've progressed past some wild accusations about the Church in general to a concentrated attack on young men who have left the order in the last decade. Not exactly what I'd expect from a Catholic girl."

I held up a hand. "Not me, Father Pelly. I'm not a girl and I'm not a Catholic . . . We're really at a standstill. I'll have to talk to Derek Hatfield and see if he'll share the FBI's ideas with me. What you need to find is someone with a secret bank account. Perhaps one of your brothers, possibly my aunt. Although if she stole the money, it certainly wasn't to use on herself. She lives very frugally. Perhaps, though, she's a fanatic about some cause I don't know anything about and stole to support it. Which might be true of any of you as well."

Rosa as a secret Torquemada appealed to me but there wasn't any real evidence of it. It was hard to imagine her feeling positive enough about anyone or anything to love it, let alone steal for it.

"As the procurator, Father Pelly, perhaps you know whether the shares were ever authenticated. If this wasn't done when you got them, it's possible they came to you as forgeries."

Pelly shook his head. "It never occurred to us. I don't know if we're too unworldly to handle assets, but it doesn't seem like the kind of thing anyone does."

"Probably not," I agreed. I asked him and Jablonski some more questions, but neither was very helpful. Pelly still seemed miffed with me over the Church and politics. Since I'd compounded my sin by not being a Catholic girl, his answers were fairly frosty. Even Jablonski commented on it.

"Why are you on such a high horse with Miss Warshawski, Gus? So she's not a Catholic. Neither is eighty-five percent of the world's population. That should make us more charitable, not less."

Pelly turned his cold stare on him, and Carroll remarked, "Let's save group criticism for chapter, Stephen."

Pelly said, "I'm sorry if I seem rude, Miss Warshawski. But this business is very worrying, especially because I was the procurator for eight years. And I'm afraid my experiences in Central America make me sensitive to criticisms about the Church and politics."

I blinked a few times. "Sensitive how?"

Carroll intervened again. "Two of our priests were shot in El Salvador last spring; the government suspected they were harboring rebels."

I didn't say anything. Whether the Church was working for the poor, as in El Salvador, or supporting the government, as in Spain, it was still, in my book, up to its neck in politics. But it didn't seem polite to pursue the argument.

Jablonski thought otherwise. "Rubbish, Gus, and you know it. You're only upset because you and the government don't see eye to eye. But if your friends have their way, you know very well that the Friary of San Tomás will have some very powerful allies." He turned to me. "That's the trouble with people like you and Gus, Miss Warshawski—when the Church is on your side, whether it's fighting racism or poverty, it's just being sensitive, not political. When it goes against your position, then it's political and up to no good."

Carroll said, "I think we're all getting a long way from Miss Warshawski's real business in coming out here. Stephen, I know we Dominicans are supposed to be preachers, but it violates some rules of hospitality to preach at a guest over lunch, even so meager a lunch as this."

He stood up and the rest of us got up also. As we walked from the refectory, Jablonski said, "No hard feelings, Miss Warshawski. I like a good fighter. Sorry if I offended you in your role as a guest."

To my surprise I found myself smiling at him. "No hard feelings, Father. I'm afraid I got a little carried away myself."

He shook hands with me briskly and walked down the hall in the opposite direction from Carroll, who said, "Good. I'm glad you and Stephen found some common ground. He's a good man, just a little aggressive sometimes."

Pelly frowned. "Aggressive! He's completely without—" He suddenly remembered to save group criticism for chapter and broke off. "Sorry, Prior. Maybe I should go back to San Tomás—that's where my mind seems to be these days."

IV

Return Engagement

IT WAS CLOSE to three when I threaded my way to my office in the South Loop. It's in the Pulteney Building, which is of the right vintage to be a national historic landmark. I sometimes think it might even qualify if it ever acquired a management interested in looking after it. Buildings around there don't fare well. They're too close to the city lockup, the slums, the peepshows and the cheap bars, so they attract clients like me: detectives on shoestring budgets, bail bondsmen, inept secretarial services.

I put the car into a lot on Adams and walked the block north to the Pulteney. The snow, or rain, or whatever it was had stopped. While the skies were still sullen, the pavement was almost dry and my beloved Magli pumps were free from further insults.

Someone had left a bourbon bottle in the lobby. I picked it up and carried it with me to throw out in my office. My long-awaited oil-tanker billionaire might show up and be put off by empty whiskey bottles in the lobby. Especially if he saw the brand.

The elevator, working for a change, clanked lugubriously down from the sixteenth floor. I stuck the bottle under one arm and slid open an ancient brass grille with the other. If I never worked out I'd stay in shape just by coming to the office every day—between running the elevator, repairing the toilet in the ladies' room on the seventh floor, and walking up and down the stairs between my fourth-floor office and the bathroom.

The elevator grudgingly stopped at the fourth floor. My office was at the east end of the corridor, the end where low rents sank even further because of the noise of the Dan Ryan L running directly underneath it. A train was clattering by as I unlocked the door.

I spend so little time in my office that I've never put much into furnishing it. The old wooden desk I'd bought at a police auction. That was it, except for two straight-backed chairs for clients, my chair, and an army-green filing cabinet. My one concession to grace was an engraving of the Uffizi over the filing cabinet.

I picked up a week's accumulation of mail from the floor and started opening it while I called my answering service. Two messages. I didn't need to get in touch with Hatfield; he'd called me and would see me in his office at nine the next morning.

I looked at a bill from a stationery company. Two hundred dollars for letterhead and envelopes? I put it in the trash and dialed the FBI. Hatfield wasn't in, of course. I got his secretary. "Yes, please tell Derek I won't be free tomorrow morning but three tomorrow afternoon will be fine." She put me on hold while she checked his calendar. I continued through the mail. The Society of Young Women Business Executives urged me to join. Among their many benefits was a group life and health insurance plan. Derek's secretary came back on the line and we dickered, compromising on two-thirty.

My second message was more of a surprise and much more welcome. Roger Ferrant had called. He was an Englishman, a reinsurance broker whom I'd met the previous spring. His London firm had underwritten a ship that blew up in the Great Lakes. I was investigating the disaster; his firm was protecting its fifty-million-dollar investment. We hadn't seen each other since a night when I'd fallen asleep—to put it politely—across from him at a posh steakhouse.

I reached him at his firm's apartment in the Hancock Building. "Roger! What are you doing in Chicago?"

"Hello, Vic. Scupperfield, Plouder sent me over here for a few weeks. Can we have dinner?"

"Is this my second chance? Or did you like my act the first time so well you want an encore?"

He laughed. "Neither. How about it? Are you free this week anytime?"

I told him I was free that very night and agreed to meet him at the Hancock Building for a drink at seven-thirty. I hung up in much better spirits—I deserved a reward for messing around in Rosa's affairs.

I quickly sorted through the rest of my mail. None of it needed answering. One envelope actually contained a check for three hundred fifty dollars. Way to pick your clients, Vic, I cheered silently. Before leaving, I typed out a few bills on the old Olivetti that had been my mother's. She subscribed firmly to the belief that IBM had stolen both the Executive and Selectric designs from Olivetti and would have been ashamed of me if I'd owned one of the Itsy-Bitsy Machine Company's models.

I quickly finished the bills, stuffed them in envelopes, turned out the lights, and locked up. Outside the street was jammed with rush-hour crowds. I jostled and darted my way through them with the ease of long experience and retrieved the Omega for another long slow drive through stop-and-go traffic.

I bore the delays meekly, swooping off the Kennedy at Belmont and detouring around to my bank with the check before going home. In a sudden burst of energy I washed the dishes before changing clothes. I kept on the yellow silk top, found a pair of black velvet slacks in the closet, and put on a black-and-orange scarf. Eye-catching but not vulgar.

Ferrant seemed to think so, too. He greeted me enthusiastically in the Scupperfield, Plouder apartment at the Hancock. "I remembered you were tough and funny, Vic, but I'd forgotten how attractive you are."

If you like thin men, which I do, Ferrant looked good himself. He had on well-tailored casual slacks with tiny pleats at the waist, and a dark green sweater over a pale yellow shirt. His dark hair, which had been carefully combed when he opened the door, fell into his eyes when I returned his hug. He pushed it back with a characteristic gesture.

I asked what brought him to Chicago.

"Business with Ajax, of course." He led me into the living room, a modernistically furnished square overlooking the lake. A large orange couch with a glass-and-chrome coffee table in front of it was flanked by chrome chairs with black fabric seats. I winced slightly.

"Hideous, isn't it?" he said cheerfully. "If I have to stay in Chicago more than a month, I'm going to make them let me get my own apartment. Or at least my own furniture. . . . Do you drink anything besides Chateau St. Georges? We have a complete liquor cabinet."

He swept open a blond-and-glass cabinet in one corner to

31

display an impressive array of bottles. I laughed: I'd drunk two bottles of Chateau St. Georges when we went to dinner together last May. "Johnny Walker Black if they have it." He rummaged through the cupboard, found a half-used bottle, and poured each of us a modest drink.

"They must hate you in London to send you to Chicago in January. And if you have to stay through February you'll know you're really on their hit list."

He grimaced. "I've been here before in winter. It must explain why you American girls are so tough. Are they as hardboiled as you in South?"

"Worse," I assured him. "They're tougher but they hide it under this veneer of soft manners, so you don't know you've been hit until you start coming to."

I sat at one end of the orange couch; he pulled up one of the chrome chairs close to me and leaned storklike over his drink, his hair falling into his eyes again. He explained that Scupperfield, Plouder, his London firm, owned three percent of Ajax. "We're not the largest stockholder, but we're an important one. So we keep a finger in the Ajax pie. We send our young fellows here for training and take some Ajax people and teach them the London market. Believe it or not, I was a young fellow once myself." Like many people in English insurance, Ferrant had started to work right after high school, or what we think of as high school. So at thirty-seven he had close to twenty years of experience in the topsy-turvy reinsurance business.

"I'm telling you that so you won't be so startled to hear I'm now a corporate officer *pro tem*." He grinned. "A lot of people at Ajax feel their noses bent because I'm so young, but by the time they have my experience, they'll be six or eight years older."

Aaron Carter, the head of Ajax's reinsurance division, had died suddenly last month of a heart attack. His most likely successor had left in September to join a rival company. "I'm just filling in until they can find someone with the right qualifications. They need a good manager, but they must find someone who knows the London market upside down."

He asked me what I was working on. I had a few routine cases going, but nothing interesting, so I told him about my aunt Rosa and the counterfeit securities. "I'd love to see her put away for securities fraud, but I'm afraid she's just an innocent bystander." On second thought, no one who ever met Rosa would think of her as innocent. Crime-free might be a better adjective.

I declined a second scotch, and we put on our coats to go into the winter night. A strong wind was blowing across the lake, driving away the clouds but dropping the temperature down to the teens. We held hands and half ran into its face to an Italian restaurant four blocks away on Seneca.

Despite its location in the convention district, the Caffe Firenze had a cheerful unpretentious interior. "I didn't know you were part Italian when I made the reservation, or I might have hesitated," Ferrant said as we turned our coats over to a plump young girl. "Do you know this place? Is the food authentic?"

"I've never heard of it, but I don't eat in this part of town too often. As long as they make their own pasta we should be fine."

I followed the maître d' to a booth against the far wall. Firenze avoided the red-checked cloth and Chianti bottles so many Italian restaurants display in Chicago. The polished wood table had linen placemats on it and a flower stuck in a Tuscan pottery vase.

We ordered a bottle of Ruffino and some *pasticcini di spinaci*, enchanting the waiter by speaking Italian. It turned out Ferrant had visited the country numerous times and spoke Italian passably well. He asked if I'd ever seen my mother's family there.

I shook my head. "My mother's from Florence, but her family was half Jewish—her mother came from a family of scholars in Pitigliano. They scattered widely at the outbreak of the war—my mother came here, her brother went to Africa, and the cousins went every which way. My grandmother died during the war. Gabriella went back once in 1955 to see her father, but it was depressing. He was the only member of her immediate family left in Florence and she said he couldn't deal with the war or the changes it brought; he kept pretending it was 1936 and the family still together. I think he's still alive but – " I made a gesture of distaste. "My dad wrote him when

33

my mother died and we got back a very unsettling letter inviting us to hear her sing. I've never felt like dealing with him."

"Was your mother a singer, then?"

"She'd trained as one. She'd hoped to sing opera. Then, when she had to flee the country, she couldn't afford to continue her lessons. She taught instead. She taught me. She hoped I'd pick it up and have her career for her. But I don't have a big enough voice. And I don't really like opera all that well."

Ferrant said apologetically that he always had tickets for the Royal Opera and enjoyed it thoroughly.

I laughed. "I enjoy the staging and the sheer—virtuosity, I guess it is—of putting an opera together. It's very strenuous work, you know. But the singing is too violent. I prefer *Lieder*. My mother always saved enough money from the music lessons to take the two of us to a couple of Lyric Opera performances every fall. Then in the summer my dad would take me to see the Cubs four or five times. The Lyric Opera is better than the Chicago Cubs, but I have to admit I've always gotten more pleasure from baseball."

We ordered dinner—fried artichoke and *pollo in galantina* for me, veal kidneys for Ferrant. The talk moved from baseball to cricket, which Ferrant played, to his own childhood in Highgate, and finally to his career in Scupperfield, Plouder.

As I was finishing my second cup of espresso, he asked me idly if I followed the stock market at all.

I shook my head. "I don't have anything to invest. Why?"

He shrugged. "I've only been here a week, but I noticed in *The Wall Street Journal* that Ajax's volume seems quite heavy compared to the other stock-insurance companies, and the price seems to be going up."

"Great. Looks like your firm picked a winner."

He signaled for the check. "We're not doing anything spectacular in the way of earnings. Not buying any companies or selling off any properties. What else makes a share price go up?"

"Sometimes institutional investors take a whimsical fancy to a stock. Insurance companies fared better during the last depression or recession or whatever than most businesses. Ajax

34

is one of the biggest—maybe the funds and the other big investors are just playing it safe . . . If you want, I could give you the name of a broker I know; she might have some other information."

"Maybe so."

We collected our coats and headed back into the wind. It was blowing harder, but fried artichokes and half a bottle of wine made it seem less penetrating. Ferrant invited me up for a brandy.

He turned the lamp by the bar on a low switch. We could see the bottles but the garish furniture was mercifully muted. I stood at the window looking down at the lake. Ice reflected the streetlights on Lake Shore Drive. By squinting I could make out the promontories farther south, which held Navy Pier and McCormick Place. In the clear winter air the South Works twelve miles away glowed red. I used to live there in an ill-built wooden row house, made distinctive by my mother's artistry.

Ferrant put his left arm around me and handed me a snifter of Martell with the right. I leaned back against him, then turned and put both arms around him, carefully holding the snifter away from his sweater. It felt like cashmere and might not take kindly to brandy. He was thin but wiry, not just an opera-loving beanpole. He slid his hand under my silk top and stroked my back, then began fumbling for the bra strap.

"It opens in front." I was having a hard time maintaining my balance and the snifter at the same time, so I put the brandy down on the window ledge behind me. Ferrant had found the front hook. I fumbled with the buttons on his pleated trousers. Making love standing up is not as easy as they make it look in the movies. We slid down onto the thick orange carpet together.

V

Frustration

WE FINISHED THE brandy and the rest of the night in a king-sized bed with a blond Scandinavian headboard. When we woke up well after eight the next morning, Ferrant and I smiled at each other with sleepy pleasure. He looked fresh and vulnerable with his dark hair hanging down in his dark blue eyes; I put an arm around him and kissed him.

He kissed me back enthusiastically, then sat up. "America is a country of terrible contrasts. They give you these wonderful outsize beds, which I'd give a month's pay for back home, then they expect you to hop out of them in the middle of the night to be at work. In London I wouldn't dream of being in the City before nine-thirty at the earliest, but here my whole staff has already been at the office for half an hour. I'd better get going."

I lay back in bed and watched him go through the male dressing ritual, which ended when he had encased his neck meekly in a gray-and-burgundy choker. He tossed me a blue paisley robe and I got up to drink a cup of coffee with him, pleased with my foresight in changing my meeting with Hatfield to the afternoon.

After Ferrant left, muttering curses against the American work ethic, I phoned my answering service. My cousin Albert had called three times, once late last night and twice this morning. The second time he'd left his office number. My pleasure in the morning began to evaporate. I put on last night's clothes, frowning at myself in the wide mirrors that served as closet doors. An outfit that looks sexy at night tends to appear tawdry in the morning. I was going to have to change for my meeting with Hatfield; I might as well go home and do it before calling Albert.

I paid dearly for parking the Omega at the Hancock Building for fourteen hours. That did nothing to cheer me up, and I earned a whistle and a yell from the traffic cop at Oak Street for swinging around the turning traffic onto the Lake Shore Drive underpass. I sobered up then. My father had drummed into my head at an early age the stupidity of venting anger with a moving car. He was a policeman and had taken guns and cars very seriously—he spent too much time with the wreckage of those who used such lethal weapons in anger.

I stopped for a breakfast falafel sandwich at a storefront Lebanese restaurant at Halsted and Wrightwood and ate it at the red lights the rest of the way up Halsted. The decimation of Lebanon was showing up in Chicago as a series of restaurants and little shops, just as the destruction of Vietnam had been visible here a decade earlier. If you never read the news but ate out a lot you should be able to tell who was getting beaten up around the world.

From North Avenue to Fullerton, Halsted is part of the recently renovated North Side, where young professionals pay two hundred fifty thousand or more for chic brick townhouses. Four blocks farther north, at Diversey, the rich have not yet stuck out rehabilitation tentacles. Most of the buildings, like mine, are comfortably run-down. One advantage is the cheap rents; the other is space to park on the street.

I stopped the Omega in front of my building and went inside to change back into the navy walking suit for my meeting with Hatfield. By then I had delayed calling Albert long enough. I took a cup of coffee into the living room and sat in the overstuffed armchair while I phoned. I studied my toes through my nylons. Maybe I'd paint the nails red. I can't stand nail polish on my fingers, but it might be sexy on my toes.

A woman answered Albert's work number. His secret lover, I thought: Rosa assumes she's his secretary, but he secretly buys her perfume and *zabiglione*. I asked for Albert; she said in a nasal, uneducated voice that "Mr. Vignelli" was in conference and would I leave a message.

"This is V. I. Warshawski," I said. "He wants to talk to me. Tell him this is the only time I'll be available today."

She put me on hold. I drank coffee and started an article in *Fortune* on chicanery at CitiCorp. I was delighted. I've never forgiven them for taking two years to answer a billing complaint. I was just getting into illegal currency manipulation when Albert came on the line, sounding more petulant than usual.

"Where have *you* been?"

I raised my eyebrows at the mouthpiece. "At an all-night sex and dope orgy. The sex was terrible but the coke was really great. Want to come next time?"

"I might have known you'd just laugh instead of taking Mama's problems seriously."

"I'm not laughing, Albert. If you read the paper, you know how hard it is to get good coke these days. But tell me, has Rosa's problem taken a turn for the worse? Just to show you I

37

mean well, I won't even charge you for my time waiting on hold."

I could visualize his fat round face puckered up in a full-scale pout as he breathed heavily into my ear. At last he said angrily, "You went to St. Albert's Priory yesterday, didn't you?"

I assented.

"What did you find out?"

"That this is going to be incredibly tough to sort out. Our best hope is that the securities had already been faked before the priory got them. I'm meeting with the FBI this afternoon and I'm going to see if they're looking into that."

"Well, Mama has changed her mind. She doesn't want you to investigate this after all."

I sat frozen for a few seconds while anger came to a focus inside my head. "What the hell do you mean, Albert? I'm not a vacuum cleaner that you switch on and off at will. You don't start me on an investigation, then call up two days later to say you've changed your mind."

I could hear paper rustling in the background, then Albert said smugly, "Your contract doesn't say that. It just says 'Termination of the case may be requested by either party, whether the requested results are obtained or not. Regardless of the state of the investigation, and regardless of whether either party disagrees with the results, the fee and expenses incurred to the time of termination shall be paid.' If you send me a bill, Victoria, I'll pay promptly."

I could smell my brain burning. "Albert. When Rosa called me on Sunday she made it sound as though her suicide would be on my head if I didn't come out and help her. What's happened since then? She find a detective she likes better? Or did Carroll call and promise her her job back if she'd get me out of the investigation?"

He said aloofly, "She told me last night she felt she was acting in a very unchristian way by getting so worried about this. She knows her name will be cleared; if it's not, she'll bear it like a Christian."

"How noble," I said sarcastically. "Rosa as a bitter martyr is a pose I know well. But the woman of sorrows is a new departure."

38

"Really, Victoria. You're acting like an ambulance chaser. Just send me a bill."

At least I had the dubious satisfaction of hanging up first. I sat fuming, cursing Rosa in Italian, then in English. Just like her to jack me around! Get me out to Melrose Park by screaming about Gabriella and my duty to my dead mother, if not to my live aunt, send me off on a wild-goose chase, then call the whole thing off. I was strongly tempted to phone her and tell her once and for all exactly what I thought of her, omitting no detail, however slight. I even looked her number up in my address book and started dialing before I realized the futility of such an act. Rosa was seventy-five. She was not going to change. If I couldn't accept that, then I was doomed to be a victim of her manipulation forever.

I sat for a while with *Fortune* open in my lap, staring across the room at the gray day outside. Last night's strong wind had blown clouds in front of it across the lake. What was Rosa's real reason for wanting the investigation to stop? She was cold, angry, vindictive—a dozen disagreeable adjectives. But not a schemer. She wouldn't call a hated niece after a ten-year hiatus just to run me through hoops.

I looked up St. Albert's Priory in the phone book and called Carroll. The call went through a switchboard. I could see the ascetic young man at the reception desk reluctantly putting down his Charles Williams to answer the phone on the sixth ring, picking up the book again before switching the call through. I waited several minutes for the prior. At last Carroll's educated, gentle voice came on the line.

"This is V. I. Warshawski, Father Carroll."

He apologized for keeping me waiting; he'd been going over the household accounts with the head cook and the receptionist had paged the kitchen last.

"No problem," I said. "I wondered if you'd spoken with my aunt since I saw you yesterday."

"With Mrs. Vignelli? No. Why?"

"She's decided suddenly that she doesn't want any investigation into the counterfeit securities, at least not on her behalf. She seems to think that worrying about them is very unchristian. I wondered if someone at the priory had been counseling her."

39

"Unchristian? What a curious idea. I don't know; I suppose it would be if she got absorbed by this problem to the exclusion of other more fundamental matters. But it's very human to worry about a fraud that might harm your reputation. And if you think of being Christian as a way to be more fully human, it would be a mistake to make someone feel guilty for having natural human feelings."

I blinked a few times. "So you didn't tell my aunt to drop the investigation?"

He gave a soft laugh. "You didn't want me to build a watch; you just wanted the time. No, I haven't talked to your aunt. But it sounds as though I should."

"And did anyone else at the priory? Talk to her, I mean."

Not as far as he knew, but he'd ask around and get back to me. He wanted to know if I had learned anything useful yet. I told him I'd be talking to Hatfield that afternoon, and we hung up with mutual promises to stay in touch.

I puttered around the apartment, hanging up clothes and putting a week's accumulation of newspapers into a stack on the back porch where my landlord's grandson would collect them for recycling. I made myself a salad with cubes of cheddar cheese in it and ate it while flicking aimlessly through yesterday's *Wall Street Journal*. At twelve-thirty I went down for the mail.

When you thought about it seriously, Rosa was an old lady. She probably had imagined she could make her problem disappear by scowling at it, the way she'd made all her problems, including her husband, Carl, disappear. She thought if she called me and ordered me to take care of it, it would go away. When the reality came a little closer after she'd talked with me, she decided it just wasn't worth the energy it would take to fight it. My problem was that I was so wound up in all the old enmities that I suspected everything she did was motivated by hatred and a need for revenge.

Ferrant called at one, partly for some light chat, and partly because of questions about Ajax's stock. "One of my responsibilities seems to be our investment division. So I got a call today from a chap named Barrett in New York. He called himself the Ajax specialist at the New York Stock Exchange. I know reinsurance, not the U.S. stock market, or even the

London stock market, so I had some trouble keeping up with him. But you remember I told you last night our stock seemed really active? Barratt called to tell me that. Called to let me know he was getting a lot of orders from a small group of Chicago brokers who had never traded in Ajax before. Nothing wrong with them, you understand, but he thought I should know about it."

"And?"

"Now I know about it. But I'm not sure what, if anything, I should do. So I'd like to meet that friend you mentioned—the one who's the broker."

Agnes Paciorek and I had met at the University of Chicago when I was in law school and she was a math whiz turned MBA. We actually met at sessions of University Women United. She was a maverick in the gray-tailored world of MBAs and we'd remained good friends.

I gave Roger her number. After hanging up I looked up Ajax in *The Wall Street Journal*. Their range for the year went from 28¼ to 55½ and they were currently trading at their high. Aetna and Cigna, the two largest stock-insurance carriers, had similar bottom prices, but their highs were about ten points below Ajax. Yesterday they'd each had a volume of about three hundred thousand, compared to Ajax's which was almost a million. Interesting.

I thought about calling Agnes myself, but it was getting close to time for me to leave to meet Hatfield. I wrapped a mohair scarf around my neck, pulled on some driving gloves, and went back out into the wind. Two o'clock is a good time to drive into the Loop. The traffic is light. I made it to the Federal Building on Dearborn and Adams in good time, left the Omega in a self-park garage across the street and walked in under the orange legs of the three-story Calder designed for Chicago's Federal Building. We pride ourselves in Chicago on our outdoor sculptures by famous artists. My favorite is the bronze wind chimes in front of the Standard Oil Building, but I have a secret fondness for Chagall's mosaics in front of the First National Bank. My artist friends tell me they are banal.

It was exactly two-thirty when I reached the FBI offices on the eighteenth floor. The receptionist phoned my name in to Hatfield, but he had to keep me waiting ten minutes just to impress me with how heavily Chicago's crime rested on his shoulders. I busied myself with a report for a client whose brother-in-law had been pilfering supplies, apparently out of bitterness from some longstanding family feud. When Hatfield finally stuck his head around the corner from the hall, I affected not to hear him until the second time he called my name. I looked up then and smiled and said I would be just a minute and carefully finished writing a sentence.

"Hello, Derek," I said. "How's crime?"

For some reason this jolly greeting always makes him grimace, which is probably why I always use it. His face has the bland handsomeness required by the FBI. He's around six feet tall with a square build. I could see him doing a hundred sit-ups and push-ups every morning with methodical uncomplaining discipline, always turning down the second martini, picking up only college girls to make sure someone with a modicum of brains would breathe in his ear how smart and how brave he was. He was dressed today in a gray-plaid suit—muted gray on slightly paler gray with the discreetest of blue stripes woven in—a white shirt whose starch could probably hold up my brassiere for a week, and a blue tie.

"I don't have a lot of time, Warshawski." He shot back a starched cuff and looked at his watch. Probably a Rolex.

"I'm flattered, then, that you wanted to make some of it available to me." I followed him down the hall to an office in the southwestern corner. Hatfield was head of white-collar crime for the Chicago Region, obviously a substantial position judging by the furniture—all wood veneer—and the location.

"That's a nice view of the metropolitan lockup," I said, looking out at the triangular building. "It must be a great inspiration for you."

"We don't send anyone there."

"Not even for overnight holding? What about Joey Lombardo and Allen Dorfmann? I thought that's where they were staying while they were on trial."

"Could you cut it out? I don't know anything about Dorfmann or Lombardo. I want to talk to you about the securities at St. Albert's."

"Great." I sat down in an uncomfortable chair covered in tan Naugahyde and put a look of bright interest on my face.

"One of the things that occurred to me yesterday was that the certificates might have been forged before they were passed on to St. Albert's. What do you know about the donor and his executors? Also, it is possible some ex-Dominican with a grudge could have been behind it. Do you have a trail on people who left the order in the last ten years?"

"I'm not interested in discussing the case with you, Warshawski. We're very well able to think of leads and follow them up. We have an excellent record here in the bureau. This forgery is a federal offense and I must request you to back out of it."

I leaned forward in my chair. "Derek, I'm not only willing but eager for you to solve this crime. It will take a cast of thousands to sort it out. You have that. I don't. I'm just here to make sure that a seventy-five-year-old woman doesn't get crushed by the crowd. And I'd like to know what you've turned up on the possibilities I just mentioned to you."

"We're following all leads."

We argued it back and forth for several more minutes, but he was adamant and I left empty-handed. I stopped in the plaza at a pay phone next to the praying mantis and dialed the *Herald-Star*. Murray Ryerson, their chief crime reporter, was in. He and I have been friends, sometimes lovers, and easy rivals on the crime scene for years.

"Hi, Murray. It's V. I. Is three o'clock too early for a drink?"

"That's no question for the crime desk. I'll connect you with our etiquette specialist." He paused. "A.M. or P.M.?"

"Now, wiseass. I'll buy."

"Gosh, Vic, you must be desperate. Can't do it now, but how about meeting at the Golden Glow in an hour?"

I agreed and hung up. The Golden Glow is my favorite bar in Chicago; I introduced Murray to it a number of years ago. It's tucked away in the DuSable Building, an 1890s skyscraper on Federal, and has the original mahogany bar that Cyrus McCormick and Judge Gary probably used to lean over.

I went to my office to check mail and messages and at four walked back up the street to the bar. Sal, the magnificent black bartender who could teach the Chicago police a thing or two about crowd control, greeted me with a smile and a majestic wave. She wore her hair in an Afro today and had on gold hoop earrings that hung to her shoulder. A shiny blue evening gown showed her splendid cleavage and five-foot-eleven frame to advantage. She brought a double Black Label to my corner booth and chatted for a few minutes before getting back to the swelling group of early commuters.

Murray came in a few minutes later, his red hair more disheveled than usual from the January wind. He had on a sheepskin coat and western boots: the urban cowboy. I said as much by way of greeting while a waitress took his order for beer; Sal only looks after her regular customers personally.

We talked about the poor showing the Black Hawks were making, and about the Greylord trial, and whether Mayor Washington would ever subdue Eddie Vrdolyak. "If Washington didn't have Vrdolyak he'd have to invent him," Murray said. "He's the perfect excuse for Washington not being able to accomplish anything."

The waitress came over. I declined a refill and asked for a glass of water.

Murray ordered a second Beck's. "So what gives, V.I.? I won't say it always spells trouble when you call up out of the blue, but it usually means I end up being used."

"Murray, I bet you a week of my pay that you've gotten more stories out of me than I have gotten clients out of you."

"A week of your pay wouldn't keep me in beer. What's up?"

"Did you pick up a story last week about some forged securities in Melrose Park? Out in a Dominican priory there?"

"Dominican priory?" Murray echoed. "Since when have you started hanging around churches?"

"It's a family obligation," I said with dignity. "You may not know it, but I'm half Italian, and we Italians stick together, through thick and thin. You know, the secret romance of the Mafia and all that. When one member of the family is in trouble, the others rally around."

Murray wasn't impressed. "You going to knock off somebody in the priory for the sake of your family honor?"

"No, but I might take out Derek Hatfield in the cause."

Murray supported me enthusiastically. Hatfield was as unco-operative with the press as he was with private investigators.

Murray had missed the story of the faked certificates.

44

"Maybe it wasn't on the wires. The feds can be pretty secretive about these things—especially Derek. Think this prior would make a good interview? Maybe I'll send out one of my babies to talk to him."

I suggested he send someone to interview Rosa, and gave him the list of possibilities I'd offered Hatfield. Murray would work those into the story. He'd probably get someone to dig up the name of the original donor and get some public exposure on his heirs. That would force Hatfield to do something—either eliminate them as being involved or publicly announce how old the dud certificates were. "Them that eat cakes that the Parsee man bakes make dreadful mistakes," I muttered to myself.

"What was that?" Murray said sharply. "Are you setting me up to do your dirty work for you, Warshawski?"

I gave him a look that I hoped implied limpid innocence. "Murray! How you talk. I just want to make sure the FBI doesn't railroad my poor frail old aunt." I signaled to Sal that we were ready to leave; she runs a tab that she sends me once a month, the only bill I ever pay on time.

Murray and I moved up north for seafood at the Red Tide. For eight dollars you can get a terrific whole Dungeness crab, which you eat sitting at a bar in a dark basement about half the size of my living room. Afterward I dropped Murray at the Fullerton L stop and went on home alone. I'm past the age where bed-hopping has much appeal.

VI

Uncle Stefan's Profession

SNOW WAS FALLING the next morning as I made my five-mile run to Belmont Harbor and back. The ice-filled water was perfectly still. Across the breakwater I could see the lake motionless, too. Not peaceful, but sullenly quiet, its angry gods held tightly by bands of cold.

A Salvation Army volunteer was stamping his feet and calling cheery greetings to commuters at the corner of Belmont and Sheridan. He gave me a smiling "God bless you" as I jogged past. Must be nice to have everything so simple and peaceful. What would he do with an Aunt Rosa? Was there any smile broad enough to make her smile back?

I stopped at a little bakery on Broadway for a cup of cappuccino and a croissant. As I ate at one of the spindly-legged tables, I pondered my next actions. I'd met with Hatfield yesterday more out of bravado than anything else—it brought me some sort of perverse pleasure to irritate his well-pressed Brooks Brothers facade. But he wasn't going to do anything for me. I didn't have the resources to pry into the Dominicans. Anyway, even if Murray Ryerson turned something up, what would I do about it if Rosa didn't want me investigating? Wasn't my obligation finished with her abrupt command to stop?

I realized that I was carrying on this internal monologue as an argument with Gabriella, who didn't seem pleased with me for bugging out so early. "Goddamn it, Gabriella," I swore silently. "Why did you make me give you that crazy promise? She hated you. Why do I have to do anything for her?"

If my mother were alive she would shrivel me on the spot for swearing at her. And then turn fierce intelligent eyes on me: So Rosa fired you? Did you go to work only because she hired you?

I slowly finished my cappuccino and went back out into a minor blizzard. Strictly speaking, Rosa had not fired me. Albert had called to say she didn't want me on the job any longer. But was that Albert or Rosa speaking? I should at least get that much clear before deciding what else to do. Which meant another trip to Melrose Park. Not today—the roads would be impossible with the snow: traffic creeping, people falling into ditches. But tomorrow would be Saturday. Even if the weather continued bad there wouldn't be much traffic.

At home I peeled off layers of shirts and leggings and soaked in a hot tub for a while. Being self-employed, I can hold my review of operations and management anywhere. This means time spent thinking in the bath is time spent working. Unfortunately, my accountant doesn't agree that this makes my water bill and bath salts tax deductible.

My theory of detection resembles Julia Child's approach to cooking: Grab a lot of ingredients from the shelves, put them in a pot and stir, and see what happens. I'd stirred at the priory, and at the FBI. Maybe it was time to let things simmer a bit and see if the smell of cooking gave me any new ideas.

I put on a wool crepe-de-chine pantsuit with a high-necked red-striped blouse and low-heeled black boots. That should be warm enough to walk in if I got stuck in the snow someplace. Wrapping my big mohair scarf around my head and neck, I went back into the storm, adding the Omega to the queue of slowly moving, sliding cars trying to get onto Lake Shore Drive at Belmont.

I crept downtown, barely able to see the cars immediately next to me, and slithered off at Jackson. Leaving the Omega next to a snowdrift behind the Art Institute, I trudged the six blocks to the Pulteney Building, which looked worse than usual in the winter weather. Tenants had tracked snow and mud into the lobby. Tom Czarnik, the angry old man who calls himself the building superintendent, refuses to mop the floor on stormy mornings. His theory is that it will just get nasty again at lunch, so why bother? I should applaud a man whose housekeeping views coincide so closely with mine, but I cursed him under my breath as my boots slid in the lobby slush. The elevator wasn't working today either, so I stomped up four flights of stairs to my office.

After turning on the lights and picking up the mail from the floor, I phoned Agnes Paciorek at her broker's office. On hold while she sold a million shares of AT&T, I looked through bills and pleas for charity. Nothing that wouldn't wait until next month. At last her brisk deep voice came on the line.

"Agnes. It's V. I. Warshawski."

We exchanged pleasantries for a few minutes, then I explained who Roger Ferrant was and said I'd given him her number.

"I know. He called yesterday afternoon. We're meeting for lunch at the Mercantile Club. Are you downtown? Want to join us?"

"Sure. Great. You find anything unusual?"

"Depends on your definition. Brokers don't think buying and selling stock is unusual but you might. I've got to run. See you at one."

The Mercantile Club sits on top of the old Bletchley Iron Building down in the financial district. It's a businessmen's

47

club, which reluctantly opened its doors to women when Mrs. Gray became president of the University of Chicago, since most of the trustees' meetings were held there. Having admitted one woman they found others sneaking through in her wake. The food is excellent and the service impeccable, although some of the old waiters refuse to work tables with women guests.

Ferrant was already sitting by the fire in the reading room where the maître d' sent me to wait for Agnes. He looked elegant in navy-blue tailoring and stood up with a warm smile when he saw me come into the room.

"Agnes invited me to gate-crash; I hope you don't object."

"By no means. You look very smart today. How are your forgeries coming?"

I told him about my useless interview with Hatfield. "And the Dominicans don't know anything, either. At least not about forgery. I need to start at the other end—who could have created them to begin with?"

Agnes came up behind me. "Created what?" She turned to Ferrant and introduced herself, a short, compact dynamo in a brown-plaid suit whose perfect stitching probably required an eight-hundred-dollar investment. Half a day's work for Agnes.

She shepherded us into the dining room where the maître d' greeted her by name and seated us by a window. We looked down at the South Branch of the Chicago River and ordered drinks. I seldom drink whiskey in the middle of the day and asked for oloroso sherry. Ferrant ordered a beer, while Agnes had Perrier with lime—the exchanges didn't close for almost two hours and she believes sober brokers trade better.

Once we were settled she repeated her initial question. I told her about the forgery. "As far as I know, the Fort Dearborn Trust discovered it because the serial numbers hadn't been issued yet. The FBI is being stuffy and close-mouthed, but I know the forgery was pretty high quality—good enough to pass a superficial test by the auditors, anyway. I'd like to talk to someone who knows something about forging—try to find out who'd have the skill to create that good a product."

Agnes cocked a thick eyebrow. "Are you asking me? I just sell 'em; I don't print 'em. Roger's problem is the type of thing

48

I'm equipped to handle. Maybe." She turned to Ferrant. "Why don't you tell me what you know at this point?"

He shrugged thin shoulders. "I told you on the phone about the call from our specialist in New York, Andy Barrett. Maybe you can start by telling me what a specialist is. He doesn't work for Ajax, I take it."

"No. Specialists are members of the New York Stock Exchange—but they're not brokers for the public. Usually they're members of a firm who get a franchise from the Exchange to be specialists—people who manage buy-and-sell orders so business keeps flowing. Barrett makes markets in your stock. Someone wants to sell a thousand shares of Ajax. They call me. I don't go down to the floor of the Chicago Exchange waving 'em around until a buyer happens along—I phone our broker in New York and he goes to Barrett's post on the floor. Barrett buys the shares and makes a match with someone who's looking for a thousand shares. If too many people are unloading Ajax at once and no one wants to buy it, he buys on his own account—he's got an ethical obligation to make markets. Once in a great while, if the market gets completely haywire, he'll ask the Exchange to halt trading in the stock until things shake out."

She paused to give us time to order, Dover sole for me, rare steaks for her and Roger. She lit a cigarette and began punctuating her comments with stabs of smoke.

"From what I gather, something of the opposite kind has been going on with Ajax the last few weeks. There's been a tremendous amount of buying. About seven times the normal volume, enough that the price is starting to go up. Not a lot—insurance companies aren't glamor investments, so you can have heavy action without too much notice being taken. Did Barrett give you the names of the brokers placing the orders?"

"Yes. They didn't mean anything to me. He's sending a list in the mail . . . I wondered, if it wouldn't be too great an imposition, Miss Paciorek, whether you'd look at the names when I get them. See if they tell you anything. Also, what should I do?"

To my annoyance, Agnes lit a second cigarette. "No, no imposition. And please call me Agnes. Miss Paciorek sounds too much like the North Shore . . . I guess what we're

49

assuming, to put the evil thought into blunt words, is that someone may be trying a covert takeover bid. If that's true, they can't have got too far—anyone with five percent or more of the stock has to file with the SEC and explain what's he doing with it. Or she." She grinned at me.

"How much stock would someone need to take over Ajax?" I asked. The food arrived, and Agnes mercifully stubbed out her cigarette.

"Depends. Who besides your firm owns sizable chunks?"

Ferrant shook his head. "I don't really know. Gordon Firth, the chairman. Some of the directors. We own three percent and Edelweiss, the Swiss reinsurers, holds four percent. I think they're the largest owners. Firth maybe owns two. Some of the other directors may have one or two percent."

"So your present management owns around fifteen percent. Someone could carry a lot of weight with sixteen percent. Not guaranteed, but that would be a good place to start, especially if your management wasn't aware it was happening."

I did some mental arithmetic. Fifty million shares outstanding. Sixteen percent would be eight million. "You'd need about five hundred million for a takeover, then."

She thought for a minute. "That's about right. But keep in mind that you don't need to come up with that much capital. Once you've bought a large block you can leverage the rest— put your existing shares up as collateral for a loan to buy more shares. Then you leverage those and keep going. Before you know it, you've bought yourself a company. That's oversimplified, of course, but that's the basic idea."

We ate in silence for a minute; then Ferrant said, "What can I do to find out for sure?"

Agnes pursed her square face as she thought about it. "You could call the SEC and ask for a formal investigation. Then you'd be sure of getting the names of the people who are really doing the buying. That's an extreme step, though. Once they're called in they're going to scrutinize every transaction and every broker. You'd want to talk to your board before you did that—some of your directors might not relish having all their stock transactions revealed to the piercing light of day."

"Well, short of that?"

"Every brokerage firm has what we call a compliance officer.

Once you get the list of firms from Barrett, you can try calling them and find out on whose behalf they're trading. There's no reason for them to tell you, though—and nothing illegal about trying to buy a company."

The waiters hovered around our table. Dessert? Coffee? Ferrant absentmindedly selected a piece of apple pie. "Do you think they'd talk to you, Miss—Agnes? The compliance officers, I mean. As I told Vic, I'm way out of depth with this stock-market stuff. Even if you coached me in what to ask, I wouldn't know if the answers I was getting were right."

Agnes put three lumps of sugar in her coffee and stirred vigorously. "It would be unusual. Let me see the list of brokers before I let you know one way or another. What you could do is call Barrett and ask him to send you a list of the names the shares were registered in when he sold them. If I know anyone really well—either the brokers or the customers—I could probably call them."

She looked at her watch. "I've got to get back to the office." She signaled for a waiter and signed the bill. "You two stay though."

Ferrant shook his head. "I'd better call London. It's after eight there—my managing director should be home."

I left with them. The snow had stopped. The sky was clear and the temperature falling. One of the bank thermometers showed 11 degrees. I walked with Roger as far as Ajax. As we said good-bye he invited me to go to a movie with him Saturday night. I accepted, then went on down Wabash to my office to finish the report on pilfered supplies.

During the slow drive home that night I pondered how to find someone who knew about forging securities. Forgers were engravers gone wrong. And I did know one engraver. At least I knew someone who knew an engraver.

Dr Charlotte Herschel, Lotty to me, had been born in Vienna, grew up in London where she ultimately received her doctor of medicine degree from London University—and lived about a mile from me on Sheffield Avenue. Her father's brother Stefan, an engraver, had immigrated to Chicago in the twenties. When Lotty decided to come to the States in 1959, she picked Chicago partly because her uncle Stefan lived here.

I had never met him—she saw little of him, just saying it made her feel more rooted to have a relative in the area.

My friendship with Lotty goes back a long way, to my student days at the University of Chicago when she was one of the physicians working with an abortion underground I was involved in. She knew Agnes Paciorek from that time, too.

I stopped at a Treasure Island on Broadway for groceries and wine. It was six-thirty when I got home and phoned Lotty. She had just come in herself from a long day at the clinic she runs on Sheffield near her apartment. She greeted my offer of dinner enthusiastically and said she would be over after a hot bath.

I cleaned up the worst ravages in my living room and kitchen. Lotty never criticizes my housekeeping, but she is scrupulously tidy herself and it didn't seem fair to drag her out for a brain-picking session on such a cold night, then have her spend it in squalor.

Chicken, garlic, mushrooms, and onions sautéed in olive oil, then flamed with brandy made an easy attractive stew. A cup of Ruffino finished the dish. By the time I had water hot for fettucine, the doorbell rang.

Lotty came up the stairs briskly and greeted me with a hug. "A lifesaver that you called, my dear. It was a long, very depressing day: a child dead of meningitis because the mother would not bring her in. She hung an amulet around her neck and thought it would bring down a fever of forty-one degrees. There are three sisters; we put them in St Vincent's for observation, but my God!"

I held her for a minute before we went into the apartment, asking if she wanted a drink. Lotty reminded me that alcohol is poison. For extreme situations she believes brandy is permissible, but she did not consider today's woes extreme. I poured myself a glass of Ruffino and put on water for her coffee.

We ate by candlelight in the dining room while Lotty unburdened herself. By the time we had finished the salad, she felt more relaxed and asked me what I was working on.

I told her about Rosa and the Dominicans and Albert's phoning me to tell me the whole thing was off.

The candlelight was reflected in her black eyes as she

narrowed them at me. "And what are you trying to prove by continuing?"

"It was Albert who phoned. Rosa may not agree," I said defensively.

"Yes. Your aunt dislikes you. She's decided—for whatever reason—to discontinue the effort to protect herself. So what are you doing? Proving that you are tougher, or smarter, or just plain better than she is?"

I thought it over. Lotty is sometimes about as pleasant as a can opener, but she braces me. I know myself better when I talk to Lotty.

"You know, I don't spend a lot of time thinking about Rosa. It's not as though she's an obsession; she doesn't control my head that much. But I feel very protective of my mother. Rosa hurt her and that makes me angry. If I can show Rosa she was wrong to stop the investigation, that I can solve this problem despite failure by the FBI and the SEC, I'll have proof that she was wrong about everything. And she'll have to believe it." I laughed and finished my glass of wine. "She won't, of course. My rational self knows that. But my feeling self thinks otherwise."

Lotty nodded. "Perfectly logical. Does your rational self have any way of solving this problem?"

"There are lots of things the FBI can do that I can't because they have so much manpower. But one thing I could look into is who actually did the forgeries. Let Derek concentrate on who planted them and which ex-Dominicans are living in luxury.

"I don't know any forgers. But it occurred to me that a forger is really a species of engraver. And I wondered about your uncle Stefan."

Lotty had been watching me with an expression of shrewd amusement. Now her face changed suddenly. Her mouth set and her black eyes narrowed. "Is this an inspired guess? Or have you spent your spare time investigating me?"

I looked at her in bewilderment.

"You wondered why you never met my uncle Stefan? Although he is my only relative living in Chicago?"

"No," I said doggedly. "I never thought about it for a minute. You've never met my aunt Rosa. Even if she weren't

53

a virago, you'd probably never have met her—friends seldom have much in common with relatives."

She continued to stare searchingly at me. I felt very hurt but could think of nothing to say that would bridge the gulf of Lotty's suspicious silence. The last time I had felt this way was the night I realized the man I had married and thought I loved was as foreign to me as Yasir Arafat. Could a friendship evaporate in the same mist as a marriage?

My throat felt tight, but I forced myself to talk. "Lotty. You've known me for close to twenty years and I've never done anything behind your back. If you think I've started now . . ." That sentence wasn't going in the right direction. "There's something you don't want me to know about your uncle. You don't have to tell me. Carry it to the grave with you. But don't act as though everything you know about me suddenly has no foundation." A light bulb went on over my head. "Oh, no. Don't tell me your uncle really is a forger?"

The set look held in Lotty's face for a few seconds, then cracked into a wry smile. "You are right, Vic. About my uncle. And about you and me. I'm truly sorry, my dear. I won't try to make excuses—there are none. But Stefan . . . When the war ended, I found there was left of my family only my brother and the distant cousins who had taken us in during the war. Hugo—my brother—and I spent what time and money we had searching for relatives. And we found Papa's brother Stefan. When Hugo decided to move to Montreal, I came to Chicago—I had an opportunity for a surgical residency at Northwestern, too good a chance to turn down." She made a throwaway gesture with her left hand. "So I set out to find Uncle Stefan. And discovered him in a federal prison at Fort Leavenworth. Currency was his specialty, although he had a social conscience: He was also forging passports for sale to the many Europeans trying to come to America at the time."

She grinned at me, the old Lotty grin. I leaned across the table and squeezed her hand. She returned the pressure, but went on talking. Detectives and doctors both know the value of talking. "I went to see him. He's likable. Like my father, but without the moral foundation. And I let him stay with me for six months when he was released—1959 that was; I was his only family, too.

"He got a job, doing custom work for a jeweler—after all, he wasn't a robber, so they weren't afraid he'd lift the sterling. As far as I know, he's never stepped over the edge again. But naturally I haven't asked."

"Naturally not. Well, I will try to find a different engraver."

Lotty smiled again. "Oh, no. Why not call him? He's eighty-two, but he still has all his wits and some besides. He might be the one person who could help you."

She would talk to him the next day and arrange a time when I could have tea with him. We had coffee and pears in the living room and played Scrabble. As usual, Lotty won.

VII

Christian Charity

THE AIR WAS clear and cold the next morning and a bright winter sun cast a strong glare back from the drifts lining the roads. Halsted had not been plowed, at least not north of Belmont, and the Omega jumped skittishly from rut to rut on the way to the Kennedy Expressway and Melrose Park.

I put on sunglasses and turned on WFMT. Satie. Unbearable. I turned it off again and started singing myself—nothing very noble, just the theme from *Big John and Sparky*. "If you go down to the woods today you'd better not go alone."

It was a little after ten when I turned north on Mannheim and made my way to Rosa's. In Melrose Park, even the side streets had been carefully cleaned. Maybe there was something to be said for suburban living after all. The path leading to her side door had been shoveled neatly, not just a path half a person wide like my building super believed in. There was even something to be said for living with Albert. Which just went to show.

Albert came to the door. The light was behind him and I could see his petulant face through the thick screen. He was surprised and angry. "What are you doing here?"

"Albert. If Rosa has stressed it once, she's stressed a hundred times the importance of families sticking together. I'm sure she'd be shocked to hear you greet me so ungraciously."

"Mama doesn't want to talk to you. I thought I made that clear the other day."

I pulled the screen door open. "Nope. You made it clear you didn't want *me* talking to *her*. That's by no means the same thing."

Albert probably outweighs me by eighty pounds, which may be why he thought it would be easy to push me back out the door. I twisted his left arm up behind him and circled around past him. I hadn't felt so good in weeks.

Rosa's harsh voice wafted down the dim hall from the kitchen, demanding to know who was at the door and why Albert didn't shut it. Didn't he know what they were paying to heat this house?

I followed the voice, Albert walking sulkily behind me. "It's me, Rosa," I said, walking into the kitchen. "I thought we ought to have a little talk about theology."

Rosa was chopping vegetables, presumably for soup, since a shinbone was browning in oil on the stove. The kitchen still had its old 1930s sink. The stove and refrigerator were old, too, small white appliances set against unpainted walls. Rosa put the pairing knife down on the counter with a snap, turned full face, and hissed angrily, "I have no wish to talk to you, Victoria!"

I pulled a kitchen chair around and sat backward on it, leaning my chin on its back. "Not good enough, Rosa. I'm not a television that you turn on and off at whim. A week ago you called me and played a tremolo passage on the family violin and dragged me out here against my will. On Thursday, suddenly your morals or ethics got the better of you. You looked at the lilies of the field and decided that it was wrong to have me toiling and spinning over your innocence." I looked at her earnestly. "Rosa, it sounds beautiful. It just doesn't sound like you."

She drew her thin mouth into a tight line. "How should you know? You were never even baptized. I would not expect you to know how a Christian behaves."

"Well, you could be right. The modern world offers few opportunities to see one in action. But you don't understand. You tugged hard on my emotions to get me out here. It's going to be even harder to get rid of me. If you had picked a private investigator out of the Yellow Pages, one who had no connection with you, it would be different. But you insisted on me and it's me you've got."

Rosa sat down. Her eyes blazed fiercely. "I have changed my mind. That is my right. You should not do anything more."

"I want to know something, Rosa. Was this your own idea? Or did someone else suggest it to you?"

Her eyes darted around the kitchen before she spoke. "Naturally I discussed it with Albert."

"Naturally. Your right-hand man and *confidant*. But who else?"

"No one!"

"No, Rosa. That little pause and the look around the room says the opposite. It wasn't Father Carroll, unless he lied to me on Thursday. Who was it?"

She said nothing.

"Who are you protecting, Rosa? Is it someone who knows about these forgeries?"

Still silence.

"I see. You know, the other day I was trying to figure an approach that I was better equipped to handle than the FBI. I came up with one, but you've just offered me a better. I'll get some surveillance on you and find out just who you talk to."

The hate in her face made me recoil physically. "So! What I should have expected from the daughter of a whore!"

Without thinking I leaned forward and slapped her on the mouth.

Slyness joined the hate in her face, but she was too proud to rub her mouth where I'd hit it. "You would not love her so much if you knew the truth."

"Thanks, Rosa. I'll be back next week for another lesson in Christian conduct."

Albert had stood silently in the kitchen doorway throughout our altercation. He walked me to the outer door. The smell of burning olive oil followed us down the hall. "You really should knock it off, Victoria. She's pretty worried."

"Why do you stick up for her, Albert? She treats you like a retarded four-year-old. Stop being such a goddamned Mama's boy. Go get yourself a girlfriend. Get your own apartment. No one's going to marry you while you're living with her."

He mumbled something inaudible and slammed the door behind me. I got into the car and sat heaving for several minutes. How dared she! She had not only insulted my mother, she had manipulated me into hitting her. I couldn't believe I'd done it. I felt sick from rage and self-disgust. But the last thing I would ever do was apologize to the old witch.

On that defiant note, I put the car into gear and headed for the priory. Father Carroll was hearing confessions and would be busy for an hour. I could wait if I wanted. I declined, leaving a message that I would call later in the weekend, and headed back to the city.

I was in no mood to do anything but fight. Back at the apartment I got out my December expenses but couldn't keep my mind on them. Finally I gathered all my stale clothes and took them down to the washing machine in the basement. I changed the sheets and vacuumed and still felt terrible. At last I gave work up as a bad idea, dug my ice skates out of the closet, and drove over to the park at Montrose Harbor. They flood an outdoor rink there and I joined a crowd of children and skated with more energy than skill for over an hour. Afterward I treated myself to a late, light lunch at the Dortmunder Restaurant in the basement of the Chesterton Hotel.

It was close to three when I got home again, tired but with the anger washed out of me. The phone was ringing as I started undoing the upper of the two locks on my door. My fingers were stiff with cold; I heard the phone ring eleven times but by the time I got the bottom lock open and sprinted across the hall to the living room, the caller had hung up.

I was meeting Roger Ferrant for a movie and dinner at six. A short nap and a long bath would restore me and even leave a little time to work on my bills.

Lotty called at four, just as I had the taps running, to ask if I wanted to go with her to Uncle Stefan's tomorrow at three-thirty. We arranged for me to pick her up at three. I was lying well submerged and slightly comatose when the phone began to ring again. At first I let it go. Then, thinking it might be Ferrant calling to change plans, I leaped from the tub, trailing a cloud of Chanel bubbles behind me. But the phone had stopped again when I reached it.

Cursing the perversity of fate, I decided I had put off work long enough, got a robe and slippers, and started in earnest. By five I had my year-end statement almost complete and December's bills ready to mail to clients, and I went to change with a feeling of awesome virtue. I put on a full peasant skirt which hit me mid-calf, knee-high red cavalier boots, and a full-sleeved white blouse. Ferrant and I were meeting at the Sullivan for the six o'clock showing of *Terms of Endearment*.

He was waiting for me when I got there, a courtesy I appreciated, and kissed me enthusiastically. I declined popcorn and Coke and we spent an agreeable two hours with half our attention on Shirley MacLaine and half on each other's bodies, making sure that various parts abandoned on Thursday morning were still where they belonged. The movie over, we agreed to complete the survey at my apartment before eating dinner.

We walked lazily up the stairs together arm in arm. I had just gotten the bottom lock unfastened when the phone started to ring again. This time I reached it by the fourth ring.

"Miss Warshawski?"

The voice was strange, a neutral voice, no accent, a hard-to-define pitch.

"Yes?"

"I'm glad to find you home at last. You're investigating the forged securities at St. Albert's, aren't you?"

"Who is this?" I demanded sharply.

"A friend, Miss Warshawski. You might almost call me an *amicus curiae*." He gave a ghostly, self-satisfied laugh. "Don't go on, Miss Warshawski. You have such beautiful gray eyes. I would hate to see them after someone poured acid on them." The line went dead.

I stood holding the phone, staring at it in disbelief. Ferrant came over to me.

"What is it, Vic?"

I put the receiver down carefully. "If you value your life, stay away from the moor at night." I tried for a light note, but my voice sounded weak even to me. Roger started to put an arm around me, but I shook it off gently. "I need to think this out on my own for a minute. There's liquor and wine in the cupboard built into the dining-room wall. Why don't you fix us something?"

He went off to find drinks and I sat and looked at the phone some more. Detectives get a large volume of anonymous phone calls and letters and you'd be a quick candidate for a straitjacket if you took them very seriously. But the menace in this man's voice had been very credible. Acid in the eyes. I shivered.

I'd stirred a lot of pots and now one of them was boiling. But which one? Could poor, shriveled Aunt Rosa have gone demented and hired someone to threaten me? The idea made me laugh a little to myself and helped restore some mental balance. If not Rosa, though, it had to be the priory. And that was just as laughable. Hatfield would like to see me out of the case, but this wasn't his kind of maneuver.

Roger came in with a couple of glasses of Burgundy. "You're white, Vic. Who was that on the phone?"

I shook my head. "I wish I knew. His voice was so—so careful. Without accent. Like distilled water. Someone wants me away from the forgeries bad enough to threaten to pour acid on me."

He was shocked. "Vic! You must call the police. This is horrible." He put an arm around me. This time I didn't push him away.

"The police can't do anything, Roger. If I called and told them—do you have any idea of the number of crank calls that are made in this city in any one day?"

"But they could send someone around to keep an eye on you."

"Sure. If they didn't have eight hundred murders to investigate. And ten thousand armed robberies. And a few thousand rapes. The police can't look after me just because someone wants to make crank phone calls."

He was troubled and asked if I wanted to move in with him until things quieted down.

"Thanks, Roger. I appreciate the offer very much. But now I have someone worried enough to do something. If I stay here, I may just catch him doing it."

We'd both lost our interest in lovemaking. We finished the wine and I made us a *frittata*. Roger spent the night. I lay awake until after three, listening to his quiet, even breathing, trying to place that accentless voice, wondering who I knew who threw acid.

VIII

At the Old Forge

SUNDAY MORNING I drove the mile to Lotty's through a succession of residential one-way streets, turning often, waiting on the blind side of intersections. No one was following me. Whoever had called last night wasn't that interested. Yet.

Lotty was waiting for me in her building entryway. She looked like a little elf: five feet of compact energy wrapped in a bright green loden jacket and some kind of outlandish crimson hat. Her uncle lived in Skokie, so I went north to Irving Park Road and over to the Kennedy, the main expressway north.

As we drove past the grimy factories lining the expressway, a few snowflakes began dancing on the windshield. The cloud cover remained high, so we didn't seem to be in for a heavy storm. Turning right on the Edens fork to the northeast suburbs, I abruptly told Lotty about the phone call I'd had last night.

"It's one thing for me to risk my life just to prove a point, but it's not fair to drag you and your uncle into it as well. The odds are it was just an angry call. But if not—you need to know the risk ahead of time. And make your own decision."

We were approaching the Dempster interchange. Lotty told me to exit east and drive to Crawford Avenue. It wasn't until I'd followed her directions and we were moving past the imposing homes on Crawford that she answered. "I can't see that you're asking us to risk anything. You may have a problem, and it may be exacerbated by your talking to my uncle. But as long as he and I don't tell anyone you've been to see him, I don't think it'll matter. If he thinks of anything you can use—well, I would not permit you in my operating room telling me what was and what was not too great a risk. And I won't do that with you, either."

We parked in front of a quiet apartment building. Lotty's uncle met us in the doorway of his apartment. He carried his eighty-two years well, looking a bit like Laurence Olivier in *Marathon Man*. He had Lotty's bright black eyes. They

61

twinkled as he kissed her. He half bowed, shaking hands with me.

"So. Two beautiful ladies decide to cheer up an old man's Sunday afternoon. Come in, come in." He spoke heavily accented English, unlike Lotty, who had learned it as a girl.

We followed him into a sitting room crammed with furniture and books. He ushered me ceremoniously to a stuffed chintz armchair. He and Lotty sat on a horsehair settee at a right angle to it. In front of them, on a mahogany table, was a coffee service. The silver glowed with the soft patina of age, and the coffee pot and serving pieces were decorated with fantastic creatures. I leaned forward to look at it more closely. There were griffins and centaurs, nymphs and unicorns.

Uncle Stefan beamed with pleasure at my interest. "It was made in Vienna in the early eighteenth century, when coffee was first becoming the most popular drink there." He poured cups for Lotty and me, offered me thick cream, and lifted a silver cover by its nymph-handle to reveal a plate of pastries so rich they bordered on erotic.

"Now you are not one of those ladies who eats nothing for fear of ruining her beautiful figure, are you? Good. American girls are too thin, aren't they, Lottchen? You should prescribe Sacher torte for all your patients."

He continued speaking about the healthful properties of chocolate for several minutes. I drank a cup of the excellent coffee and ate a piece of hazelnut cake and wondered how to change the subject gently. However, after pouring more coffee and urging more cakes on me, he abruptly took the plunge himself.

"Lotty says you wish to talk about engraving."

"Yes, sir." I told him briefly about Aunt Rosa's problems. I own a hundred shares of Acorn, a young computer company, given me in payment for an industrial espionage case I'd handled for them. I pulled the certificate out of my handbag and passed it to Uncle Stefan.

"I think most shares are printed on the same kind of paper. I'm wondering how difficult it would be to forge something like this well enough to fool someone who was used to looking at them."

He took it silently and walked over to a desk that stood in

front of a window. It, too, was an antique, with ornately carved legs and a green leather top. He pulled a magnifying glass from a narrow drawer in the middle, turned on a bright desk lamp, and scrutinized the certificate for more than a quarter of an hour.

"It would be difficult," he pronounced at last. "Perhaps not quite as difficult as forging paper money successfully." He beckoned me over to the desk; Lotty came, too, peering over his other shoulder. He began pointing out features of the certificate to me: The paper stock, to begin with, was a heavy-grade parchment, not easy to obtain. "And it has a characteristic weave. To fool an expert, you would need to make sure of this weave. They make the paper like this on purpose, you see, just to make the poor forger's life more difficult." He turned to grin wickedly at Lotty, who frowned in annoyance.

"Then you have the logo of the issuing company, and several signatures, each with a stamp over it. It is the stamp that is most difficult; that is almost impossible to replicate without smearing the ink of the signature. Have you seen those fake shares of your aunt's? Do you know what they did wrong?"

I shook my head. "All I know is that the serial numbers were ones that the issuing companies had never used. I don't know about these other features."

He snapped off the desk lamp and handed me back the certificate. "It's a pity you haven't seen them. Also, if you knew how the forger intended to use them, that would tell you how good, how—convincing—they had to be."

"I've thought about that. The only real use for a phony share would be as collateral. They're always examined closely by the banks at the time of sale.

"In this case, though, some real stocks were stolen. So the thief just needed to convince some priests and their auditors that they still had their assets. That way it wouldn't be like an ordinary theft where you'd know just when the stuff was taken and who had had access to it since you last saw it."

"Well, I'm sorry I can tell you nothing else, young lady. But surely you will have another piece of cake before you go."

I sat back down and took a piece of apricot-almond torte. My arteries were screaming in protest as I ate a bite. "Actually, sir, there is something else you might know. The forgeries could have been done anytime in the last ten years. But suppose, for the sake of argument, they were made relatively recently. How could I find out who did them? Assuming he— or she—worked in the Chicago area?"

He was gravely silent for a long minute. Then he spoke quietly. "Lottchen has told you about my past, how I created twenty-dollar bills. Masterpieces, really," he said with a return of his more jovial manner. "Considering I made all my own equipment.

"There are really two breeds of forger, Miss Warshawski. Independent artisans like me. And those who work for an organization. Now here you have someone who has done the work at another person's request. Unless you believe that the same person who created the new stole and disposed of the old. Really, what you want is not the—the master engraver, but his client. Am I not right?"

I nodded.

"Well, I cannot help you with finding this engraver. We independent artisans tend not to—to make public our handiwork and I am not part of a network of forgers. But perhaps I could help you find the client."

"How?" Lotty asked before I could.

"By making up such a piece and letting it be known that I have one for sale."

I thought about it. "It might work. But you'd be running a terrible risk. Even with my most persuasive intervention, it would be hard to convince the feds that your motives were pure. And remember that the people who ordered these things might be violent—I've already had a threatening phone call. If they found out you were doublecrossing them, their justice would be even harder to take than a stint at Fort Leavenworth."

Uncle Stefan leaned over and clasped one of my hands. "Young lady, I am an old man. Although I enjoy life, my fear of death has passed. And such an occupation would be rejuvenating for me."

Lotty interrupted with some vigorous arguments of her own. Their discussion got quite heated and moved into German, until Lotty said disgustedly in English, "On your grave we will put a marker reading 'He died stubborn.'"

After that, Uncle Stefan and I discussed practical details. He would need to keep my Acorn certificate and get some others. He would find any supplies he needed and send me the bills. To be on the safe side, in case my anonymous caller really meant business, he wouldn't phone me. If he needed to talk to me, he'd run an ad in the *Herald-Star*. Unfortunately, he couldn't promise very speedy results.

"You must resign yourself to weeks, perhaps many weeks, not days, my dear Miss Warshawski."

Lotty and I left amid mutual protestations of goodwill—at least between Uncle Stefan and me. Lotty was a little frosty. As we got into the car she said, "I suppose I could call you in to consult on geriatric cases. You could think of criminal enterprises that would bring adventure and the flush of youth back to people worried about making ends meet on Social Security."

I drove over to Route 41, the old highway connecting Chicago and the North Shore. Nowadays it offered a quiet, pretty drive past stately homes and the lake. "I'm sorry, Lotty. I didn't go there with anything more than the hope that your uncle might know who's who in Chicago forging . Personally, I think his idea is a long shot. If he can do the job and make some contacts, how likely is it he'll come up with the right people? But it's a clever idea, and better than anything I can think of. Anyway, I'd certainly rather have a charming criminal as my only Chicago relative than an honest bitch; if you're too upset, I'll trade you Rosa for Stefan."

Lotty laughed at that and we made the drive back to Chicago peaceably, stopping on the far North Side for a Thai dinner. I dropped Lotty at her apartment and went on home to call my answering service. A Father Carroll had phoned, and so, too, had Murray Ryerson from the *Star*.

I tried the priory first. "They told me you were by here yesterday, Miss Warshawski. I'm sorry I couldn't see you then. I don't know if you've heard, but we had some rather extraordinary news this morning: We found the original certificates."

I stood momentarily stunned. "That *is* extraordinary," I finally said. "Where did they turn up?"

"They were on the altar this morning when we began celebrating mass." Since well over a hundred people had legitimate business in the priory chapel on Sunday mornings, no one could possibly say who might or might not have gone there early and returned the stolen goods. Yes, the FBI had sent someone out to take possession, but Hatfield had called at three to say that these shares were genuine. The FBI was keeping them awhile to run lab tests on them. And Carroll didn't know now if they'd ever get them back.

Out of curiosity I asked if Rosa had been to mass that morning. Yes, and looking grimly at anyone who tried to talk to her, Carroll assured me. Her son stayed away, but he usually did. As we started to hang up, he remembered my question about whether anyone at the priory had talked to Rosa about pulling out of the investigation. He had asked the fathers whom Rosa would most likely listen to and none of them had talked to her.

I called Murray next. He wasn't as full of the returned certificates as I expected. More recent news occupied his attention.

"I talked to Hatfield twenty minutes ago. You know what an arrogant, uncommunicative bastard he is. Well, I couldn't get shit out of him about the returned stocks and I asked every question in my arsenal and more besides. I got him in a corner finally and he as good as admitted the FBI is dropping the investigation. Putting it on the back burner, he said, cliché hack that he is. But that means dropping it."

"Well, if the real things have turned up, they don't need to worry so much."

"Yeah, and I believe in the Easter bunny. Come on, Vic!"

"Okay, wordly-wise newspaperman. Who's applying the screws? The FBI isn't scared of anyone except maybe J. Edgar's ghost. If you think someone's backing them off, who is it?"

"Vic, you don't believe that any more than I do. No organization is exempt from pressure if you know where the right nerves are. If you know something you're not telling I'll—I'll—" he broke off unable to think of an effective threat.

"And another thing. What was that crap you gave me about your poor frail old aunt? I sent one of my babies out to talk to her yesterday afternoon and some fat goon who claimed he was the son practically broke my gal's foot in the door. Then the Vignelli woman joined him in the hall and treated her to some high-level swearing on newspapers in general and the *Star* in particular."

I laughed softly. "Okay, Rosa! Two points for our side."

"Goddamn it, Vic, why'd you sic me onto her?"

"I don't know," I said irritably. "To see if she'd be as nasty to anyone else as she is to me? To see if you could learn something she wouldn't tell me? I don't know. I'm sorry your poor little protégée had her feelings hurt, but she's going to have to learn to take it if she plans to survive in your game." I started to tell Murray that I, too, had been warned off the investigation, then held back. Maybe someone had brushed back the FBI. And maybe that someone had called me as well. If the FBI respected them, so should I. I bade Murray an absentminded good-night and hung up.

IX

Final Trade

THE SNOW HELD off overnight. I got up late to do my virtuous five miles, running north and west through the neighborhood. I didn't think anyone was watching me, but if they were, it was sensible to vary my route.

A little later I followed the same procedure in my car, looping the Omega north and west through the side streets, then hitting the Kennedy from the west at Lawrence. I seemed to be clean. Thirty miles south on the expressway, past the city limits, is the town of Hazel Crest. You cannot buy handguns in Chicago, but a number of suburbs do a flourishing legal business in them. At Riley's, on 161st Street, I showed them my private investigator's license and my certificate that proved I'd passed the state's exam for private security officers. These enabled me to waive the three-day waiting period and also to register the gun in Chicago; private citizens can't register handguns here unless they bought them before 1979.

67

I spent the rest of the day finishing up a few outstanding problems—serving a subpoena to a bank vice-president hiding unconvincingly in Rosemont, and showing a small jewelry store how to install a security system.

And I kept wondering who was backing off first Rosa and then the FBI. It wouldn't help to park in front of Rosa's and watch her. What I really needed was a tap on her phone. And that was beyond my resources.

I tried thinking about it from the other end. Who had I talked to? That was easy: the prior, the procurator, and the student master. I'd also told Ferrant and Agnes what I was doing. None of these five seemed a likely candidate for threatening either me or the FBI.

Of course, Jablonski could be that type of antiabortion fanatic who thinks it's a worse sin to have an abortion than to kill someone who promotes freedom of choice, but he hadn't struck me as particularly crazy. Despite Pelly's protests, the Catholic Church does carry a lot of clout in Chicago. But even if it could pressure the FBI out of the investigation, why would it want to? Anyway, a priory in Melrose Park was on the fringes of the Church power structure. And why would they steal their own stock certificates? Even assuming they were in touch with forgers the whole idea was too far out. I went back to my original theory—my phone call had come from a crank, and the FBI was backing out because it was understaffed and overworked.

Nothing happened to make me change my mind during the next several days. I wondered vaguely how Uncle Stefan was doing. If it weren't for the fact that there really had been a forgery, I would have put the whole thing out of my mind.

On Wednesday I had to go to Elgin to testify in a case being tried in the state appeals court there. I stopped in Melrose Park on my way back to town, partly to see Carroll, partly to see if a visit to the priory might tickle my threatening caller back to life. If it didn't, it would prove nothing. But if I heard from him again, it might show he was watching the priory.

It was four-thirty when I reached St. Albert's, and the friars were filing into the chapel for vespers and evening mass. Father Carroll came out of his office as I stood hesitating and gave me a welcoming smile, inviting me to join them for evening prayer.

I followed him into the chapel. Two rows of raised stalls faced each other in the middle of the room. I went with him to the back row on the left side. The seats were divided by arms raised between them. I sat down and slid back in the seat. Father Carroll gave me a service book and quietly pointed out the lessons and prayers they would be using, then knelt to pray.

In the winter twilight, I felt as though I had slipped back five or six centuries in time. The brothers in their white robes, the candlelight flickering on the simple wooden altar to my left, the few people coming in from the outside to worship in the public space divided from the main chapel by a carved wooden screen—all evoked the medieval Church. I was the discordant note in my black wool suit, my high heels, my makeup.

Father Carroll led the service, singing in a clear, well-trained voice. The whole service was sung antiphonally between the two banks of stalls. It's true, as Rosa said, that I'm no Christian, but I found the service satisfying.

Afterward, Carroll invited me back to his office for tea. Almost all tea tastes like stewed alfalfa to me, but I politely drank a cup of the pale green brew and asked him if he'd heard anything more from the FBI.

"They tested the shares for fingerprints and a lot of other things—I don't know what. They thought there might be dust or something on them that would show where the things had been stored. I guess they didn't find anything, so they're going to bring them back tomorrow." He grinned mischievously. "I'm making them give me an armed escort over to the Bank of Melrose Park. We're getting those things into a bank vault."

He asked me to stay for dinner, which was being served in five minutes. Memories of Kraft American cheese restrained me. On an impulse I invited him to eat with me in Melrose Park. The town has a couple of excellent Italian restaurants. Somewhat surprised, he accepted.

"I'll just change out of my robe." He smiled again. "The young brothers like to go out in them in public—they like people to look at them and know they're seeing a foreign breed. But we older men lose our taste for showing off."

He returned in ten minutes in a plaid shirt, black slacks, and a black jacket. We had a pleasant meal at one of the little restaurants on North Avenue. We talked about singing; I complimented him on his voice and learned he'd been a student at the American Conservatory before entering the priesthood. He asked me about my work and I tried to think of some interesting cases.

"I guess the payoff is you get to be your own boss. And you have the satisfaction of solving problems, even if they're only little problems most of the time. I was just out in Elgin today, testifying at the state court there. It brought back my early days with the Chicago public defender's office. Either we had to defend maniacs who ought to have been behind bars for the good of the world at large, or we had poor chumps who were caught in the system and couldn't buy their way out. You'd leave court every day feeling as though you'd just helped worsen the situation. As a detective, if I can get at the truth of a problem, I feel as though I've made some contribution."

"I see. Not a glamorous occupation, but it sounds very worthwhile . . . I'd never heard Mrs. Vignelli mention you. Until she called last week, I didn't know she had any family besides her son. Are there other relatives?"

I shook my head. "My mother was her only Chicago relative—my grandfather and she were brother and sister. There may be some family on my uncle Carl's side. He died years before I was born. Shot himself, actually—very sad for Rosa." I fiddled with the stem on my wineglass, tempted to ask him if he knew what lay behind Rosa's dark insinuations about Gabriella. But even if he knew, he probably wouldn't tell me. And it seemed vulgar to bring up the family emnity in public.

After I took him back to the priory I swung onto the Eisenhower back to Chicago. A little light snow had begun falling. It was a few minutes before ten; I turned on WBBM, Chicago's news station, to catch news and a weather forecast.

I listened vaguely to reports of failed peace initiatives in Lebanon, continued high unemployment, poor retail sales in December despite Christmas shopping. Then Alan Swanson's crisp voice continued:

Tonight's top local story is the violent death of a Chicago stockbroker. Cleaning woman Martha Gonzales found the body of broker Agnes Paciorek in one of the conference rooms in the offices of Feldstein, Holtz and Woods, where Miss Paciorek worked. She had been shot twice in the head. Police have not ruled out suicide as a cause of death. CBS news correspondent Mark Weintraub is with Sergeant McGonnigal at the Fort Dearborn Tower offices of Feldstein, Holtz and Woods.

Swanson switched over to Weintraub. I almost swerved into a ditch at Cicero Avenue. My hands were shaking and I pulled the car over to the side. I turned off the engine. Semis roared past, rattling the little Omega. The car cooled, and my feet began growing numb inside their pumps. "Two shots in the head and the police still haven't ruled out suicide," I muttered. My voice jarred me back to myself; I turned the motor on and headed back into the city at a sober pace.

WBBM played the story at ten-minute intervals, with few new details. The bullets were from a twenty-two-caliber pistol. The police finally decided to eliminate suicide since no gun was found by the body. Miss Paciorek's purse had been recovered from a locked drawer in her desk. I heard Sergeant McGonnigal saying in a voice made scratchy by static that someone must have intended to rob her, then killed her in rage because she didn't have a purse.

On impulse I drove north to Addison and stopped in front of Lotty's apartment. It was almost eleven: no lights showed. Lotty gets her sleep when she can—her practice involves a lot of night emergencies. My trouble would keep.

Back at my own apartment, I changed from my suit into a quilted robe and sat down in the living room with a glass of Black Label whiskey. Agnes and I went back a long way together, back to the Golden Age of the sixties, when we thought love and energy would end racism and sexism. She'd come from a wealthy family, her father a heart surgeon at one of the big suburban hospitals. They'd fought her about her friends, her life-style, her ambitions, and she'd won every battle. Relations with her mother became more and more strained. I would have to call Mrs. Paciorek, who disliked me since I represented everything she didn't want Agnes to be. I'd have to hear how they always knew this would happen, working downtown where the niggers are. I drank another glass of whiskey.

I'd forgotten all about laying some bait for my anonymous phone caller until the telephone interrupted my maudlin mood. I jumped slightly and looked at my watch: eleven-thirty. I picked up a Dictaphone from my desk and turned it to "Record" before picking up the receiver.

It was Roger Ferrant, feeling troubled about Agnes's death. He'd seen it on the ten o'clock news and tried calling me then. We commiserated a bit; then he said hesitantly, "I feel responsible for her death."

The whiskey was fogging my brain slightly. "What'd you do—send a punk up to the sixtieth floor of the Fort Dearborn Tower?" I switched off the Dictaphone and sat down.

"Vic, I don't need your tough-girl act. I feel responsible because she was staying late working on this possible Ajax takeover. It wasn't something she had time for during the day. If I hadn't called her—"

"If you hadn't called her, she would have been there late working on another project," I interrupted him coldly. "Agnes often finished her day late—the lady worked hard. And if it comes to that, you wouldn't have called her if I hadn't given you her number, so if anyone's responsible, it's me." I took another swallow of whiskey. "And I won't believe that."

We hung up. I finished my third glass of scotch and put the bottle away in the built-in cupboard in the dining room, draped my robe over a chair back, and climbed naked into bed. Just as I turned out the bedside light, something Ferrant had said rang a bell with me. I called him back on the bedside phone.

"It's me, Vic. How did you know Agnes was working late on your project tonight?"

"I talked to her this afternoon. She said she was going to stay late and talk to some of her broker pals; she didn't have time to get to it during the day."

"In person or on the phone?"

"Huh? Oh, I don't know." He thought about it. "I can't remember exactly what she said. But it left me with the impression that she was planning to see someone in person."

"You should talk to the police, Roger." I hung up and fell asleep almost immediately.

X

Mixed Grill

NO MATTER HOW often I wake up with a headache, I never remember it the next time I'm putting away five or six ounces of whiskey. Thursday morning a dry mouth and pounding head and heart woke me at five-thirty. I looked disgustedly at myself in the bathroom mirror. "You're getting old, V.I., and unattractive. When your face has cracks in it the morning after five ounces of scotch, it's time to stop drinking."

I squeezed some fresh orange juice and drank it in one long swallow, took four aspirins, and went back to bed. The ringing phone woke me again at eight-thirty. A neutral young male voice said he was connected with Lieutenant Robert Mallory of the Chicago police department and would I be able to come downtown that morning and talk to the lieutenant.

"It's always a pleasure for me to talk to Lieutenant Mallory," I replied formally, if somewhat thickly, through the miasma of sleep. "Perhaps you could tell me what this is about."

The neutral young man didn't know, but if I was free at nine-thirty, the lieutenant would see me then.

My next call was to the *Herald-Star*. Murray Ryerson hadn't yet come in for the day. I called his apartment, and felt vindictive pleasure at getting him out of bed. "Murray, what do you know about Agnes Paciorek?"

He was furious. "I can't believe you got me out of bed to ask me that. Go buy the fucking morning edition." He slammed the phone down.

Angry myself, I dialed again. "Listen, Ryerson. Agnes Paciorek was one of my oldest friends. She got shot last night. Now Bobby Mallory wants to talk to me. I'm sure he's not calling for deep background on University Women United, or Clergy and Laity Concerned About Vietnam. What was in her office that makes him want to see me?"

"Hang on a second." He put the receiver down; I could hear his feet padding away down the hall, then water running and a woman's voice saying something indistinguishable. I ran into the kitchen and put a small pot of water on the stove, ground

73

beans for one cup of coffee, and brought cup, water, and filter back to my bedside phone—all before Murray returned.

"I hope you can hold off Jessica or whatever her name is for a few seconds."

"Don't be catty, Vic. It isn't attractive." I heard springs creaking, then a muffled "ouch" from Murray.

"Right," I said dryly. "Now tell me about Agnes."

Paper rustled, springs creaked again, and Murray's smothered voice whispered, "Knock it off, Alice." Then he put the mouthpiece in front of his lips again and began reading from his notes.

"Agnes Paciorek was shot at about eight last night. Two twenty-two bullets in the brain. Office doors not locked—cleaning women lock behind when they finish sixtieth floor, usually at eleven o'clock. Martha Gonzales cleans floors fifty-seven through sixty, got to floor at her usual time, nine-fifteen, saw nothing unusual on premises, got to conference room at nine-thirty, saw body, called police. No personal attack—no signs of rape or struggle. Police presume attacker took her completely by surprise or possibly someone she knew . . . That's the lot. You're someone she knew. They probably just want to know where you were at eight last night. By the way, since you're on the phone, where were you?"

"In a bar, waiting for a report from my hired gun." I hung up and looked sourly around the room. The orange juice and aspirin had dissipated the headache, but I felt rotten. I wasn't going to have time for running if I had to be in Mallory's office by nine-thirty, and a long, slow run was what I needed to get the poisons out of my system. I didn't even have time for a long bath, so I steamed myself under the shower for ten minutes, put on the crepe-de-chine pant-suit, this time with a man-tailored shirt of pale lemon, and ran down the stairs two at a time to my car.

If the Warshawski family has a motto, which I doubt, it's "Never skip a meal," perhaps in Old Church Slavonic, wreathed around a dinner plate with knife and fork rampant. At any rate, I stopped at a bakery on Halsted for coffee and a ham croissant and headed for Lake Shore Drive and the Loop. The croissant was stale, and the ham might have been rancid, but I plowed into it bravely. Bobby's little chats can go on for hours. I wanted to fortify myself.

Lieutenant Mallory had joined the police the same year as my dad. But my father, his better in brains, never had a lot of ambition, certainly not enough to buck the prejudice against Polish cops in an all-Irish world. So Mallory had risen and Tony had stayed on the beat, but the two remained good friends. That's why Mallory hates talking to me about crime. He thinks Tony Warshawski's daughter should be making a better world by producing happy healthy babies, not by catching desperadoes.

I pulled into the visitors' parking lot at the Eleventh Street station at nine-twenty-three. I sat in the car to relax for a few minutes, finish my coffee, clear my mind of all thoughts. For once, I had no guilty secrets. It should be a straightforward conversation.

At nine-thirty I made my way past the high wooden admissions desk where pimps were lining up to redeem last night's haul of hookers, and went down the hallway to Mallory's office. The place smelled a lot like St. Albert's priory. Must be the linoleum floors. Or maybe all the people in uniform.

Mallory was on the phone when I got to the cubicle he calls an office. His shirt sleeves were rolled up and the muscular arm that waved me in strained the white fabric. Before entering, I helped myself to coffee from a pot in the corner of the hall, then sat in an uncomfortable folding chair across the desk while he finished his call. Mallory's face betrays his moods. He turns red and blustery on days when I'm on the periphery of some crime; relaxed and genial means he's thinking of me as his old buddy Tony's daughter. Today he looked at me gravely as he hung up the phone. Trouble. I took a swallow of coffee and waited.

He flicked a switch on the intercom on his desk and waited silently while someone answered his summons. A young black officer, resembling Neil Washington from *Hill Street Blues*, came in shortly with a steno pad in one hand and a cup of coffee for Mallory in the other. Mallory introduced him as Officer Tarkinton.

"Miss Warshawski is a private investigator," Mallory

75

informed Tarkinton, spelling the name for him. "Officer Tarkinton is going to keep a record of our conversation."

The formality and the display of officialdom were supposed to intimidate. I drank some more coffee, puzzled.

"Were you a friend of Agnes Marie Paciorek?"

"Bobby, you're making me feel like I ought to have my attorney here. What's going on?"

"Just answer the questions. We'll get to the reasons quickly enough."

"My relations with Agnes aren't a secret. You can get the details from anyone who knows both of us. Unless you tell me what's behind this, I'm not answering any questions."

"When did you first meet Agnes Paciorek?"

I drank some more coffee and said nothing.

"You and Paciorek are described as sharing an alternate lifestyle. This same witness says you are responsible for introducing the dead woman to unconventional behavior. Do you want to comment on that?"

I felt my temper rising and controlled it with an effort. It's a typical police tactic in this type of interrogation—get the witness mad enough to start mouthing off. And who knows what self-constructed pitfalls you'll wander into? I used to see it all the time in the public defender's office. I counted to ten in Italian and waited.

Mallory clenched his fist tightly around the edge of his metal desk. "You and Paciorek were lesbians, weren't you?" Suddenly his control broke and he smashed his fist on the desk top. "When Tony was dying you were up at the University of Chicago screwing around like a pervert, weren't you? It wasn't enough that you demonstrated against the war and got involved with that filthy abortion underground. Don't think we couldn't have pulled you in on that. We could have, a hundred times over. But everyone wanted to protect Tony. You were the most important thing in the world to him, and all the time— Jesus Christ, Victoria. When I talked to Mrs. Paciorek this morning, I wanted to puke."

"Are you charging me with something, Bobby?"

He sat smoldering.

"Because if you're not, I'm leaving." I got up, putting an

76

empty Styrofoam cup on the corner of his desk, and started out the door.

"No you don't, young lady. Not until we get this straightened out."

"There's nothing to straighten out," I said coldly. "First of all, under the Illinois criminal code, lesbianism between consenting adults is not an indictable offense. Therefore it is none of your goddamned business whether or not Ms. Paciorek and I were lovers. Second, my relations with her are totally unconnected with your murder investigation. Unless you can demonstrate some kind of connection, I have absolutely nothing to say to you."

We locked gazes for an angry minute. Then Bobby, his face still set in hurt hard lines, asked Officer Tarkinton to leave. When we were alone he said in a tight voice, "I should have gotten someone else to handle the interrogation. But goddamn it, Vicki . . ."

His voice trailed off. I was still angry, but I felt grudging sympathy for him. "You know, Bobby, what hurts me is that you talk to Mrs. Paciorek, whom you never met before in your life, and believe a shopping list of calumny from her without even asking me, and you've known me since I was born."

"Okay, talk. I'm asking. Talk to me about the Paciorek girl."

I picked up the Styrofoam cup and looked inside. It was still empty. "Agnes and I met when we were both students in the college. I was prelaw and she was a math major who ultimately decided to get an MBA. I'm not going to try to describe to you what it felt like in those days—you don't have much sympathy for the causes that consumed us. I think sometimes that I'll never feel so—so alive again."

A wave of bittersweet memory swept over me and I closed my eyes tightly to keep tears at bay. "Then the dream started falling apart. We had Watergate and drugs and the deteriorating economy, and racism and sexual discrimination continued despite our enthusiasm. So we all settled down to deal with reality and earn a living. You know my story. I guess my ideals died the hardest. It's often that way with the children of immigrants. We need to buy the dream so bad we sometimes can't wake up.

"Well, Agnes's story was a little different. You met the parents. First of all, her father is a successful cardiac surgeon, pulls in a good half million a year at a conservative guess. But more important, her mother is one of the Savages. You know, old Catholic money. Convent of the Sacred Heart for prep school, then the deb balls and all the other stuff. I don't know exactly how the very rich live, just differently from you and me.

"Anyway, Agnes was born fighting it. She fought it through twelve years at Sacred Heart, and came to the U of C against their harshest opposition. She borrowed the money because they wouldn't pay to send her to a Jewish commie school. So it wasn't too surprising that she got swept up in all the causes of the sixties. And for both of us, feminism was the most important, because it was central to us."

I was talking more to myself than to Bobby; I wasn't sure how much he could really hear of what I was saying.

"Well, after Tony died, Agnes used to invite me up to Lake Forest for Christmas and I got to know the Pacioreks. And Mrs. Paciorek decided to hang all Agnes's weird behavior on me. It took her off the hook, you see—she wasn't a failure as a parent. Agnes, who figured as sweet and impressionable in this scenario, had fallen under my evil influence.

"Well, buy that or not as you choose, but keep in mind that sweet impressionable people don't build up the kind of brokerage business Agnes did.

"Anyway, Agnes and I were good friends at the University. And we stayed good friends. And in its way that was a small miracle. When our rap group followed the national trend and split between radical lesbians and, well, straights, she became a lesbian and I didn't. But we remained very good friends—an achievement for that era, when politics divided marriages and friends alike. It seems pointless now, but it was very real then."

Like a lot of my friends, I'd resented suddenly being labeled straight because of my sexual preferences. After all, we'd been fighting the straights—the prowar, antiabortion, racist world. Now overnight we were straights, too? It all seems senseless now. The older I get, the less politics means to me. The only thing that seems to matter is friendship. And Agnes and I had been good friends for a long time. I could feel tears behind my eyes and squeezed them tightly again. When I looked up at Bobby he was frowning at the desk top, drawing circles on it with the back of a ballpoint pen.

"Well, I've told you my story, Bobby. Now explain why you needed to hear it."

He continued to stare at the desk. "Where were you last night?"

My temper began rising again. "Goddamn it, if you want to charge me with murder, come out and do it. I'm not accounting for my movements otherwise."

"From the way the body looked, we believe she was seeing someone she expected, not a chance intruder." He pulled a leather-covered date book from the middle desk drawer. He flipped it open and tossed it to me. For Wednesday, January 18, Agnes had written: "V.I.W.," heavily underscored, followed by several exclamation points.

"Looks like a date, doesn't it." I tossed the book back to him. "Have you established that I'm her only acquaintance with those initials?"

"There aren't too many people in the metropolitan area with those initials."

"So the current theory reads that she and I were lovers and we had a falling-out? Now she's been living with Phyllis Lording for three years and I've been involved with God-knows-who-all since we left school, besides being married once—oh, yeah, I guess the theory would say I divorced Dick to keep Agnes happy. But despite all that, suddenly we decided to have a grand lovers' quarrel and because I'm trained in self-defense and carry a gun at times, I won by putting a couple of bullets through her head. You said hearing about me from Mrs. Paciorek made you want to puke; frankly, Bobby, listening to what goes on in the alleged minds of the police makes me feel like I've wandered into a really low-grade porn shop. Talk about puking . . . Anything else you want to know?" I stood up again.

"Well, you tell me why she wanted to see you. And were you there last night?"

I stayed on my feet. "You should have started with your last question. I was in Melrose Park last night with the Reverend

79

Boniface Carroll, O.P., Prior of St. Albert's Dominican Priory, from about four-thirty to about ten. And I don't know why Agnes wanted to talk to me—assuming I'm the one she wanted to talk to. Try Vincent Ignatius Williams."

"Who's he?" Bobby demanded, startled.

"I don't know. But his initials are V.I.W." I turned and left, ignoring Bobby's voice as it came bellowing down the corridor after me. I was furious; my hands were shaking with rage. I stood by the door of the Omega taking in deep gulps of icy air, slowly expelling it, trying to calm myself.

Finally I climbed into the car. The dashboard clock read eleven. I headed the Omega north into the Loop, parking at a public lot not too far from the Pulteney. From there I walked three blocks to Ajax's headquarters.

Their glass-and-steel skyscraper occupies sixty of the ugliest stories in Chicago. Located at the northwestern corner of Michigan and Adams, it overwhelms the Art Institute opposite. I've often wondered why the Blairs and the McCormicks allowed a monster like Ajax so near their favorite charity.

Uniformed security guards patrol Ajax's gray lobby. Their job is to keep miscreants like me from attacking officers like Roger Ferrant. Even after they'd checked with him and found he was willing to see me, they made me fill out a form for a visitor's pass. By that time my temper was so brittle that I scribbled a note under my signature promising not to mug any of their executives in the hallway.

Ferrant's office lay on the lake side of the fifty-eighth floor, which proved the importance of his temporary position.

An angular secretary in a large antechamber informed me that Mr. Ferrant was engaged and would see me shortly. Her desk, facing the open door, kept her from seeing Lake Michigan. I wondered if that was her own idea, or if Ajax management didn't think secretaries could be trusted to work if they saw the outside world.

I sat in a large, green-covered plush armchair and flicked through the morning's *Wall Street Journal* while I waited. The headline in "Heard on the Street" caught my eye. The *Journal* had picked up the rumor of a potential takeover for Ajax. The Tisch brothers and other likely insurance-company owners had been interviewed, but all of them professed total ignorance. Ajax chairman Gordon Firth was quoted as saying:

> Naturally we're watching the share price with interest, but no one has approached our shareholders with a friendly offer.

And that seemed to be all they knew in New York.

At a quarter to twelve the door to the inner office opened. A group of middle-aged men, mostly overweight, came out talking in a subdued hubbub. Ferrant followed, straightening his tie with one hand and pushing his hair out of his eyes with the other. He smiled, but his thin face was troubled.

"Have you eaten? Good. We'll go to the executive dining room on sixty."

I told him that was fine and waited while he put on his suit jacket. We rode in silence to the top of the building.

In the executive dining and meeting rooms, Ajax compensated for the stark unfriendliness of the lobby. Brocade drapes were looped back over gauze hangings at the windows. Walls were paneled in dark wood, possibly mahogany, and the recessed lighting picked up strategically placed bits of modern sculpture and painting.

Ferrant had his own table near a window, with plenty of space between him and any eavesdropping neighbors. As soon as we were seated, a black-uniformed waiter popped out of the ground to waft luncheon menus in front of us and ask for our drink orders. Last night's scotch was adding to the discomfort of my morning with Mallory. I ordered orange juice. I flipped indifferently through the menu. When the waiter came back with our drinks, I found I didn't have any appetite.

"Nothing for me now."

Ferrant looked at his watch and said apologetically that he was on a short timetable and would have to eat.

Once the waiter was gone, I said abruptly, "I spent the morning with the police. They think Agnes was expecting someone last night. You said the same thing. Did she tell you anything—anything at all that would help identify the one she was waiting for?"

"Barrett sent me the names of brokers here in Chicago

who've been trading in Ajax. It came in Monday's mail and I met Agnes for lunch on Tuesday and gave it to her then, along with the list of those the shares had been registered to. She said she knew a partner in one of the firms pretty well and would call him. But she didn't tell me who."

"Did you keep a copy of the names?"

He shook his head. "I've kicked myself a hundred times over for that. But I don't have the American photocopy habit. I always thought it was stupid, generated mounds of useless paper. Now I'm changing my mind. I can get Barrett to send me another copy, but I won't get it today."

I drummed my fingers on the table. Useless to be irritated about that. "Maybe her secretary can dig it up for me . . . When she talked to you yesterday, did she mention my name at all?"

He shook his head. "Should she have?"

"She had my initials in her date book. With Agnes, that means—meant—a reminder to herself. She didn't write down her appointments; she relied on her secretary to keep track of them. So my initials meant she wanted to talk to me." I'd been too angry with Mallory to explain that to him, too angry, as well, to tell him about Ferrant and Ajax.

"The police came up with an extraterrestrial theory about Agnes and me being lovers and my shooting her out of spite or revenge or something. It didn't make me too confiding. But I can't help wondering . . . You saw the story in this morning's *Journal*?"

He nodded.

"Well, here you've got a possible takeover bid. None of the principals—if there are any—step into the open. Agnes starts prying. She wants to talk to me, but before she does that she ends up dead."

He looked startled. "You don't really think her death has anything to do with Ajax, do you?"

The waiter brought him a club sandwich and he began eating automatically. "It really troubles me to think my questions might have sent that poor girl to her death. You pooh-poohed me last night for feeling responsible. Christ! I feel ten times as responsible now." He put his sandwich down and leaned across the table. "Vic, no company takeover is more valuable than a person's life. Leave it be. If there is a connection—if you stir up the same people—I just couldn't bear it. It's bad enough to feel responsible for Agnes. I scarcely knew her. But I just don't want to worry about that with you, too."

You can't touch someone in the executive dining room; every corporate officer I ever met was a born-again gossip. Word would spread through all sixty floors by nightfall that Roger Ferrant had brought his girlfriend to lunch and held hands with her.

"Thanks, Roger. Agnes and I—we're grown women. We make our own mistakes. No one else has to take responsibility for them. I'm always careful. I think you owe taking care of yourself to the friends who love you, and I don't want to cause my friends any grief . . . I'm not sure I believe in immortality or heaven or any of those things. But I do believe, with Roger Fox, that we all have to listen to the voice within us, and how easily you can look at yourself in the mirror depends on whether you obey that voice or not. Everyone's voice gives different counsel, but you can only interpret the one you hear."

He finished his drink before answering. "Well, Vic, add me to the list of friends who don't want to grieve over you." He got up abruptly and headed for the exit, leaving his sandwich half eaten on the table.

XI

Acid Test

THE FORT DEARBORN Trust, Chicago's largest bank, has buildings on each of the four corners of Monroe and LaSalle. The Tower, their most recent construction, is a seventy-five-story building on the southwest side of the intersection. Its curved, aqua-tinted glass sides represent the newest trend in Chicago architecture. The elevator banks are built around a small jungle. I skirted trees and creeping vines until I found the elevators to the sixtieth floor, where Feldstein, Holtz and Woods, the firm in which Agnes had been a partner, occupied the north half. I'd first been there when the firm moved in three years ago. Agnes had just been made a partner and

Phyllis Lording and I were helping her hang pictures in her enormous new office.

Phyllis taught English at the University of Illinois-Chicago Circle. I'd called her from the Ajax dining room before coming over to the Fort Dearborn Tower. It was a painful conversation, Phyllis trying unsuccessfully not to cry. Mrs. Paciorek was refusing to tell her anything about the funeral arrangements.

"If you're not married, you don't have any rights when your lover dies," she said bitterly.

I promised to come see her that evening and asked if Agnes had said anything, either about Ajax or why she wanted to see me.

"She told me she'd had lunch with you last Friday, you and some Englishman . . . I know she said he'd brought up an interesting problem . . . I just can't remember anything else now."

If Phyllis didn't know, Agnes's secretary might. I hadn't bothered phoning ahead to Feldstein, Holtz and Woods, and I arrived on a scene of extraordinary chaos. The inside of a brokerage firm always looks like a hurricane's just been through; brokers carve perilous perches for themselves inside mountains of documents—prospectuses, research reports, annual reports. The wonder is that they ever work through enough paper to know anything about the companies they trade in.

A murder investigation superimposed on this fire hazard was unbearable, even for someone with my housekeeping standards. Gray dusting powder covered the few surfaces not crowded with paper. Desks and terminals were jammed into the already overflowing space so work could go on while police cordoned off parts of the floor they thought might yield clues.

As I walked through the open area towards Agnes's office, a young patrolman stopped me, demanding my business. "I have an account here. I'm going to see my broker." He tried to stop me with further questions, but someone barked an order at him from the other side of the room and he turned his back on me.

Agnes's office was roped off, even though the murder had taken place on the other side of the floor. A couple of detectives were going through every piece of paper. I figured they might finish by Easter.

Alicia Vargas, Agnes's young secretary, was huddled miserably in a corner with three word-processor operators; the police had commandeered her rosewood desk as well. She saw me coming and jumped to her feet.

"Miss Warshawski! You heard the news. This is terrible, terrible. Who would do a thing like that?"

The word-processor operators all sat with their hands in their laps, green cursors blinking importunately on blank screens in front of them. "Could we go someplace to talk?" I asked, jerking my head toward the eavesdroppers.

She collected her purse and jacket and followed me at once. We rode the elevator back down to the coffee shop tucked into one corner of the lobby jungle. My appetite had come back. I ordered corned beef on rye—extra calories to make up for skipping lunch at the executive dining room.

Miss Vargas's plump brown face was swollen from crying. Agnes had picked her out of the typing pool five years ago when Miss Vargas was eighteen and on her first job. When Agnes was made partner, Miss Vargas became her personal secretary. The tears marked genuine grief, but probably also concern for her uncertain future. I asked her whether any of the senior partners had talked to her about her job.

She shook her head sadly. "I will have to talk to Mr. Holtz, I know. They will not think of it until then. I am supposed to be working for Mr. Hampton and Mr. Janville"—two of the junior partners—"until things are straightened out." She scowled fiercely, keeping back further tears. "If I must go back to the pool, or working for many men, I—I, well I will have to find a job elsewhere."

Privately I thought that was the best thing for her to do, but being in a state of shock is not the best time to plan. I set my energies instead to calming her down and asking her about Agnes's interest in the putative Ajax takeover.

She didn't know anything about Ajax. And the brokers' names given Agnes by Ferrant? She shook her head. If they hadn't come in the mail, she wouldn't have seen them in the normal course of things. I sighed in exasperation. I'd have to

85

get Roger to ask Barrett for a duplicate list if it didn't turn up in the office.

I explained the situation to Miss Vargas. "There's a strong possibility that one of the people on the list might have been coming to see Agnes last night. If so, that would be the last person to see her alive. It might even be the murderer. I can get another copy of the list, but it'll take time. If you can look through her papers and find it, it'd be a help. I'm not sure what will identify it. It should be on letterhead from Andy Barrett, the Ajax specialist. May even be part of a letter to Roger Ferrant."

She agreed readily enough to look for the list, although she didn't hold out much hope of finding it in the mass of papers in Agnes's office.

I settled the bill and we went back to the disaster area. The police pounced on Miss Vargas suspiciously: Where had she been? They needed to go over some material with her. She looked at me helplessly; I told her I'd wait.

While she talked to the police I nosed out Feldstein, Holtz's research director, Frank Bugatti. He was a young, hard-hitting MBA. I told him I'd been a client of Miss Paciorek. She'd been looking into insurance stocks for me.

"I hate to seem like a vulture—I know she's only been dead a few hours. But I saw in this morning's paper that someone might be trying to take over Ajax. If that's true, the price should keep going up, shouldn't it? Maybe this is a good time to get into the stock. I was thinking of ten thousand shares. Agnes was going to check with you and see what you know about it."

At today's prices, a customer buying ten thousand shares had a good half million to throw around. Bugatti treated me with commensurate respect. He took me into an office made tiny by piles of paper and told me all he knew about a potential Ajax takeover: nothing. After twenty minutes of discoursing on the insurance industry and other irrelevancies, he offered to introduce me to one of the other partners who would be glad to do business with me. I told him I needed some time to adjust to the shock of Miss Paciorek's death, but thanked him profusely for his help.

Miss Vargas was back at her makeshift desk when I returned

to the floor. She shook her head worriedly when I appeared. "I find no list of the kind you're looking for. At least not on top of her desk. I'll keep looking if the police let me back in her office"—she made a contemptuous face—"but maybe you should get the names elsewhere if you can."

I agreed and called Roger from her phone. He was in a meeting. I told the secretary this was more important than any meeting he could be in and finally bullied her into bringing him to the phone. "I won't keep you, Roger, but I'd like another copy of those names you gave Agnes. Can you call Barrett and ask him to express mail them to you? Or to me? I could get them on Saturday if he sent them out tomorrow morning."

"Of course! I should have thought of that myself. I'll call him right now."

Miss Vargas was still staring at me hopefully. I thanked her for her help and told her I'd be in touch. When I walked past Agnes's roped-off office I saw the detectives still toiling away at papers. It made me glad to be a private investigator.

That was about the only thing I was glad about all day. It was four o'clock and snowing when I left the Dearborn Tower. By the time I picked up the Omega the traffic had congealed; early commuters trying to escape expressway traffic had immobilized the Loop.

I wished I hadn't agreed to stop in on Phyllis Lording. I'd started the day exhausted; by the time I'd left Mallory's office at eleven I was ready for bed.

As it turned out, I wasn't sorry I went. Phyllis needed help dealing with Mrs. Paciorek. I was one of her few friends who knew Agnes's mother and we talked long and sensibly about the best way to treat neurotics.

Phyllis was a quiet, thin woman several years older than Agnes and me. "It's not that I feel possessive about Agnes. I know she loved me—I don't need to own her dead body. But I have to go to the funeral. It's the only way to make her death real."

I understood the truth of that and promised to get the details from the police if Mrs. Paciorek wouldn't reveal them to me.

Phyllis's apartment was on Chestnut and the Drive, a very posh neighborhood just north of the Loop overlooking Lake Michigan. Phyllis also felt depressed because she knew she couldn't afford to keep the place on her salary as a professor. I sympathized with her, but I was pretty sure Agnes had left her a substantial bequest. She'd asked me to lunch one day last summer shortly after she'd redone her will. I wondered idly if the Pacioreks would try to overturn it.

It was close to seven when I finally left, turning down Phyllis's offer of supper. I had been too overloaded with people for one day. I needed to be alone. Besides, Phyllis believed eating was just a duty you owed your body to keep it alive. She maintained hers with cottage cheese, spinach, and an occasional boiled egg. I needed comfort food tonight.

I drove slowly north. The thickly falling snow coagulated the traffic even after rush hour. All food starting with *p* is comfort food, I thought: pasta, potato chips, pretzels, peanut butter, pastrami, pizza, pastry . . . By the time I reached the Belmont exit I had quite a list and had calmed the top layer of frazzle off my mind.

I needed to call Lotty, I realized. By now she would have heard the news about Agnes and would want to discuss it. Remembering Lotty made me think of her uncle Stefan and the counterfeit securities. That reminded me in turn of my anonymous phone caller. Alone in the snowy night his cultured voice, weirdly devoid of any regional accent, seemed full of menace. As I parked the Omega and headed into my apartment building, I felt frail and very lonely.

The stairwell lights were out. This was not unusual—our building super was lazy at best, drunk at worst. When his grandson didn't come round, a light often went unchanged until one of the tenants gave up in exasperation and took care of it.

Normally, I would have made my way up the stairs in the dark but the night ghosts were too much for me. I went back to the car and pulled a flashlight from the glove compartment. My new gun was inside the apartment, where it could do me the least good. But the flashlight was heavy. It would double as a weapon if necessary.

Once in the building I followed a trail of wet footprints to the second floor, where a group of De Paul students lived. The melted snow ended there. Obviously I'd let my nerves get the better of me, a bad habit for a detective.

I started up the last flight at a good clip, playing the light across the worn shiny stairs. At the half landing to the third floor, I saw a small patch of wet dirt. I froze. If someone had come up with wet feet and wiped the stairs behind him, he might have left just such a small, streaky spot.

I flicked off the light and wrapped my muffler around my neck and face with one arm. Ran up the stairs fast, stooping low. As I neared the top I smelled wet wool. I flung myself at it, keeping my head tucked down on my chest. I met a body half again as big as mine. We fell over in a heap, with him on the bottom. Using the flashlight I smashed where I thought his jaw should be. It connected with bone. He gave a muffled shriek and tore himself away. I pulled back and started to kick when I sensed his arm coming up toward my face. I ducked and fell over in a rolling ball, felt liquid on the back of my neck underneath the muffler. Heard him tearing down the stairs, half slipping.

I was on my feet starting to follow when the back of my neck began burning as though I'd been stung by fifty wasps. I pulled out my keys and got into the apartment as quickly as I could. Double-bolting the door behind me, I ran to the bathroom shedding clothes. I kicked off my boots but didn't bother with my stockings or trousers and leaped into the tub. Turning the shower on full force, I washed myself for five minutes before taking a breath.

Soaking wet and shivering I climbed out of the tub on shaking legs. The mohair scarf had large round holes in it. The collar of the crepe-de-chine jacket had dissolved. I twisted around to look at my back in the mirror. A thin ring of red showed where the skin had been partially eaten through. A long fat finger of red went down my spine. Acid burn.

I was shaking all over now. Shock, half my mind thought clinically. I forced myself out of wet slacks and pantyhose and wrapped up in a large towel that irritated my neck horribly. Tea is good for shock, I thought vaguely, but I hate tea; there wasn't any in my house. Hot milk—that would do, hot milk with lots of honey. I was shaking so badly I spilled most of it on the floor trying to get it into a pan, and then had a hard time getting the burner lighted. I stumbled to the bedroom, pulled the quilt from the bed, and wrapped up in it. Back in

89

the kitchen I managed to get most of the milk into a mug. I had to hold the cup close to my body to keep from spilling it all over me. I sat on the kitchen floor draped in blanketing and gulped down the scalding liquid. After a while the shakes eased. I was cold, my muscles were cramped and aching, but the worst was over.

I got stiffly to my feet and walked on leaden legs back to the bedroom. As best I could I rubbed Vaseline onto the burn on my back, then got dressed again. I piled on layers of heavy clothes and still felt chilly. I turned on the radiator and squatted in front of it as it banged and hissed its way to heat.

When the phone rang I jumped; my heart pounded wildly. I stood over it fearfully, my hands shaking slightly. On the sixth ring I finally answered it. It was Lotty.

"Lotty!" I gasped.

She had called because of Agnes, but demanded at once to know what the trouble was. She insisted on coming over, brusquely brushing aside my feeble protests that the attacker might still be lurking outside.

"Not on a night like this. And not if you broke his jaw."

She was at the door twenty minutes later. "So, *Liebchen*. You've been in the wars again." I clung to her for a few minutes. She stroked my hair and murmured in German and I finally began to warm up. When she saw that I'd stopped shivering she had me take off my layers of swaddling. Her strong fingers moved very gently along my neck and upper spine, cleaning off the Vaseline and applying a proper dressing.

"So, my dear. Not very serious. The shock was the worst part. And you didn't drink, did you? Good. Worst possible thing for shock. Hot milk and honey? Very good. Not like you to be so sensible."

Talking all the while she went out to the kitchen with me, cleaned the milk from the floor and stove, and set about making soup. She put on lentils with carrots and onions and the rich smell filled the kitchen and began reviving me.

When the phone rang again, I was ready for it. I let it ring three times, then picked it up, my recorder switched on. It was my smooth-voiced friend. "How are your eyes, Miss Warshawski? Or Vic, I should say—I feel I know you well."

"How is your friend?"

"Oh, Walter will survive. But we're worried about you, Vic. You might not survive the next time, you know. Now be a good girl and stay away from Rosa and St. Albert's. You'll feel so much better in the long run." He hung up.

I played the tape back for Lotty. She looked at me soberly. "You don't recognize the voice?"

I shook my head. "Someone knows I was at the priory yesterday, though. And that can only mean one thing: One of the Dominicans has to be involved."

"Why, though?"

"I'm being warned off the priory," I said impatiently. "Only they know I was there." A terrible thought struck me and I began shivering again. "Only they, and Roger Ferrant."

XII

Funeral Rites

LOTTY INSISTED ON spending the night. She left early in the morning for her clinic, begging me to be careful. But not to drop the investigation. "You're a Jill-the-Giant-Killer," she said, her black eyes worried. "You are always taking on things that are too big for you, and maybe one day you will take on one big thing too many. But that is your way. If you weren't living so, you would have a long unhappy life. Your choice is for the satisfied life, and we will hope it, too, is a long one."

Somehow these words did not cheer me up.

After Lotty left, I went down to the basement where each tenant has a padlocked area. With aching shoulders I pulled out boxes of old papers and knelt on the damp floor sorting through them. At last I found what I wanted—a ten-year-old address book.

Dr. and Mrs. Thomas Paciorek lived on Arbor Drive in Lake Forest. Fortunately their unlisted phone number hadn't changed since 1974. I told the person who answered that I would speak to either Dr. or Mrs. Paciorek, but was relieved to get Agnes's father. Although he'd always struck me as a cold, self-absorbed man, he'd never shared his wife's personal animosity toward me. He believed his daughter's problems stemmed from her own innate willfulness.

"This is V. I. Warshawski, Dr. Paciorek. I'm very sorry about Agnes. I'd like to come to her funeral. Can you tell me when it will be?"

"We're not making a public occasion of it, Victoria. The publicity around her death has been bad enough without turning her funeral into a media event." He paused. "My wife thinks you might know something about who killed her. Do you?"

"If I did, you can be sure I would tell the police, Dr. Paciorek. I'm afraid I don't. I can understand why you don't want a lot of people or newspapers around, but Agnes and I were good friends. It matters a lot to me to pay my last respects to her."

He hemmed and hawed, but finally told me the funeral would be Saturday at Our Lady of the Rosary in Lake Forest. I thanked him with more politeness than I felt and called Phyllis Lording to let her know. We arranged to go together in case the Knights of Columbus were posted at the church door to keep out undesirables.

I didn't like the way I was feeling. Noises in my apartment were making me jump, and at eleven, when the phone rang, I had to force myself to pick it up. It was Ferrant, in a subdued mood. He asked if I knew where Agnes's funeral was being held, and if I thought her parents would mind his coming.

"Probably," I said. "They don't want me there and I was one of her oldest friends. But come anyway." I told him the time and place and how to find it. When he asked if he could accompany me, I told him about Phyllis. "She probably isn't up to meeting strangers at Agnes's funeral."

He invited me to dinner, but I turned that down, too. I didn't really believe Roger would hire someone to throw acid at me. But still . . . I had eaten dinner with him the same day I'd made my first trip to the priory. It was the next day that Rosa decided to back out of the case. I wanted to ask him, but it sounded too much like Thomas Paciorek asking me on my honor as a Girl Scout if I'd helped kill his daughter.

I was scared, and I didn't like it. It was making me distrust my friends. I didn't know where to start looking for an acid thrower. I didn't want to be alone, but didn't know Roger well enough to be with him.

At noon, as I walked skittishly down Halsted to get a sandwich, an idea occurred to me that might solve both my immediate problems. I phoned Murray from the sandwich shop.

"I need to talk to you," I said abruptly when he came to the phone. "I need your help."

He must have sensed my mood, because he didn't offer any of his usual wisecracks, agreeing to meet me at the Golden Glow at five.

At four-thirty I changed into a navy wool pantsuit, and stuck a toothbrush, the gun, and a change of underwear in my handbag. I checked all the locks, and left by the back stairs. A look around the building told me my fears were unwarranted; no one was lying in wait for me. I also checked the Omega carefully before getting in and starting it. Today at least I was not going to be blown to bits.

I got stuck in traffic on the Drive and was late to the Golden Glow. Murray was waiting for me with the early edition of the *Herald-Star* and a beer.

"Hello, V. I. What's up?"

"Murray, who do you know who throws acid on people he doesn't like?"

"No one. My friends don't do that kind of thing."

"Not a joke, Murray. Does it ring a bell?"

"Who do you know had acid thrown at them?"

"Me." I turned around and showed him the back of my neck where Lotty had dressed the burn. "He was trying for my eyes but I was expecting it and turned away in time. The thrower's name is probably Walter, but the man who got him to throw it—that's who I want."

I told him about the threats, and the fight, and described the voice of the man who had called. "Murray, I'm scared. I don't scare easily, but—Jesus Christ! the thought of some maniac out there trying to blind me! I'd rather take a bullet in the head."

He nodded soberly. "You're stepping on the feet of someone with bunions, V. I., but I don't know whose. Acid." He shook his head. "I'd be sort of tempted to say Rodolpho Fratelli, but the voice doesn't sound right—he's got that heavy, grating voice. You can't miss it."

Fratelli was a high-ranking member of the Pasquale family. "Maybe someone who works for him?" I asked.

He shrugged. "I'll get someone to look into it. Can I do a story on your attack?"

I thought about it. "You know, I haven't been to the police. I guess I'm too angry with Bobby Mallory." I sketched my interview with him for Murray. "But maybe it will make my anonymous caller a little more cautious if he sees there's a big universe out there keeping an eye open for him . . . The other thing is—I'm kind of embarrassed to ask this, but the truth is, I'm not up to a night alone. Can I crash with you?"

Murray looked at me for a few seconds, then laughed. "You know, Vic, it's worth the earful I'll get canceling my date just to hear you plead for help. You're too fucking tough all the time."

"Thanks, Murray. Glad to make your day." I wasn't liking myself too well when he went off to the telephone. I wondered what column this went under: taking prudent precautions, or being chicken?

We went to dinner at the Officers' Mess, a romantic Indian restaurant on Halsted, and then dancing at Bluebeard's. As we were climbing into bed at one, Murray told me he'd sicced a couple of reporters on digging up information about acid throwers.

I got up early Saturday and left Murray still asleep—I needed to change for Agnes's funeral. All was still quiet at my apartment, and I began to think I was letting fear get far too much the better of me.

Changing into the navy walking suit, this time with a pale gray blouse and navy pumps, I took off to collect Lotty and Phyllis. It was only 10 degrees out, and the sky was overcast again. I was shivering with cold by the time I got back into the car—I needed to replace my mohair shawl.

Lotty was waiting in her doorway dressed in black wool, for once dignified enough to be a doctor. She didn't say much on the drive down to Chestnut Street. When we got to the condo, she got out to fetch Phyllis, who didn't look as if she'd slept or eaten in the two days since I'd seen her last. The skin on her pale, fine-boned face was drawn so tightly I thought it might crack, and she had bluish shadows under her eyes. She was

94

wearing a white wool suit with a pale yellow sweater. I had a vague idea that those were mourning colors in the Orient. Phyllis is a very literary person and she would pay tribute to a dead lover with some kind of mourning that only another scholar would understand.

She smiled at me nervously as we headed back north toward Lake Forest. "They don't know I'm coming, do they?" she asked.

"No."

Lotty took exception to that. Why was I acting in a secretive way, which could only precipitate a scene when Mrs. Paciorek realized who Phyllis was.

"She's not going to do that. Graduates of Sacred Heart and St. Mary's don't have scenes at their daughters' funerals. And she won't take it out on Phyllis—she'll know I was the real culprit. Besides, if I'd told her ahead of time who I was bringing she might have instructed the bouncer not to seat us."

"Bouncer?" Phyllis asked.

"I guess they call them ushers in churches." That made Phyllis laugh and we made the rest of the drive considerably more at ease.

Our Lady of the Rosary was an imposing limestone block on top of a hill overlooking Sheridan Road. I slid the Omega into a parking lot at its foot, finding a niche between an enormous black Cadillac and an outsize Mark IV. I wasn't sure I'd ever find my car again in this sea of limos.

As we climbed a steep flight of stairs to the church's main entrance, I wondered how the elderly and infirm made it to mass. Perhaps Lake Forest Catholics were never bed- or wheelchair-ridden, but wafted directly to heaven at the first sign of disability.

Agnes's brother Phil was one of the ushers. When he saw me his face lit up and he came over to kiss me. "V.I.! I'm so glad you made it. Mother told me you weren't coming."

I gave him a quick hug and introduced him to Lotty and Phyllis. He escorted us to seats near the front of the church. Agnes's coffin rested on a stand in front of the steps leading up to the altar. As people came in they knelt in front of the coffin for a few seconds. To my surprise, Phyllis did so before joining us in the pew. She knelt for a long time and finally crossed herself and rose as the organ began playing a voluntary. I hadn't realized she was a Catholic.

One of the ushers, a middle-aged man with a red face and white hair, escorted Mrs. Paciorek to her place in the front row. She was wearing black, with a long black mantilla pinned to her head. She looked much as I remembered her: handsome and angry. Her glance at the coffin as she entered her pew seemed to say: "I told you so."

I felt a tap on my shoulder and looked up to see Ferrant, elegant in a morning coat. I wondered idly if he'd packed morning clothes just on the chance of there being a funeral in Chicago and moved over to make room for him.

The organ played Fauré for perhaps five minutes before the procession entered. It was huge and impressive. First came acolytes, one swinging a censer, one carrying a large crucifix. Then the junior clergy. Then a magnificent figure in cope and miter, carrying a crosier—the cardinal archbishop of Chicago, Jerome Farber. And behind him, the celebrant, also in cope and miter. A bishop, but not one I recognized. Not that I know many bishops by sight—Farber is in the papers fairly regularly.

I realized after the ceremony had begun that one of the junior priests was Augustine Pelly, the Dominican procurator. That was odd—how did he know the Pacioreks?

The requiem mass itself was chanted in Latin, with Farber and the strange bishop doing a very creditable job. I wondered how Agnes would have felt about this beautiful, if archaic, ritual. She was so modern in so many ways. Yet the magnificence might have appealed to her.

I made no attempt to follow the flow of the service through risings and kneelings. Nor did Lotty and Roger. Phyllis, however, participated completely, and when the bell sounded for communion I wasn't surprised that she edged her way past us and joined the queue at the altar.

As we were leaving the church, Phil Paciorek stopped me. He was about ten years younger than Agnes and me and had had a mild crush on me in the days when I used to frequent the Lake Forest house. "We're having something to eat at the house. I'd like it if you and your friends came along."

I looked a question at Lotty, who shrugged as if to say it

would be a mistake either way, so I accepted. I wanted to find out what Pelly was doing here.

I hadn't been to the Paciorek house since my second year in law school. I sort of remembered it as being near the lake, but made several wrong turns before finding Arbor Road. The house looked like a Frank Lloyd Wright building with a genetic malfunction—it had kept reproducing wings and layers in all directions until someone gave it chemotherapy and stopped the process.

We left the car among a long line of others on Arbor Road and went into one of the boxes that seemed to contain the front door. When I used to visit there, Agnes and I had always come in from the side door where the garage and stables were.

We found ourselves in a black-and-white marbled foyer where a maid took Lotty's coat and directed us to the reception. The bizarre design of the house meant going up and down several short marble staircases that led nowhere, until we had made two right turns, which took us to the conservatory. This room had been inspired by the library at Blenheim Palace. Almost as big, it contained a pipe organ as well as bookstacks and some potted trees. I wasn't sure why they called it a conservatory instead of a music room or a library.

Phil spotted us at the door and came over to greet us. He was finishing a combined M.D.-Ph.D. program at the University of Chicago. "Dad thinks I'm crazy," he grinned. "I'm going into neurobiology as a researcher, instead of neurosurgery where the money is. I think Cecelia is the only one of his children who has turned out satisfactorily." Cecelia, the second daughter after Agnes, was standing near the organ with Father Pelly and the strange bishop. At thirty she already looked like Mrs. Paciorek, including an imposing bosom under her expensive black suit.

I left Phil talking to Phyllis and skirted my way through the crowd to the organ. Cecelia refused to shake hands and said, "Mother told us you weren't coming." This was the same thing Phil had said when I met him at the church, except that he was pleased and Cecelia was angry.

"I haven't talked to her, Cecelia. I spoke with your dad yesterday and he invited me."

"She said she phoned you."

I shook my head. Since she wasn't going to introduce me, I said to the strange bishop, "I'm V. I. Warshawski, one of Agnes's old school friends. Father Pelly and I have met out at the Friary of Albertus Magnus." I half held out my hand, but dropped it when the bishop made no corresponding gesture. He was a lean, gray-haired man of perhaps fifty, sporting a purple episcopal shirt with a gold chain draped across it.

Pelly said, "This is the Right Reverend Xavier O'Faolin."

I whistled mentally. Xavier O'Faolin was a Vatican functionary, in charge of the Vatican's financial affairs. He'd been in the papers quite a bit last summer when the scandal broke over the Banco Ambrosiano and Roberto Calvi's tangled problems. The Bank of Italy believed O'Faolin might have had a hand in Ambrosiano's vanishing assets. The bishop was half Spanish, half Irish, from some Central American country, I thought. Heavy friends, Mrs. Paciorek had.

"And you were both old friends of Agnes's?" I asked a bit maliciously.

Pelly hesitated, waiting for O'Faolin to say something. When the bishop didn't speak, Pelly said austerely, "The bishop and I are friends of Mrs. Paciorek's. We met in Panama when her husband was stationed there."

The army had put Dr. Paciorek through medical school; he'd done his stint for them in the Canal Zone. Agnes had been born there and spoke Spanish quite well. I'd forgotten that. Paciorek had come a long way from a man too poor to pay his own tuition.

"So she takes an interest in your Dominican school in Ciudad Isabella?" It was an idle question, but Pelly's face was suddenly suffused with emotion. I wondered what the problem was— did he think I was trying to revive the Church-in-politics argument at a funeral?

He struggled visibly with his feelings and at last said stiffly, "Mrs. Paciorek is interested in a wide range of charities. Her family is famous for its support of Catholic schools and missions."

"Yes, indeed." The archbishop finally spoke, his English so heavily accented as to be almost incomprehensible. "Yes, we owe much to the goodwill of such good Christian ladies as Mrs. Paciorek."

Cecelia was biting her lips nervously. Perhaps she, too, was afraid of what I might say or do. "Please leave now, Victoria, before Mother realizes you're here. She's had enough shocks because of Agnes."

"Your father and brother invited me, Ceil. I'm not gate-crashing."

I pushed my way through a mink and sable farm glistening with diamonds to the other side of the room where I'd last seen Dr. Paciorek. About halfway there I decided the best route lay on the outside of the room through the corridor made by the potted plants. Skirting sideways against the main flow of traffic, I made my way to the edge. A few small knots of people were standing beyond the trees, talking and smoking desultorily. I recognized an old school friend of Agnes's from Sacred Heart, lacquered hard and encrusted with diamonds. I stopped and exchanged stilted pleasantries.

As Regina paused to light a fresh cigarette, I heard a man speaking on the other side of the orange tree we stood under. "I fully support Jim's policy in Interior. We had dinner last week in Washington and he was explaining what a burden these diehard liberals are making of his life."

Someone else responded in the same vein. Then a third man said, "But surely there are adequate measures for dealing with such opposition." Not an unusual conversation for a right-wing bastion of wealth, but it was the third speaker's voice that held me riveted. I was certain I'd heard it on the phone two nights ago.

Regina was telling me about her second daughter, now in eighth grade at Sacred Heart, and how clever and beautiful she was. "That's wonderful, Regina. So nice to see you again."

I circled the orange tree. A large group stood there, including the red-faced man who'd been ushering at the church, and O'Faolin. Mrs. Paciorek, whom I hadn't seen earlier, was standing in the middle, facing me. In her late fifties, she was still an attractive woman. When I knew her, she followed a rigorous exercise regimen, drank little, and didn't smoke. But years of anger had taken their toll on her face. Under the beautifully coiffed dark hair it was pinched and lined. When she saw me, the furrows in her forehead deepened.

99

"Victoria! I specifically asked you not to come. What are you doing here?"

"What are you talking about? Dr. Paciorek asked me to the service, and Philip invited me to come here afterward."

"When Thomas told me yesterday that you were coming I phoned you three times. Each time I told the person who answered to make sure you knew you were not welcome at my daughter's funeral. Now don't pretend you don't know what I'm talking about."

I shook my head. "Sorry, Mrs. Paciorek. You spoke with my answering service. I was too busy to phone in for messages. And even if I'd gotten your orders, I would still have come: I loved Agnes too much to stay away from her funeral."

"Loved her!" Her voice was thick with anger. "How dare you make filthy innuendos in this house."

"Love? Filthy innuendos?" I echoed, then laughed. "Oh. You're still stuck on the notion that Agnes and I were lovers. No, no. Just good friends."

At my laughter her face suffused with crimson. I was afraid she might have a stroke on the spot. The red-faced white-haired man stepped forward and took my arm. "My sister made it clear you're not wanted here. I think it's time you left." His heavy voice was not that of my threatening caller.

"Sure," I said. "I'll just find Dr. Paciorek and say goodbye to him." He tried to propel me toward the door but I shook his hand loose with more vigor than grace. I left him rubbing it and paused in the crowd behind Mrs. Paciorek, straining for the smooth, accentless voice of my caller. I couldn't find it. At last I gave up, found Dr. Paciorek, made some routine condolences, and collected Phyllis and Lotty.

XIII

Late Trades

FERRANT DROPPED BY late in the afternoon with a copy of Barrett's list. He was grave and formal and declined an offer of a drink. He didn't stay long, just looked over the brokers with me, told me none of those registered as buying the stock were Ajax customers, and left.

None of the firms listed were familiar to me, nor were the names of the stock registrants. In fact, most of the registrants were the brokers themselves. Barrett's cover letter to Roger explained that this was typically the case right after a stock changed hands—it generally took a month or so for the actual owner's name to be filed.

One company appeared several times: Wood-Sage, Inc. Its address was 120 S. LaSalle. Three of the brokers also had addresses there, a fact that seemed more interesting than it really was. When I looked it up on my detailed map of the Loop, I discovered that it was the Midwest Stock Exchange.

There wasn't much I could do with the list until Monday, so I put it in a drawer and concentrated on the NFL Pro Bowl. I sent out for a pizza for supper and spent the night restlessly, the Smith & Wesson loaded next to my bed.

Sunday's *Herald-Star* had a nice little story about my acid burn on the front page of *ChicagoBeat*. They'd used a picture taken last spring at Wrigley Field, a bright eye-catching shot. Readers who made it to Section III couldn't avoid seeing me. The personal ads included numerous thanksgivings to St. Jude, several lovers seeking reconciliations, but no message from Uncle Stefan.

Monday morning, I stuck my gun in a shoulder holster under a loose tweed jacket and drove the Omega into the Loop to begin a day at the brokerage houses. At the offices of Bearden & Lyman, Members of the New York Stock Exchange, I told the receptionist I had six hundred thousand dollars to invest and wanted to see a broker. Stuart Bearden came out to meet me personally. He was a dapper man in his middle forties, wearing a charcoal pinstripe suit and a David Niven mustache.

He led me through a maze of cubicles where earnest young people sat with phones in one hand, typing on their computer terminals with the other, to his own office in the far corner of the floor. He brought me coffee and treated me with the deference half a million dollars commands. I liked it. I'd have to tell more people I was rich.

Calling myself Carla Baines, I explained to Stuart that Agnes Paciorek had been my broker. I was getting ready to place an order for several thousand shares of Ajax when she'd warned me away from the stock. Now that she was dead I was looking

101

for a new broker. What did Bearden & Lyman know about Ajax? Would they agree with Ms. Paciorek's advice?

Bearden didn't blink or blench on hearing Agnes's name. Instead, he told me what a tragedy her death was; what a tragedy, too, that you couldn't feel safe working in your own office at night. He then punched away at his computer and told me the stock was trading at 54⅜. "It's been going up the last few weeks. Maybe Agnes had some inside news that the stock is cresting. Are you still interested?"

"I'm not in any hurry to invest. I guess I should make up my mind about Ajax in the next day or so, though. Do you think you could scout around and let me know if you hear anything?"

He looked at me closely. "If you've been thinking about this move for some time, you must know there's a lot of talk about a covert takeover bid. If that's the situation, the price will probably continue to go up until the rumor is confirmed one way or another. If you're going to buy, you should do it now."

I spread my hands. "That's why I don't understand Ms. Paciorek's advice. That's why I came here—to see if you knew why she'd warn me *not* to buy."

Bearden called his research director. The two had a short conversation. "Our staff hasn't heard anything to counter-indicate a buy order. I'd be very happy to take it for you this morning."

I thanked him but said I needed to do some more research before I made a decision. He gave me his card and asked me to let him know in a day or two.

Bearden & Lyman was on the fourteenth floor of the Stock Exchange. I rode the elevator down eleven floors to my next quarry: Gill, Turner & Rotenfeld.

By noon, having talked myself dry in three different broker-age offices, I beat a discouraged retreat to the Berghoff for lunch. Ordinarily I don't like beer, but their homemade dark draft is an exception. A stein and a plate of sauerbraten helped recoup my strength for the afternoon. Everyone had given me essentially the same information I'd gotten from Stuart Bearden. They knew the rumors about Ajax and they urged me to buy. None of them showed any dismay on hearing either Agnes's name or my interest in Ajax. I wondered if I'd taken the wrong approach. Maybe I should have used my own name.

Maybe I was barking up an empty tree. Perhaps a late-night burglar, intent on computer terminals, had found Agnes and shot her.

I continued to prove that a woman with six hundred thousand dollars to invest gets red-carpet treatment. I'd talked to no one but senior partners all morning and Tilford & Sutton was no exception: Preston Tilford would see me personally.

Like the firms I'd visited that morning, this one was medium-sized. The names of twenty or so partners were on the outer door. A receptionist directed me down a short hallway and through the trading room where a score of frantic young brokers manned phones and terminals. I picked my way through the familiar stacks of debris to Tilford's office in the far corner.

His secretary, a pleasant, curly-haired woman in her late forties, told me to go in. Tilford was nervous, his finger-nails bitten down to the quick. This was not necessarily a sign of guilty knowledge, at least not guilty knowledge about Agnes—most of the brokers I'd seen today were high-strung. It must be nerve-racking following all that money up and down.

He doodled incessantly as I pitched my tale to him. "Ajax, hmm?" he said when I'd finished. "I don't know. I have—had a lot of respect for Agnes's judgment. It so happens we're not recommending anyone to buy now, either, Ms., uh, Baines. Our feeling is that these takeover rumors have been carefully placed by someone trying to manipulate the stock. The bottom could crash out at any time. Now, if you're looking for a growth stock, I have several here that I could recommend for you."

He pulled a stack of prospectuses from a desk drawer and shuffled through them with the speed of a professional card dealer. I left with two hot prospects tucked into my bag and a promise to call again soon. On my way to number seven, I called my answering service and told them to take messages if anyone phoned asking for Carla Baines.

At four-thirty, I'd finished with Barrett's list. Except for Preston Tilford, everyone had recommended buying Ajax. He was also the only one who discounted the takeover rumors. That didn't prove anything one way or another about him. It might mean only that he was a shrewder broker than the rest—after all, only one man in one brokerage firm had recommended against buying Baldwin when its stock was soaring, and he was the only one out of the entire universe of security analysts who had been correct. Still, Tilford's recommendation against Ajax was the sole unusual incident of the day. So that was where I had to start.

Back home I changed out of my business clothes into jeans and a sweater. Pulled on my low-heeled boots. Before charging into action, I called the University of Chicago and undertook the laborious process of tracking down Phil Paciorek. Someone finally referred me to a lab where he was working late.

"Phil, it's V.I. There was someone at your house yesterday whose name I'd like to know. Trouble is, I don't know what he looks like, only how his voice sounds." I described the voice as best I could.

"That could be a lot of different people," he said dubiously.

"No accent at all," I repeated. "Probably a tenor. You know, most people have some kind of regional accent. He doesn't. No midwestern nasal, no drawl, no extra Boston r's."

"Sorry, V.I. Doesn't ring a bell. If something occurs to me, I'll call you, but that's too vague."

I gave him my phone number and hung up. Gloves, pea jacket, picklocks and I was set. Cramming a peanut butter sandwich into my coat pocket, I clattered down the stairs into the cold January night. Back at the Stock Exchange, a security guard in the hall asked me to sign in. He didn't want any identification so I put down the first name that came to me: Derek Hatfield. I rode to the fifteenth floor, got off, checked the stairwell doors to see that they weren't the kind that lock behind you, and settled down there to wait.

At nine o'clock a security guard came up the stairs from the floor below. I slid back into the hallway and found a ladies' room before he got to the floor. At eleven, the floor lights went out. The cleaning women, calling to each other in Spanish, were packing up for the night.

After they left, I waited another half hour in case anyone had forgotten anything. Finally leaving the stairwell, I walked down the hall to the offices of Tilford & Sutton, my boots clopping softly on the marble floor. I'd brought a flashlight, but fire-exit lights gave enough illumination.

104

At the outer door I shone my flashlight around the edges to make sure there was no alarm. Offices in a building with internal security guards usually don't have separate alarms, but it's better to be safe than sorry. Pulling my detective's vade mecum from my pocket, I tried a series of picklocks until I found one that worked.

No windows opened onto the outer office. It was completely dark, except for the green cursors flashing urgent messages on blank computer screens. I shivered involuntarily and ran a hand across the burn spot on the back of my neck.

Using my light as little as possible, I picked my way past desks and mounds of papers to Preston Tilford's office. I wasn't sure how often the security guards visited each floor and didn't want to risk showing a light. Tilford's door was locked, too, and took a few minutes of fumbling in the dark. I'd learned to pick locks from one of my more endearing clients in the public defender's office, but had never achieved the quickness of a true professional.

Tilford's door was solid wood, so I didn't have to worry about light shining through a panel as I did with the outer door. Closing it softly, I flipped a switch and took my bearings. One desk, two filing cabinets. Try everything first to see what's locked and look in the locked drawers.

I worked as quickly as I could, keeping my gloves on, not really sure what I was trying to find. The locked file cabinet contained files for Tilford's private customers. I picked a couple at random for close scrutiny. As far as I could tell, they were all in order. Not knowing what should be in a customer statement made it hard to know what to look for—high debit balances, maybe. But Tilford's customers seemed to keep on top of their accounts. I handled the pages carefully, leaving them in their original order, and refiled them neatly. I looked at the names one by one to see if any of his customers sounded familiar. Other than a handful of well-known Chicago business names I didn't see any I knew personally until I came to the P's. Catherine Paciorek, Agnes's mother, was one of Preston's clients.

My heart beating a little faster, I pulled out her file. It, too, was in order. Only a small amount of the fabled Savage fortune amassed by Agnes's grandfather was handled at Tilford &

Sutton. I noticed that Mrs. Paciorek had purchased two thousand shares of Ajax on December 2. That made me raise my eyebrows a little. Hers was a blue-chip portfolio with few transactions. In fact, Ajax was the only company she'd traded in 1983. Worth pursuing further?

I could find no other clients trading in Ajax stock. Yet Tilford had registered many more than Catherine Paciorek's two thousand shares. I frowned and turned to the desk.

This was carefully built, of dark mahogany, and the lock in the middle drawer was tough. I ended up scratching the surface as I fumbled with the picklocks. I stared at it in dismay, but it was too late now to worry.

Tilford kept an unusual collection in his private space: Besides a half-empty bottle of Chivas, which wasn't too surprising, he had a fine collection of hard-core porn. It was the kind of stuff that makes you feel we should work toward Shaw's idea of a disembodied mind. I grimaced, flipping through the whole stack to make sure nothing more interesting was interleafed.

After that, I figured Tilford owed me a drink and helped myself to some of the Chivas. In the bottom drawer I uncovered file folders of more clients, perhaps his ultrapersonal, supersecret accounts. There were nine or ten of these, including an organization called Corpus Christi. I dimly remembered reading something about it recently in *The Wall Street Journal*. It was a Roman Catholic lay group, made up primarily of wealthy people. The current pope liked it because it was conservative on such important points as abortion and the importance of clerical authority, and it supported right-wing governments with close Church ties. The pope liked the group so much, according to the *Journal*, that he'd appointed some Spanish bishop as its leader and had him—the Spaniard—reporting directly to him—the pope. This miffed the archbishop of Madrid because these lay groups were supposed to report to their local bishops. Only Corpus Christi had a lot of money and the pope's Polish missions took a lot of money, and no one was saying anything directly, but the *Journal* did some discreet reading between the ledger lines.

I flipped through the file, looking at transactions for the Corpus Christi account. It had started in a small way the previous March. Then it began an active trading program, which ran to several million dollars by late December. But no record existed of what it was trading in. I wanted it to be Ajax.

Tilford & Sutton was supposed to have taken largish positions in Ajax, according to Barrett. Yet the two thousand shares Mrs. Paciorek bought in December were the only trace of Ajax activity I'd seen in the office. Where were copies of Corpus Christi's statement showing what it was actually buying and selling? And why wasn't it in the file, as was the case with the other customers? Tilford's office didn't include a safe. Using my flashlight as little as possible, I surveyed the other offices. A large modern safe stood in a supply room, its door to be opened by someone who knew which eighteen numbers to punch on the electronic lock. Not me. If Corpus Christi's records were in there, they were in there for good.

The bells at the nearby Methodist Temple chimed the hour: two o'clock. I took the Corpus Christi and Mrs. Paciorek files out to the main room and hunted around for a photocopier. A large Xerox machine stood in the corner. It took a while to warm up. Using my flashlight surreptitiously, I copied the contents of the two files. To separate the pages I had to take off my gloves. I stuffed them in my back pocket.

I had just finished when the night watchman came by and looked in through the glass panel. Like a total imbecile, I had left Tilford's office door ajar. As the watchman fumbled with his keys, I hit the off button and looked around desperately for a hiding place. The machine had a paper cupboard built in underneath. My five-feet-eight frame fit badly, but I squeezed in and pulled the door as nearly shut as I could.

The watchman turned on the overhead lights. Through a crack in the door I watched him go into Tilford's office. He spent long enough in there to decide the place had been burglarized. His voice crackled dimly as he used his walkie-talkie to call for reinforcements. He made a circuit of the outer room, shining his flashlight in corners and closets. Apparently he thought the Xerox machine held nothing but its own innards: He walked past it, stopped directly in front of me, then returned to the inner office.

Hoping he would stay there until help arrived, I gently shoved the door open. Silently easing my cramped body onto

107

the floor, I crawled on hands and knees to the near wall where a window overlooked a fire escape. I slid the window open as quietly as possible and climbed out into the January night.

The fire escape was covered with ice. I almost ended my career forever as I skidded across its narrow iron platform, saving myself with a grab at the burning-cold railing. I'd been holding both the originals and photocopies of Tilford's documents, as well as my flashlight. These flew across the ice as I seized the guardrail. Cursing to myself, I crawled precariously across the platform retrieving documents, stuffing them into my jeans waistband with numbed fingers. I pulled the gloves from my back pocket and put them on while skidding my way down as quickly as possible to the floor below.

The window was locked. I hesitated only seconds, then kicked it in. Brushing glass fragments away with my sweat-shirted arm, I soon had a hole big enough to climb through.

I landed on top of a desk covered with files. These scattered in my wake. I kept bumping into desks and cabinets as I tried running to the far door. How could people get to their desks in the morning with so much clutter blocking their paths? I cracked the outer door, heard nothing, and made my way down the hall. I was about to open the stairwell door when I heard feet pounding on the other side.

Turning back down the hall, I tried every door. Miraculously one opened under my hand. I stepped inside onto something squishy and was hit in the nose by someone with a stick. Fighting back, I found myself wrestling a large mop.

Outside I could hear the voices of two patrolmen agreeing in low murmurs about which parts of the floor to guard. Trying to move quietly, I edged my way to the wall of the supply closet and ran into a coatrack. Clothes were hanging from it: the regulation smocks of the cleaning women. I fumbled in the dark, pulled my jeans off, stuck my documents inside the waistband of my tights, and pulled on the nearest smock. It came barely to my knees, and was miles too large in the shoulders, but it covered me.

Hoping I was not covered with paper, glass shards, or blood, and praying that these patrolmen had not dandled me on their knees thirty years ago, I swung open the closet door.

The policemen were about twenty feet from me, their backs

108

turned. "You!" I screamed, donning Gabriella's thick accent. They swirled around. "What goes on here, eh? I am calling manager!" I started off in righteous indignation to the elevator.

They were on me in an instant. "Who are you?"

"Me? I am Gabriella Sforzina. I work here. I belong. But you? What you doing here, anyway?" I started shouting in Italian, trusting none of them knew the words to "Madamina" from *Don Giovanni*.

They looked at each other uncertainly. "Take it easy, lady. Take it easy." The speaker was in his late forties, not far from pension time, not wanting any trouble. "Someone broke into one of the offices upstairs. We think he left by the fire escape. You haven't seen anyone on this floor, have you?"

"What?" I shrieked, adding in Italian, "Why do I pay taxes, eh, that's what I want to know—for bums like you to let burglars in while I'm working? So I can be raped and murdered?" I obligingly translated into English for them.

The younger one said, "Uh, look, lady. Why don't you just go on home." He scribbled a note on a pad and ripped off the sheet for me. "Just give that to the sergeant at the door downstairs and he'll let you out."

It was only then that I realized my gloves were lying with my jeans on the floor of the supply closet.

XIV

Fiery Aunts, Mourning Mothers

LOTTY WAS NOT amused. "You sound just like the CIA," she snapped, when I stopped by the clinic to tell her my adventure. "Breaking into people's offices, stealing their files."

"I'm not stealing the files," I said virtuously. "I wrapped them up and mailed them back first thing this morning. What troubles me from a moral standpoint is the jacket and gloves I left there—technically their loss is a business expense. Yet will the IRS turn me in if I itemize? I should call my accountant."

"Do that," she retorted. Her Viennese accent was evident, as always when Lotty was angry. "Now leave. I'm busy and have no wish to talk to you in such a mood."

The break-in had made the late editions. Police speculated

that the watchman interrupted the thief before he took anything of value, since nothing of value was missing. My prints are on file at the Eleventh Street station, so I hoped none showed up that I couldn't reasonably account for as part of my business visit to Tilford's office.

What would they make of Derek Hatfield's name on the Stock Exchange's sign-in register, I wondered. I had to figure out some way of finding out if they questioned Hatfield about it.

Whistling through my teeth, I started the Omega and headed out to Melrose Park. Despite Lotty's ill humor I was pleased with myself. Typical criminal failing—you carry off a coup, then have to brag about it. Sooner or later one of your bragees tells the police.

Snow was beginning to fall as I turned onto Mannheim Road. Small dry spitballs, Arctic snow, no good for snowmen. I was wearing long underwear under my navy pantsuit and hoped that would be enough protection against a minus 28 wind chill. Some time today I'd have to find an Army-Navy Surplus and get another pea jacket.

The Priory of Albertus Magnus loomed coldly through the driving pellets. I parked the car out of the wind as far as possible and fought my way to the priory entrance. The wind sliced through suit and underwear and left me gasping for air.

Inside the high-vaulted, stale hallway the sudden silence was palpable. I rubbed my arms and stamped my feet and warmed myself before asking the anemic ascetic at the reception desk to find Father Carroll for me. I hoped I was too early for evening prayers and too late for classes or confessions.

About five minutes later, as the building's essential chill began making me shiver, Father Carroll himself came down the hall. He was moving quickly, yet not hurrying, a man in control of his life and so at peace.

"Miss Warshawski. How nice to see you. Have you come about your aunt? She's back today, as she probably told you."

I blinked a few times. "Back? Back here, you mean? No, she hadn't told me. I came . . . I came to see if you could give me any information about a Catholic lay organization called Corpus Christi."

"Hmm." Father Carroll took my arm. "You're shivering—

110

let's get to my office and have a cup of tea. You can have a nice chat with your aunt. Father Pelly and Father Jablonski are there, too."

I followed him meekly down the hall. Jablonski, Pelly, and Rosa were sitting at a deal table in Pelly's outer office, drinking tea. Rosa's steel-colored hair was as stiffly waved as though made, in fact, from cast iron. She wore a plain black dress with a silver cross at the throat. She was listening attentively to Pelly as Carroll and I came in. At the sight of me her face changed. "Victoria! What are you doing here?"

The hostility was so obvious that Carroll looked astounded. Rosa must have noticed this, but her hatred was too fierce for her to care about externals; she continued to glare at me, her thin bosom heaving. I walked around the table to her and kissed the air by her cheek. "Hello, Rosa. Father Carroll says they've brought you back—as the treasurer, I hope? How splendid. I know Albert must be ecstatic, too."

She looked at me malevolently. "I know well I cannot make you be quiet, or stop you harassing me. But perhaps in the presence of these holy fathers you will at least not strike me."

"I don't know, Rosa. Depends on what the Holy Spirit prompts you to say to me. Don't bet on anything, though."

I turned to Carroll. "I'm Rosa's brother's only surviving granddaughter. When she sees me, it always chokes her up like this . . . Could I trouble you for that cup of tea?"

Glad of something to do to cover the tension, Carroll bustled with an electric kettle behind me. When he handed me a cup I asked, "Does this mean you've found who was responsible for the forgeries?"

He shook his head, his pale brown eyes troubled. "No. Father Pelly persuaded me, though, that Mrs. Vignelli really could not have been involved. We know how valuable her work is, and how much it means to her—it seemed unnecessarily cruel to make her sit at home for months or years."

Pelly put in, "Actually, we're not sure they will ever clear the matter up. The FBI seems to have lost interest. Do you know anything about it?" He looked questioningly at me.

I shrugged. "I get all my news from the daily papers. I haven't seen anything in there about the FBI dropping the investigation. What has Hatfield said to you?"

Carroll answered, "Mr. Hatfield hasn't told us anything. But since the real stocks turned up, they don't seem to be as interested in the investigation."

"Could be. Derek doesn't talk too much to me." I sipped some of the pale green tea. It was warming; that was the best that could be said for it. "I really came out here for a different reason. A friend of mine was shot last week. Saturday I learned Father Pelly was a friend of hers, too. Perhaps the rest of you knew her—Agnes Paciorek?"

Carroll shook his head. "Of course, we've all been praying for her this week. But Augustine was the only person out here who knew her personally. I don't think we can tell you much about her."

"I didn't come about her. Or not directly about her. She was shot while tracking down some information for an Englishman I introduced her to. That would make me feel responsible even if we hadn't been good friends. I think she was looking at something connected with a Catholic lay organization called Corpus Christi. I wanted to know if you could tell me anything about it."

Carroll smiled gently. "I've heard of it, but I couldn't tell you much about it. They like to operate secretly—so even if I were a member I couldn't tell you anything."

Rosa said venomously, "And why do you want to know, Victoria? To sling mud at the Church?"

"More mud? Sorry, Rosa. Just because I'm not a Catholic doesn't mean I go around persecuting the Church."

"No? Then why do you involve yourself in protest meetings on abortion? I saw you at that demonstration last year outside the diocesan offices."

"Rosa! Don't tell me you were out there with the fetus worshippers! Were you the old woman who spat at a girl in a wheelchair?"

Rosa's teacup clattered from the deal table to the uncarpeted linoleum floor. The institutional mug was too heavy to break, but tea spilled everywhere. She leaped to her feet, ignoring the tea dripping down the front of her black dress. *"Figlia di puttana!"* she shouted. "Mind your own business. Leave the business of good Catholics alone."

112

Carroll looked shocked, whether from the unexpected outburst or because he understood Italian I couldn't tell. He took Rosa's arm. "Mrs. Vignelli. You're letting yourself get overexcited. Maybe the strain of this terrible suspicion has been too much for you. I'm going to call your son and ask him to come pick you up."

He told Jablonski to get some towels and sat Rosa down in the room's one armchair. Pelly squatted on the floor next to her. He smiled chidingly. "Mrs. Vignelli. The Church admires and supports those who support her, but even ardor can be a sin if not held in check and used properly. A good Catholic welcomes all questions about the Church and the faith. Even if you suspect your niece of scoffing at you and your faith, treat her with charity. If you turn the other cheek long enough, that's how you'll win her. If you abuse her, you'll only drive her away."

Rosa folded thin lips into an invisible line. "You're right, Father. I spoke without thinking. You will forgive me, Victoria: I am old and small things affect me too much."

The charade of piety made me faintly ill. I smiled sardonically and told her that was fine; I could make allowances for her enfeebled state.

A young brother came in with an armful of towels. Rosa took these from him and cleaned herself, floor, and table with her usual angry efficiency. She smiled bleakly at Father Carroll. "Now. If you will let me use the phone I will call my son."

Pelly and Carroll ushered her into the inner office; I sat in one of the folding chairs at the table. Jablonski was eyeing me with lively curiosity.

"Do you usually rub your aunt the wrong way?"

I smiled. "She's old. Little things get to her."

"She's extremely difficult to work with," he said abruptly. "We've lost a lot of part-time people over the years because of her—no one can do anything perfectly enough for her. For some reason she listens to Gus, but he's the only one who can make her see reason. She even snaps at Boniface, and you have to be pretty thin-skinned not to get along with him."

"Why keep her then? What's all the anxiety to bring her back?"

"She's one of those indispensable battle-axes," he grimaced.

113

"She knows our books, she works hard, she's efficient—and we pay her very little. We'd never get anyone with her skill or dedication for what we can afford to give her."

I grinned to myself: served Rosa right for all her anti-feminist attacks to be the victim of wage discrimination herself.

She came out with Pelly, backbone as straight as ever, ignoring me pointedly as she said good-bye to Jablonski. She was going to wait for Albert in the entrance hall, she announced. Pelly took her elbow solicitously and escorted her out the door. The only man who could get along with Rosa. What a distinction. For a fleeting moment I wondered what her life had been like when Uncle Carl was alive.

Carroll came back into the outer office a few seconds later. He sat down and looked at me for a while without talking. I wished I hadn't let myself get caught up in Rosa's anger.

When he spoke, it wasn't about my aunt. "Do you want to tell me why you're asking about Corpus Christi and Agnes Paciorek?"

I chose my words carefully. "The Ajax Insurance Company is one of the country's largest property-casualty insurers. One of their officers came to me a couple of weeks ago concerned that a covert takeover bid might be in the offing. I talked to Agnes about it—as a broker she had ready access to trading news.

"The night she died, she called the man from Ajax to tell him she was meeting with someone who might have information about the stock. At the least, that person was the last who saw her alive. Since he—or she—hasn't come forward, it might even be the person who killed her."

Now came the tricky part. "The only clue I have is some notes she scribbled. Some of the words made it clear she was thinking about Ajax when she wrote them. Corpus Christi appeared on that list. It wasn't a memo or anything like that—just the cryptic comments you make when you're writing while you think. I have to start someplace, so I'm starting with these notes."

Carroll said, "I really can't tell you much about the organization. Its members guard their privacy zealously. They take literally the injunction about doing your good works in secret. They also take quasi-monastic vows, those of poverty and

114

obedience. They have some kind of structure with the equivalent of an abbot in all the locations where they have members, and their obedience is to the abbot, who may or may not be a priest. He usually is. Even so, he'd be a secret member, carrying out his parish duties as his regular work."

"How can they take vows of poverty? Do they live in communes, or monasteries?"

He shook his head. "But they give all their money to Corpus Christi, whether it's their salary or inheritance or stock-market earnings or whatever. Then the order gives it back to them according to their level of need, and also the kind of life-style they need to maintain. Say you were a corporate lawyer. They'd probably let you have a hundred thousand dollars a year. You see, they don't want any questions about why your living standard is so much lower than that of your fellow lawyers."

Pelly came back into the room at that point. "Lawyers, Prior?"

"I was trying to explain to Miss Warshawski how Corpus Christi works. I don't really know too much about it. Do you, Gus?"

"Just what you hear around. Why do you want to know?"

I told him what I'd told Carroll.

"I'd like to see those notes," Pelly said. "Maybe they'd give me some idea what the connection was in her mind."

"I don't have them with me. But the next time I come out I'll bring them." If I remembered to put something down on paper.

It was nearly four-thirty when I got back to the Eisenhower and the snow was coming down as furiously as ever. It was dark now, too, and nearly impossible to see the road. Traffic moved at about five miles an hour. Every now and then, I'd pass some poor soul who'd slid off the side completely.

As I neared the Belmont exit, I debated whether to go home and leave my next errand for an easier day. Two angry ladies in one afternoon was a little hard on the system. But the sooner I talked to Catherine Paciorek the sooner I'd get her out of my life.

I continued north. It was seven by the time I reached the Half Day Road exit.

Away from the expressway arteries the roads were unplowed. I almost got stuck a few times on Sheridan Road, and came to a complete halt just after turning onto Arbor. I got out and looked thoughtfully at the car. No one in the Paciorek house was likely to give me a push. "You'd better be moving by the time I come back," I warned the Omega, and set off to do the last half mile on foot.

I moved as quickly as possible through the deep snow, glad of earmuffs and gloves, but wishing desperately for a coat. I let myself into the garage and rang the bell at the side entrance. The garage was heated and I rubbed my hands and feet in the warmth while I waited.

Barbara Paciorek, Agnes's youngest sister, answered the door. She had been about six when I last saw her. A teenager now, she looked so much like Agnes had when I first met her that a small shock of nostalgia ran through me.

"Vic!" she exclaimed. "Did you drive all the way up from Chicago in this terrible weather? Is Mother expecting you? Come on in and get warm." She led me in through the back hallway, past the enormous kitchen where the cook was hard at work on dinner. "Daddy's stuck at the hospital—can't get home until they plow the side roads, so we're going to eat in about half an hour. Can you stay?"

"Sure, if your mother wants me."

I followed her across vaguely remembered hallways until we reached the front part of the house. Barbara led me into what the Pacioreks called the family room. Much smaller than the conservatory, perhaps only twenty or thirty feet across, the room held a piano and an enormous fireplace. Mrs. Paciorek was doing needlepoint in front of the fire.

"Look who's dropped in, Mother," Barbara announced as though she was bringing a pleasant surprise.

Mrs. Paciorek looked up. A frown creased her handsome forehead. "Victoria. I won't pretend I'm happy to see you; I'm not. But there is something I wanted to discuss with you and this saves me the trouble of phoning. Barbara! Leave, please."

The girl looked surprised and hurt at her mother's hospitality. I said, "Barbara, there's something you could do for me if you'd be good enough. While your mother and I are talking, could you find a filling station with a tow truck? My Omega is

116

stuck about a half mile down the road. If you call now, they should have a truck free by the time I leave."

I sat in a chair near the fire across from Mrs. Paciorek. She put her needlepoint aside with a tidy anger reminiscent of Rosa. "Victoria, you corrupted and destroyed the life of my oldest child. Is it any wonder that you are not welcome in this house?"

"Catherine, that is pig swill, and you know it."

Her face turned red. Before she could speak, I regretted my rudeness—today was my day for tangling with angry women.

"Agnes was a fine person," I said gently. "You should be proud of her. And proud of her success. Very few people achieve what she did, and almost no women. She was smart and she had guts. She got a lot of that from you. Be proud—feel pleased. Grieve for her."

Like Rosa, she had lived with her anger too long to want to give it up. "I won't flatter you by arguing with you, Victoria. It was enough for Agnes to know I believed in something for her to believe the opposite. Abortion. The war in Vietnam. Worst of all, the Church. I thought I had seen my family name degraded in every possible way. I didn't realize how much I could have forgiven until she announced in public that she was a homosexual."

I opened my eyes very wide. "In public! She actually announced it right in the middle of LaSalle Street? Out where every taxi driver in Chicago could hear her?"

"I know you think you're being very funny. But she might as well have screamed it in the middle of LaSalle Street. Everyone knew about it. And she was proud of it. Proud of it! Archbishop Farber even agreed to talk to her, to make her understand the degradation she was subjecting her body to. Her own family as well. And she laughed at him. Called him names. The kinds of things *you* would think of. I could tell you had led her into that, just as you led her into all her other horrible activities. And then—to bring that—that creature, that vile thing to my daughter's funeral."

"Just out of curiosity, Catherine, what did Agnes call Archbishop Farber?"

Her face turned alarmingly red again. "It's that kind of thing. That kind of attitude. You have no respect for people."

117

I shook my head. "Wrong. I have a lot of respect for people. I respected Agnes and Phyllis for example. I don't know why Agnes chose lesbian relations. But she loved Phyllis Lording, and Phyllis loved her, and they lived very happily together. If five percent of married couples brought each other that much satisfaction the divorce rate wouldn't be what it is . . . Phyllis is an interesting woman. She's a substantial scholar; if you read her book *Sappho Underground* you might get some understanding of what she and Agnes were all about in their life together."

"How can you sit there and talk about this—perversion and dare compare it with the sacrament of marriage?"

I rubbed my face. The fire was making me a little light-headed and sleepy. "We're never going to agree about this. Maybe we should just agree not to discuss it anymore. For some reason, it brings you solace to be furious at Agnes's way of living, and it brings you further pleasure to blame it on me. I guess I don't really care that much—if you want to be that blind about your daughter's character and personality and how she made her choices, that's your problem. Your views don't affect the truth. And they only make one person miserable: you. Maybe Barbara some. Perhaps Dr. Paciorek. But you're the main sufferer."

"Why did you bring her to the funeral?"

I sighed. "Not to piss you off, believe it or not. Phyllis loved Agnes. She needed to see her funeral. She needed that ritual . . . Why am I talking? You're not listening to what I'm saying, anyway. You just want to fuel your rage. But I didn't come all the way out here in a snowstorm just to talk about Phyllis Lording, although I enjoyed that. I need to ask you about your stock transactions. Specifically, how you came to buy two thousand shares of Ajax last month."

"Ajax? What are you talking about?"

"The Ajax Insurance Company. You bought two thousand shares on December second. Why?"

Her face had turned pale; the skin looked papery in the firelight. It seemed to me a cardiac surgeon would talk to his wife about the strain her wild mood changes put on her heart. But they say you notice least about the ones you're closest to.

Her iron control came through for her. "I don't expect you

118

to understand what it's like to have a lot of money. I don't know what two thousand shares of Ajax are worth—"

"Almost a hundred twenty thousand at today's prices," I put in helpfully.

"Yes. Well, that's a fraction of the fortune my father left in my care. It's very possible my accountants thought it was a good year-end investment. For transactions that small they wouldn't bother to consult me."

I smiled appreciatively. "I can understand that. What about Corpus Christi? You're an influential Catholic. What can you tell me about them?"

"Please leave now, Victoria. I'm tired and it's time for my dinner."

"Are you a member, Catherine?"

"Don't call me Catherine. Mrs. Paciorek is appropriate."

"And I would prefer you to call me Miss Warshawski . . . Are you a member of Corpus Christi, Mrs. Paciorek?"

"I never heard of it."

There didn't seem to be anything left to discuss at that point. I started to leave, then thought of something else and stopped in the doorway. "What about the Wood-Sage corporation? Know anything about it?"

Maybe it was just the firelight, but her eyes seemed to glitter strangely. "Leave!" she hissed.

Barbara was waiting for me at the end of the hallway where it angled off toward the back of the house. "Your car's in the garage, Vic."

I smiled at her gratefully. How could she have grown up so sane and cheerful with such a mother? "How much do I owe you? Twenty-five?"

She shook her head. "Nothing. I—I'm sorry Mother's so rude to you."

"So you're making up for it by towing my car?" I took out my billfold. "You don't have to do that, Barbara. What your mother says to me doesn't affect how I feel about you." I pushed the money into her hand.

She smiled with embarrassment. "It was only twenty."

I took the extra five back.

"Do you mind if I ask you something? Were you and Agnes, like Mother keeps saying—" she broke off, blushing furiously.

119

"Were your sister and I lovers? No. And while I love many women dearly, I've never had women lovers. It makes your mother happier, though, to think that Agnes couldn't make her own decisions."

"I see. I hope you're not angry, that you don't mind . . ."

"Nope. Don't worry about it. Phone me sometime if you want to talk about your sister. She was a good lady. Or give Phyllis Lording a call. She'd appreciate it very much."

XV

The Fire Next Time

IT WAS SO late when I got home that I didn't check with my answering service until the next morning. They told me then that Roger had called several times, and Murray Ryerson had also left a message. I tried Murray first.

"I think I found your friend Walter. A man calling himself Wallace Smith was treated last Thursday at St Vincent's for a broken jaw. He paid cash for the visit, which astounded the staff because he was there overnight and the bill came to more than a thousand dollars. Still, you know what they say—the best medical care today costs no more than the cheapest nuclear submarine."

"His address a fake?"

"I'm afraid so. Turned out to be a vacant lot in New Town. But we got a good description from the night nurse in the emergency room. Big surly guy with black curly hair, bald in front. No beard. I gave it to my gofer at the police. He said it sounded like Walter Novick. He's a stevedore and usually uses a knife. Might explain why he didn't do so well with acid."

I didn't say anything and Murray added penitently, "Sorry. Not funny, I guess. Anyway, he's a free lance, but he's done a lot of work for Annunzio Pasquale."

I felt an unaccustomed surge of fear. Annunzio Pasquale. Local mob figure. Murder, torture, you name it: yours for the asking. What could I possibly have done to arouse the interest of such a man?

"You there, Vic?"

"Yes. For a few more hours, anyway. Send irises to my funeral; I've never cared much for lilies."

"Sure, kid. You be careful who you open doors to. Look both ways before you cross Halsted . . . Maybe I'll run a little story on this—might make the mean streets a bit safer for you."

"Thanks, Murray," I said mechanically, and hung up. Pasquale. It had to be the forgeries. Had to be. If you wanted to create money and push it into circulation, who's the first person you'd hire? A Mafia man. Ditto for securities.

I don't frighten easily. But I'm not the Avenger—I can't take on organized crime with my own bare hands. If Pasquale really was involved with the forgeries I'd graciously concede the round. Except for one thing. My life had been threatened gratuitously. Not just my life—my eyesight, my livelihood. If I gave in to that, I'd never have a moment's peace with myself again.

I frowned at a stack of newspapers on the coffee table. There might be a way. If I could talk to Pasquale. Explain where our interests diverged. Explain that the matter of the securities would blow up in his face and just to leave that alone. I'd turn the other cheek if he would withdraw his protection from Novick.

I wondered how I could best get this message to the don. An ad in the *Herald-Star* would do the trick, but might bring the law down on me hard and heavy, too. Hatfield would love to be able to hold me on an obstructing federal justice charge.

I called a woman I know in the D.A.'s office. "Maggie— V. I. Warshawski. I need a favor."

"I'm on my way to court, V.I. Can it wait?"

"This won't take long—I just want to know some of Don Pasquale's fronts—restaurants, laundries, anyplace I might be able to get discreetly in touch with him."

A long silence at the other end. "You're not so hard up you'd work for him, are you?"

"No way, Maggie—I don't think I could stand up in court to an interrogation by you."

Another pause, then she said, "I guess I'm happier not knowing why you want to know. I'll call you when I'm free— maybe about three this afternoon."

I wandered restlessly around the apartment. I was sure it wasn't Pasquale who'd been on the phone to me. I'd seen him in the Federal Building once or twice, heard him speak in a thick Italian accent. Besides, say Pasquale was ultimately responsible for the forged stocks, responsible for creating them, he couldn't be the one who got them into the priory safe. Maybe he lived in Melrose Park, maybe he went to church at the priory. Even so, he'd have to have bought off a lot of people there to get at the safe. Boniface Carroll or Augustine Pelly as front men for the Mafia? Ludicrous.

Of course, there was always Rosa. I snorted with laughter at the image of Rosa as a Mafia moll. She'd keep Annunzio in line good and proper—yes, no pasta for you tonight, Annunzio, unless you burn my niece with acid.

I suddenly thought of my cousin Albert. I hadn't even included him in the picture before; he was so much in Rosa's shadow. But . . . he was a CPA and the mob could always use good CPAs. And here he was, fat, forty, unmarried, dominated by this truly awful mother. Maybe that would rouse some antisocial spirit in him—it would in me. What if Rosa had called me without his knowing it? Then afterward he talked her into sending me away. For some bizarre reason he had stolen St. Albert's stocks and replaced them with counterfeits, but when the investigation heated up he replaced them. He could have gotten the combination to the safe at any time from Rosa.

I continued to work up a case against Albert while cooking curried eggs with peas and tomatoes for lunch. I didn't know my cousin very well. Almost anything could go on behind that bloated, amorphous exterior.

Roger Ferrant called again while I was halfway through the curried eggs. I greeted him cheerfully.

"Vic. You're sounding more like yourself again. I want to talk to you."

"Sure. Have you learned something new about your Ajax takeover?"

"No, but there's something else I want to discuss with you. Can we have dinner tonight?"

On an impulse, still preoccupied with Albert, I not only

122

agreed but even offered to cook. After hanging up I cursed myself—that meant cleaning up the damned kitchen.

Feeling slightly aggrieved, I scrubbed out a collection of stale pots and plates. Made the bed. Trudged through unshoveled sidewalks to the grocery, where I bought a pot roast and cooked it like beef Bourguignon, with onions, mushrooms, salt pork, and of course, Burgundy. To show Roger I didn't suspect him anymore—or at least not at the moment—I decided to serve dinner wine in the red Venetian glasses my mother had brought from Italy. She had originally carried out eight, carefully wrapped in her underwear, but one of them broke several years ago when my apartment was ransacked. I now keep them in a locked cupboard in the back of my clothes closet.

When Maggie called at four-thirty, I realized one side benefit of heavy housework—it definitely keeps your mind off your troubles. I'd been too busy to think about Don Pasquale all afternoon.

Her voice on the phone brought the clutch of fear back to my stomach.

"I just took a brief glance through his files. One of his favorite meeting places is Torfino's in Elmwood Park."

I thanked her with as much heartiness as I could muster.

"Don't," she said soberly. "I don't think I'm doing you any favor telling you this. All I'm doing is speeding you on your way. I know you'd find it out for yourself—one of your newspaper pals would be glad to send you to your funeral just to generate a snappy story." She hesitated. "You were always a maverick when you were on the public defender's roster—I hated appearing against you because I never knew what outrageous defense you might rig up. I know you're a good investigator, and I know you have a lot of pride. If you're onto something that leads to Pasquale, call the police, call the FBI. They've got the resources to handle the Mob, and even they're fighting a losing battle."

"Thanks, Maggie," I said weakly. "I appreciate the advice. I really do. I'll think about it."

I got the number of Torfino's restaurant. When I called and asked for Don Pasquale, the voice at the other end said brusquely he'd never heard of such a man and hung up.

123

I dialed again. When the same voice answered, I said, "Don't hang up. If you should ever happen to meet Don Pasquale, I'd like to give him a message."

"Yes?" Grudgingly.

"This is V. I. Warshawski. I'd like a chance to talk to him." I spelled my last name slowly, giving him my phone number, and hung up.

By now my stomach was jumping in earnest. I wasn't sure I'd be able to handle either Roger or dinner, let alone a combination of the two. To relax, I went into the living room and picked out scales on my mother's old piano. Deep diaphragm breaths. Now, scales on a descending "Ah." I worked vigorously for forty-five minutes, starting to feel some resonance in my head as I loosened up. I really should practice regularly. Along with the red glasses, my voice was my legacy from Gabriella.

I felt better. When Roger arrived at seven with a bottle of Taittinger's and a bunch of white spider mums, I was able to greet him cheerfully and return his polite kiss. He followed me to the kitchen while I finished cooking. I wished now I hadn't cleaned up this morning. The place was such a mess I'd have to wash up again tomorrow.

"I lost track of you at Agnes's funeral," I told him. "You missed a good old scene with some of her relatives."

"Just as well. I'm not much of a scene person."

I dressed a salad and handed it to him and pulled the roast from the oven. We went into the dining room. Roger uncorked the champagne while I dished out the dinner. We ate without talking for a while, Roger staring at his place. At last I said, "You said there was something you wanted to discuss—not anything very pleasant, I take it."

He looked up at that. "I told you I'm not interested in scenes. And I'm afraid what I want to discuss has the makings of a row."

I set down my wineglass. "I hope you're not going to try to talk me into laying off my investigation. That would lead to a first-class fight."

"No. I can't say I'm crazy about it. It's the way you do it, that's all. You've closed me out of any discussion about that— or anything you're doing. I know we haven't spent that much time together so maybe I don't have the right to have expectations about you, but you've been damned cold and unfriendly the last few days. Since Agnes was shot, in fact, you've been really bitchy."

"I see . . . I seem to have stirred up some people who are a lot bigger than me. I'm afraid, and I don't like that. I don't know who I can trust, and that makes it hard to be open and friendly with people, even good friends."

His face twitched angrily. "What the hell have I done to deserve that?"

I shrugged. "Nothing. But I don't know you that well, Roger, and I don't know who you talk to. Listen. I guess I am being bitchy—I don't blame you for getting mad. I got involved in a problem that was puzzling but didn't seem too dangerous— my aunt's thing with the fake stock shares—and the next thing I knew someone tried pouring acid in my eyes." He looked shocked. "Yes. Right on this very landing. Someone who wants me away from the priory.

"I don't really think that's you. But I don't know where it's coming from, and that makes me draw away from people. I know it's bitchy, or I'm bitchy, but I can't help it. And then Agnes's being shot . . . I do feel kind of responsible, because she was working on your problem, and I sent you to her. Even if her being shot doesn't have anything to do with Ajax, which maybe it doesn't, I still feel responsible. She was working late, and probably meeting someone involved in the takeover. I know that's not very clear, but do you understand?"

He rubbed a hand through his long forelock. "But, Vic, why couldn't you say any of this to me? Why did you just draw back?"

"I don't know. It's how I operate. I can't explain it. It's why I'm a private eye, not a cop or a fed."

"Well, could you at least tell me about the acid?"

"You were here the night I got the first threatening phone call. Well, they tried making good on it last week. I anticipated the attack and broke the guy's jaw and took the acid on my neck instead of my face. Still, it was very—well, shocking. I thought I heard the man who made the phone call talking at Agnes's funeral. But when I tried to find him, I couldn't." I

125

described the voice and asked Roger if he remembered meeting anyone like that.

"His voice . . . it was like someone who didn't grow up speaking English and is disguising an accent. Or someone whose natural accent would be a strong drawl or something regional that he's trying to cover."

Roger shook his head. "I can't differentiate American accents too well, anyway . . . But, Vic, why couldn't you tell me this? You didn't really think I was responsible for it, did you?"

"No. Not really, of course. I just have to solve my own problems. I don't plan to turn into a clinging female who runs to a man every time something doesn't work out right."

"Do you think you could find some middle way between those two extremes? Like maybe talking your problems over with someone and still solving them yourself?"

I grinned at him. "Nominating yourself, Roger?"

"It's a possibility, yes."

"I'll think about it." I drank some more champagne. He asked me what I was doing about Ajax. I didn't think I should spread my midnight adventure at Tilford & Sutton too far—a story like that is very repeatable. So I just said I'd done a little digging. "I came across the name of a holding company, Wood-Sage. I don't know that they're involved in your problem, but the context was a bit unusual. Do you think you could talk to your specialist and see if he's heard of them? Or to some of your corporate investment staff?"

Roger half bowed across the table. "Oh, wow! Legman for V. I. Warshawski. What's the male equivalent of a gangster's moll?"

I laughed. "I don't know. I'll get you fitted out with a machine gun so you can do it in the best Chicago style."

Roger reached a long arm across the table and squeezed my free hand. "I'd like that. Something to tell them about in the box at Lloyd's . . . Just don't shut me out, V.I. Or at least tell me why you're doing it. Otherwise I start imagining I'm being rejected and get complexes and other Freudian things."

"Fair enough." I disengaged my hand and moved around the table to his chair. I don't blame men for loving long hair on women; there was something erotic and soothing about running my fingers through the long mop that kept falling into Ferrant's eyes.

Over the years I've noticed that men hate secrets or ambiguities. Sometimes I even feel like pampering them about it. I kissed Roger and loosened his tie, and after a few minutes' uncomfortable squirming on the chair, led him into the bedroom.

We spent several agreeable hours there and fell asleep around ten o'clock. If we hadn't gone to bed so early, my deepest sleep wouldn't have been over by three-thirty. I might have been sleeping too heavily for the smoke to wake me.

I sat up in bed, irritated, momentarily thinking I was back with my husband, one of whose less endearing habits was smoking in bed. However, the acrid smell in no way resembled a cigarette.

"Roger!" I shook him as I started scrambling around in the dark for a pair of pants. "Roger! Wake up. The place is on fire!"

I must have left a burner on in the kitchen, I thought, and headed toward it with some vague determination to extinguish the blaze myself.

The kitchen was in flames. That's what they say in the newspapers. Now I knew what they meant. Living flames enveloped the walls and snaked long orange tongues along the floor toward the dining room. They crackled and sang and sent out ribbons of smoke. Party ribbons, wrapping the floor and the hallway.

Roger was behind me. "No way, V.I.!" he shouted above the crackling. He grabbed my shoulder and pulled me toward the front door. I seized the knob to turn it and drew back, scorched. Felt the panels. They were hot. I shook my head, trying to keep panic at bay. "It's on fire, too!" I screamed. "Fire escape in the bedroom. Let's go!"

Back down the hall, now purple and white with smoke. No air. Crawl on the ground. On the ground past the dining room. Past the remains of the feast. Past my mother's red Venetian glasses, wrapped with care and taken from Italy and the Fascists to the precarious South Side of Chicago. I dashed into the dining room and felt for them through the smog, knocking

127

over plates, the rest of the champagne, finding the glasses while Roger yelled in anguish from the doorway.

Into the bedroom, wrapping ourselves in blankets. Shutting the bedroom door so opening the window wouldn't feed the hungry flames, the flames that devoured the air. Roger was having trouble with the window. It hadn't been opened in years and the locks were painted shut. He fumbled for agonizing seconds while the room grew hotter and finally smashed the glass with a blanketed arm. I followed him through the glass shards out into the January night.

We stood for a moment gulping in air, clinging to each other. Roger had found his pants and was pulling them on. He had bundled up all the clothes he could find at the side of the bed and we sorted out the leavings. I had my jeans on. No shirt. No shoes. One of my wool socks and a pair of bedroom slippers had come up in the bundle. The freezing iron cut into my feet and seemed to burn them. The slippers were moth-eaten, but the leather was lined with old rabbit fur and cut out the worst of the cold. I wrapped my naked top in a blanket and started down the slippery, snow-covered steps, clutching the glasses in one hand and the icy railing in the other.

Roger, wearing untied shoes, trousers, and a shirt, came hard on my heels. His teeth were chattering. "Take my shirt, Vic."

"Keep it," I called over my shoulder. "You're cold enough as it is. I've got the blanket . . . We need to wake up the kids in the second-floor apartment. Your legs are so long, you can probably hang over the edge of the ladder and reach the ground—it ends at the second floor. If you'll take my mother's goblets and carry them down, I'll break in and get the students."

He started to argue, chivalry and all that, but saw there wasn't time. I wasn't going to lose those glasses and that was that. Grabbing the snow-covered rung at the end of the escape with his bare hands, he swung over the edge. He was about four feet from the ground. He dropped off and stretched up a long arm for the goblets. I hooked my legs over one of the rungs and leaned over. Our fingertips just met.

"I'm giving you three minutes in there, Vic. Then I'm coming after you."

I nodded gravely and went to the bedroom window on the second story. While I pounded and roused two terrified youths from a mattress on the floor, half my mind was working out a puzzle. Fire at the front door, fire in the kitchen. I might have started a kitchen fire by mistake, but not one at the front door. So why was the bottom half of the building not on fire while the top half was?

The students—a boy and a girl in the bedroom, another girl on a mattress in the living room—were confused and wanted to pack their course notes. I ordered them roughly just to get dressed and move. I took a sweatshirt from a stack of clothes in the bedroom and put it on and bullied and harassed them out the window and down the fire escape.

The fire engines were pulling up as we half slid, half jumped, into the snow below. For once I was grateful to our building super for not shoveling better—the snow made a terrific cushion.

I found Roger in front of the building with my first-floor neighbors, an old Japanese couple named Takamoku. He'd gone in for them through a ground-floor window. The fire engines were drawing an excited crowd. What fun! A midnight fire. In the flashing red lights of the engines and the blue of the police cars, I watched avid faces gloating while my little stake in life burned.

Roger handed me my mother's wineglasses and I cradled them, shivering, while he put an arm around me. I thought of the other five, locked in my bedroom, in the heat and flames. "Oh, Gabriella," I muttered, "I'm so sorry."

XVI

No One is Lucky Forever

THE PARAMEDICS HUSTLED us off to St. Vincent's hospital in a couple of ambulances. A young intern, curly-haired and exhausted, went through some medical rituals. No one was badly hurt, although Ferrant and I both were surprised to find burns and cuts on our hands—we'd been too keyed up during our getaway to notice.

The Takamokus were badly shocked by the fire. They had

lived quietly in Chicago after being interned during World War II, and the destruction of their tiny island of security was a harsh blow. The intern decided to admit them for a day or two until their daughter could fly from Los Angeles to make housing arrangements for them.

The students were excited, almost unbearably so. They couldn't stop talking and yelling. Nervous reaction, but difficult to bear. When the authorities came in at six to question us, they kept shouting and interrupting each other in their eagerness to tell their tale.

Dominic Assuevo was with the fire department's arson unit. He was a bull-shaped man—square head, short thick neck, body tapering down to surprisingly narrow hips. Perhaps an ex-boxer or ex-football player. With him were a uniformed fireman and Bobby Mallory.

I'd been sitting in a torpor, anguished at the wreck of my apartment, unwilling to think. Or move. Looking at Bobby, I knew I'd need to pull my wits together. I took a deep breath. It almost didn't seem worth the effort.

The weary intern gave exhausted consent for the police to question us—except for the Takamokus, who had already been wafted into the hospital's interior. We moved into a tiny office near the emergency room, the hospital security-staff room, obligingly vacated by two drowsing security guards. The eight of us made a tight fit, the investigators and one of the students standing, the rest in the room's few chairs.

Mallory looked at me in disgust and said, "If you knew what you looked like, Warshawski. Half naked and your boyfriend no better. I never thought I'd see the day I'd be glad Tony was dead, but I'm thankful he can't see you now."

His words acted like a tonic. The dying war horse staggers to its feet when it hears a bugle. Police accusations usually rouse me.

"Thank you, Bobby. I appreciate your concern."

Assuevo intervened quickly. "I want the full story on what happened tonight. How you became aware of the fire, what you were doing."

"I was asleep," I explained. "The smoke woke me up. Mr. Ferrant was with me; we realized the kitchen was on fire, tried the front door and found it was on fire, too. We got out by the fire escape—I roused these kids, he got Mr. and Mrs. Takamoku. That's all I know."

Roger confirmed my story. We both vowed that the people we'd gotten up had been sound asleep at the time. Could they have been faking it? Assuevo wanted to know.

Ferrant shrugged. "They could have been, but they seemed pretty deep in sleep to me. I wasn't concerned about that kind of thing, Mr. Assuevo. Just to get them up and out."

After thrashing that out, Assuevo went on to explore our feelings about the landlord—did any of us bear a grudge, what kind of problems had we had with the apartment, how had the landlord responded. To my relief, even the overwrought students sensed where those questions were going.

"He was a landlord," one of the girls said, the thin, long-haired one who'd been in the living room. The other two chimed in their agreement. "You know, the place was clean and the rent was cheap. We didn't care about anything else."

After a few more minutes of that, Assuevo murmured with Bobby near the door. He came back and told the students they could leave.

"Why don't you go, too?" I said to Roger. "It's time you were getting down to Ajax, isn't it?"

Ferrant gripped my shoulder. "Don't be an ass, V.I. I'll call my secretary in a bit—it's only seven o'clock. We'll see this out together."

"Thank you, Mr. Ferrant," Assuevo said swiftly. "Since you were in the apartment at the time of the fire, we would have to ask you to stay, anyway."

Bobby said, "Why don't you explain how you two know each other and why."

I looked coldly at Mallory. "I can see where this is headed, and I don't like it one bit. If you are going to imply in any way that either Mr. Ferrant or I knew anything about the fire, we are going to insist on charges being brought before we answer any questions. And my attorney will have to be present."

Roger scratched his chin. "I'll answer any questions that'll help solve this problem—I assume everyone agrees the apartment was set on fire by an arsonist—but if you're charging me with breaking any laws, I'd better call the British consul."

131

"Oh, get off your high horse, both of you. I just want to know what you were doing tonight."

I grinned at him. "No, you don't, Bobby: It'd make you blush."

Assuevo stepped in again. "Someone tried to kill you, Ms. Warshawski. They broke the lock on the front door to get into the building. They poured kerosene on your apartment door and set fire to it. You want my opinion, you're lucky to be alive. Now the lieutenant and I gotta make sure, Ms. Warshawski, that there aren't some bad guys"—his eyebrows punctuated the remark to let me know that "bad guys" was facetious— "out there who are trying for you personally. Maybe it's just someone with a grudge against the landlord, and he goes after you as a sideline. But maybe it's against you, okay? And so maybe Mr. Ferrant here"—sketching a gesture at Roger—"is assigned to make sure you stay in the apartment tonight. So don't be such an angry lady. The lieutenant and I, we're just doing our job. Trying to protect you. Unless maybe you set the fire yourself, huh?"

I looked at Roger. He pushed the hair out of his eyes and tried straightening a nonexistent tie before speaking. "I can see you have to look into that, Mr. Assuevo. I've done my share of fire-claim investigations and I assure you, I know you have to explore every possibility. While you're doing that, though, maybe we can try to find out who actually set that fire." He turned to me. "Miss Warshawski, you don't think it could be the same person who threw—"

"No," I interrupted him firmly, before he could complete the sentence. "Not at all."

"Then who? If it was personally directed—no, not the people who shot Agnes?" Roger looked at Mallory. "You know, Miss Paciorek was murdered recently while looking into a takeover attempt for me. Now Miss Warshawski's trying to pick up that investigation. This is something you really need to look into."

Roger, you goon, I thought. Did that just occur to you? Mallory and Assuevo were talking in unison. "Threw what?" Bobby was demanding, while Assuevo said, "Who's Miss Paciorek?"

When they quieted down, I said to Bobby, "Do you want to explain Agnes Paciorek to Mr. Assuevo, Lieutenant?"

"Don't ride me, Warshawski," he warned. "We've had our discussion on that. If you or Mr. Ferrant has some hard evidence to show she was killed because she was looking into those Ajax buyers, give it to me and I'll follow it to the end. But what you've told me so far doesn't add up to more than the kind of guilt we always find with friends and relations—she was killed because I didn't do this or that or because I asked her to stay late or whatever. You have anything to add to that, Mr. Ferrant?"

Roger shook his head. "But she told me she was staying late to talk to someone about the sales."

Bobby sighed with exaggerated patience. "That's just what I mean. You're the college-educated one, Vicki. You explain to him about logic and moving from one argument to the other. She was working late on Ajax and she got shot. Where's the connection?"

"Ah," Assuevo said. "That stockbroker who was killed. My sister's husband's niece is a cousin of her secretary . . . Do you think there's a connection with the fire, Ms. Warshawski?"

I shrugged. "Tell me something about the arson. Does it have a signature you recognize?"

"It could be the work of any professional. Quick, clean, minimum fuel, no prints—not that we expect prints in the middle of January. No evidence left behind. It was *organized*, Ms. Warshawski. Organized. So we want to know who is organizing against you. Maybe the enemies of Ms. Paciorek?"

Mallory looked at me thoughtfully. "I know you, Vicki. You're just arrogant enough to go stirring that pot without telling me. What have you found?"

"It's not arrogance, Bobby. You made some really disgusting accusations the morning after Agnes died. I figure I don't owe you one thing. Not one name, not one idea."

His round face turned red. "You don't talk to me that way, young lady. If you obstruct the police in the performance of their duties, you can be arrested. Now what have you found out?"

"Nothing. I know who the Chicago brokers were for the big

133

blocks of Ajax sales the last six-seven weeks. You can get those from Mr. Ferrant here. That's what I know."

His eyes narrowed. "You know the firm of Tilford and Sutton?"

"Stockbrokers? Yeah, they're on Mr. Ferrant's list."

"You ever been to their offices?"

"I don't have anything to invest."

"You wouldn't have been there two nights ago, would you, *investigating* their Ajax sales?"

"At night? Stockbrokers do business during the day. Even I know that . . ."

"Yeah, clown. Someone broke into their offices. I want to know if it was you."

"There were eight or nine brokers on Mr. Ferrant's list. Were they all broken into?"

He smashed his fist on the table to avoid swearing. "It was you, wasn't it?"

"Why, Bobby? You keep telling me there's nothing to investigate there. So why would I break in to investigate something that doesn't exist?"

"Because you're pigheaded, arrogant, spoiled. I always told Tony and Gabriella they should have more children—they spoiled you rotten."

"Well, too late to cry about that now . . . Look, I've had a rough night. I want to find some place to crash and then try to get my life going again. Can I go back to the apartment and see if any of my clothes are salvageable?"

Assuevo shook his head. "We got a lot more to discuss here, Ms. Warshawski. I need to know what you're working on."

"Oh, yeah," Bobby put in. "Ferrant here started to ask if it was the same person who threw something, and you cut him off. Who threw what?"

"Oh, some kids on Halsted threw a rock at the car the other night—random urban violence. I don't think they'd set fire to my apartment just because they missed the car."

"You chase them?" Assuevo demanded. "You hurt them in some way?"

"Forget it," Bobby told him. "It didn't happen. She doesn't chase kids. She thinks she's Paladin or the Lone Ranger. She's stirred up something big enough to hire a professional torch,

134

and now she's going to be a heroine and not say anything about it." He looked at me, his gray eyes serious, his mouth set in a tight line. "You know, Tony Warshawski was one of my best friends. Anything happens to you, his and Gabriella's ghosts will haunt me the rest of my life. But no one can talk to you. Since Gabriella died, there isn't a person on this planet can get you to do something you don't want to do."

I didn't say anything. There wasn't anything I could say.

"C'mon, Dominic. Let's go. I'm putting a tail on Joan of Arc here; that's the best we can do right now."

After he left, the exhaustion swept over me again. I felt that if I didn't leave now I'd pass out in the chair. Still wrapped in the blanket, I forced myself to my feet, accepting Roger's helping hand gratefully. In the hallway, Assuevo lingered a moment to talk to me. "Ms. Warshawski. If you know *anything* about this arson attempt, and do not tell us, you are liable for criminal prosecution." He stabbed my chest with his finger as he talked. I was too tired even to become angry. I stood holding my glasses and watched him trot to catch up with Bobby.

Roger put an arm around me. "You're all done in, old girl. Come back to the Hancock with me and take a hot bath."

As we reached the outer door, he felt in his pockets. "I left my wallet on your dresser. No money for a cab. You have any?"

I shook my head. He ran across the parking lot to where Bobby and Assuevo were climbing into Bobby's police car. I staggered drunkenly after him. Roger demanded a lift back to my apartment so he could try to rummage for some money. And possibly some clothes.

The ride back down Halsted was strained and quiet. When we got to the charred remains of my building, Assuevo said, "I just want you to be very clear that that building may not be safe. Any accidents, you're on your own."

"Thanks," I said wearily. "You guys are a big help."

Roger and I picked our way across ice mountains formed by the frozen jets of water from the fire trucks. It was like walking through a nightmare—everything was familiar, yet distorted. The front door, broken open by the firefighters, hung crazily on its hinges. The stairs were almost impassable, covered with ice and grime and bits of walls that had fallen in.

At the second-floor landing, we decided to separate. The stairs and floor might take the weight of one person, but not two. Locked in my stubborn desire to cling to my mother's two surviving wineglasses, I allowed Roger to go ahead and stood holding them, shivering in my slippers, wrapped in the blanket.

He picked his way cautiously up to the third floor. I could hear him going into my apartment, heard the occasional thud of a brick or piece of wood falling, but no crashes or loud cries. After a few minutes he came back to the hallway. "I think you can come up, Vic."

I clutched the wall with one hand and stepped around the ice. The last few stairs I had to do on hands and knees, moving the glasses up a step, then myself, and so to the landing.

The front of my apartment had essentially been destroyed. Standing in the hall, you could look directly into the living room through holes in the walls. The area around the front door had been incinerated, but by stepping through a hole in the living-room wall you could stand on supporting beams.

Such furniture as I owned was destroyed. Blackened by fire and soaked with water, it was irrecoverable. I tried picking out a note on the piano and got a deadened twang. I bit my lip and resolutely moved past it toward the bedroom. Because bedroom and dining room were on either side of the main hall and the main path of the fire, the damage there was less. I'd never sleep in that bed again, but it was possible, by sorting carefully, to find some wearable clothes. I pulled on a pair of boots, donned a smoke-filled sweater, and rummaged for an outfit that would carry me through the morning.

Roger helped me pack what seemed restorable into two suitcases, prying open their frozen locks.

"What we don't take now I might as well kiss good-bye—the neighborhood will be poking through the remains before too long."

I waited until we were ready to leave before looking in the cupboard at the back of my closet. I was too afraid of what I'd find. Fingers shaking, I pried the door off its sagging hinges. The glasses were wrapped carefully in pieces of old sheet. I unrolled these slowly. The first one I picked had a jagged piece

136

broken from it. I bit my lower lip again to keep it in order and unwrapped the other four. They seemed to be all right. I held them up to the dim morning light and twirled them. No cracks or bubbles.

Roger had been standing silently. Now he picked his way across the debris. "All well?"

"One's broken. Maybe someone could glue it, though—it's just one big piece." The only other valuables in the cupboard were Gabriella's diamond drop earrings and a necklace. I put these in my pocket, rewrapped the glasses and placed them in one suitcase, and put on the shoulder holster with my Smith & Wesson in it. I couldn't think of anything else I desperately needed to keep. Unlike Peter Wimsey, I collect no first editions. Such kitchen gadgets as I owned could be replaced without too much grief.

As I started lugging the suitcases to the hole in the living-room wall, the phone rang. Roger and I looked at each other, startled. It never occurred to us that Ma Bell could keep the wires humming after a fire. I managed to find the living-room extension buried under some plaster.

"Yes?"

"Miss Warshawski?" It was my smooth-voiced friend. "You were lucky, Miss Warshawski. But no one is lucky forever."

XVII

The Fallen Knight

WE DROVE DOWN to the Hancock in the Omega. I let Roger out with my baggage and went to find street parking. By the time I staggered back to his apartment I knew I wasn't going to be able to do anything until I got some sleep. Pasquale, Rosa, Albert, and Ajax whirled muzzily through my brain, but walking was so difficult that thinking was impossible.

Roger let me in and gave me a set of keys. He had showered. His face was gray with fatigue, but he didn't think he could take the day off with so many rumors flying around about the takeover—management was meeting daily, mapping strategy.

He held me tightly for a few minutes. "I didn't say much at the hospital because I was afraid I might ruin your story. But please, Vic, please don't run off into anything stupid today. I like you better in one piece."

I hugged him briefly. "All I care about right now is getting some sleep. Don't worry about me, Roger. Thanks for the place to stay."

I was too tired to bathe, too tired to undress. I just managed to pull my boots off before falling into bed.

It was past four when I woke again, stiff and foggy but ready to start moving again. I realized with distaste that I stank and my clothes stank, too. A small utility room next to the bathroom held a washing machine. I piled in jeans, underwear, and everything in the suitcases that didn't require dry cleaning. A long soak in the bathtub and I felt somewhat more human.

As I waited for my jeans to dry I called my answering service. No message from Don Pasquale, but Phil Paciorek had phoned and left his on-call number. I tried it, but he apparently was handling some emergency surgery. I gave Ferrant's number to the hospital and tried Torfino's restaurant again. The same gritty voice I'd talked to the day before continued to disclaim all knowledge of Don Pasquale.

The early evening editions had arrived in the downstairs lobby. I stopped in the coffee shop to read them over a cappuccino and a cheese sandwich. The fire had made the *Herald-Star*'s front page—ARSON ON THE NORTH SIDE— in the lower left corner. Interview with the De Paul students. Interview with the Takamokus' worried daughter. Then, in a separate paragraph with its own subhead: "V. I. Warshawski, whose apartment was the focal point of the fire, has been investigating a problem involving forged securities at the Priory of Albertus Magnus in Melrose Park. Ms. Warshawski, the victim of an acid-throwing mugger two weeks ago, was not available for comment on a connection between her investigation and the fire."

I ground my teeth. Thanks a bunch, Murray. The *Herald-Star* had already run the acid story, but now the police were bound to read it and see the connection. I drank some more cappuccino, then flipped to the personal section of the classifieds. A small message was waiting for me: "The oak has sprouted." Uncle Stefan and I had agreed on this since he'd been working with my certificates of Acorn stock. I had last looked at the personals on Sunday; today was Thursday. How long had the ad been running?

Roger was home when I got back to the apartment. He told me apologetically that he was all done in; could I manage dinner alone while he went to bed?

"No problem. I slept all day." I helped him into bed and gave him a backrub. He was asleep by the time I left the room.

I pulled on long underwear and as many sweatshirts as I could manage, then walked back to Lake Shore Drive to retrieve my car. A wind blowing across the lake cut through my pullovers and long underwear. Tomorrow I'd definitely stop at Army-Navy Surplus for a new pea jacket.

I wondered about the tail Bobby claimed he was going to slap on me. No one had followed me to my car. Looking in the rearview mirror, I didn't see any waiting cars. And no one would loiter on the street in this wind. I decided it must have been bravado—or someone had countermanded Bobby.

The Omega started only after severe grumbling. We sat and shivered together, the car refusing to produce any heat. A five-minute warm-up finally persuaded the transmission to groan into gear.

While side streets were still piled with snow, Lake Shore Drive was clear. After a few turgid blocks, the car moved north briskly. At Montrose the heater finally kicked grudgingly into life. At the Evanston border I had stopped shivering and was able to pay more attention to traffic and road conditions.

The night was clear; on Dempster the heavy rush-hour traffic was moving well. I spun off onto Crawford Avenue and made it to Uncle Stefan's a few minutes before seven. Before leaving the car, I jammed the Smith & Wesson into the front of my jeans where the butt dug into my abdomen—the pullovers made a shoulder holster impractical.

Whistling through my teeth, I rang Uncle Stefan's bell. No answer. I shivered in the entryway a few minutes, and rang again. It hadn't occurred to me that he wouldn't be home. I could wait in the car, but the heater wasn't very efficient. I rang the other bells until someone buzzed me in—one in every building, letting the muggers and buggers in.

Uncle Stefan's apartment was on the fourth floor. On my way up, I passed a pretty young woman coming down with a baby and a stroller. She looked at me curiously. "Are you going to visit Mr. Herschel? I've been wondering whether I should look in on him—I'm Ruth Silverstein—I live across the hall. When I take Mark for a walk at four, he usually comes out to give us cookies. I didn't see him this afternoon."

"He could have gone out."

I could see her flush in the stairway light. "I'm home alone with the baby, so maybe I pay more attention to my neighbors than I should. I usually hear him leave—he walks with a cane, you know, and it makes a particular kind of noise on the stairs."

"Thanks, Mrs. Silverstein." I trotted up the last flight of stairs, frowning. Uncle Stefan was in good health, but eighty-two years old. Did I have any right to break in on him? Did I have a duty to do so? What would Lotty say?

I pounded loudly on the heavy apartment door. Put an ear to the panel and heard nothing. No, a faint buzz of noise. The TV or radio. Shit.

I went back down the stairs two at a time, propped open the outer door with a glove, and jogged across the slippery sidewalk to the Omega. My picklocks were in the glove compartment.

As I dashed back into the building, I watched Mrs. Silverstein and Mark disappear into a small grocery store up the block. I might have ten minutes to get the door open.

The trick about prying open other people's doors is to relax and go by feel. Uncle Stefan had two locks, a deadbolt and a regular Yale. I worked the deadbolt first. It clicked and I realized with dismay that it had been open when I started on it; I'd just double-locked the door. Trying to breathe loosely I chivvied it the other way. It had just slid back when I heard Mrs. Silverstein come into the building. At least, judging from the sounds, that's who it was; someone talking briskly to a baby about the nice chicken Daddy would have when he got back from his late meeting. The stroller bumped its way to the fourth-floor landing. The lower lock clicked back and I was inside.

I picked my way past an Imari umbrella stand into the ornately decorated living room. In the light of a brass lamp I could see Uncle Stefan lying across the leather desk, its green dyed red-brown by a large congealing pool of blood. "Oh,

140

Christ!" I muttered. While I felt the old man's wrist, all I could think of was how furious Lotty would be. Unbelievably, a faint pulse still fluttered. I leaped over chairs and footstools and pounded on the Silverstein door. Mrs. Silverstein opened it at once—she'd just come home, coat still on, baby still in stroller.

"Get an ambulance as fast as you can—he's seriously injured."

She nodded matter-of-factly and bustled into the interior of her apartment. I went back to Uncle Stefan. Grabbing blankets from a tidy bed in a room off the kitchen, wrapping him, lowering him gently on the floor, raising his feet onto an intricately cut leather footstool, and then waiting. Waiting.

Mrs. Silverstein had sensibly asked for paramedics. When they heard about shock and blood loss, they set up a couple of drips—plasma and glucose. They were taking him to Ben Gurion Memorial Hospital, they told me, adding that they would make a police report and could I wait in the apartment, please.

As soon as they were gone, I phoned Lotty.

"Where are you?" she demanded. "I read about the fire and tried phoning you."

"Yes, well, that can wait. It's Uncle Stefan. He's been seriously wounded. I don't know if he'll live. They're taking him to Ben Gurion."

A long silence at the other end, then Lotty said very quietly, "Wounded? Shot?"

"Stabbed, I think. He lost a lot of blood, but they missed the heart. It had clotted by the time I found him."

"And that was when?"

"About ten minutes ago . . . I waited to call until I knew what hospital he'd be going to."

"I see. We'll talk later."

She hung up, leaving me staring at the phone. I prowled around the living room, waiting for the police, trying not to touch anything. As the minutes passed, my patience ran out. I found a pair of gloves in a drawer in the tidy bedroom. They were several sizes too large, but they kept me from leaving prints on the papers on the desk. I couldn't find any stock certificates at all—not forged, not my Acorn shares.

The room, while crowded with furniture, held few real hiding places. A quick search revealed nothing. Suddenly it occurred to me that if Uncle Stefan had made a forged stock certificate, he'd have to have tools lying around, tools the police would be just as happy not seeing. I sped up my search and found parchment, blocks, and tools in the oven. I bundled them up into a paper bag and went to find Mrs. Silverstein.

She came to the door, cheeks red, hair frizzled from heat; she must have been cooking. "Sorry to bother you again. I've got to wait here for the police and I'll probably have to go to the station with them. Mr. Herschel's niece will be by later for some things. Would you mind if I told her to ring your bell and pick this bag up from you?"

She was happy to help. "How is he? What happened?"

I shook my head. "I don't know. The paramedics didn't say anything. But his pulse was steady, even though it was weak. We'll hope for the best."

She invited me in for a drink but I thought it best not to give the police any ideas connecting the two of us and waited for them across the way. Two middle-aged men finally arrived, both in uniform. They came in with guns drawn. When they saw me, they told me to put my hands on the wall and not to move.

"I'm the person who called you. I'm just as surprised by all this as you are."

"We'll ask the questions, honey." The speaker had a paunch that obscured his gunbelt. He patted me down clumsily, but found the Smith & Wesson without any trouble. "You got a license for this, girlie?"

"Yup," I said.

"Let's see it."

"Mind if I take my hands off the wall? Hampers any movements."

"Don't be a wiseass. Get the license and get it fast." This was the second cop, leaner, with a pockmarked face.

My purse was on the floor near the door—I'd dropped it without thinking when I saw Uncle Stefan and hadn't bothered to pick it up. I pulled out by billfold and took out my P.I. license and my permit for the gun.

The stout cop looked them over. "Oh, a private eye. What are you doing here in Skokie, girlie?"

I shook my head. I hate suburban police. "The bagels in Chicago aren't as good as the ones they make out here."

Fat cop rolled his eyes. "We picked up Joan Rivers, Stu . . . Listen, Joan. This ain't Chicago. We want to put you away, we can, won't worry us none. Now just tell us what you were doing here."

"Waiting for you guys. Clearly a mistake."

The lean cop slapped my face. I knew better than to react—up here resisting arrest could stick and I'd lose my license. "Come on, girlie. My partner asked you a question. You going to answer it?"

"You guys want to charge me? If so, I'll call my lawyer. If not, no questions."

The two looked at each other. "Better call your lawyer, girlie. And we'll be hanging onto the gun. Not really a lady's weapon."

XVIII

In the Slammer

THE D.A. WAS mad at me. That didn't bother me too much. Mallory was furious—he'd read about the acid in the *Herald-Star*. I was used to Mallory's rage. When Roger learned I'd spent the night in a Skokie lockup, his worry turned to frustrated anger. I thought I could handle that. But Lotty. Lotty wouldn't speak to me. That hurt.

It had been a confused night. Pockmark and Fatso booked me around nine-thirty. I called my lawyer, Freeman Carter, who wasn't home. His thirteen-year-old daughter answered. She sounded like a poised and competent child, but there wasn't any way of telling when she'd remember to give her father the message.

After that we settled down for some serious questioning. I decided not to say anything, since I really didn't have much of a story I wanted to tell. I couldn't tell the truth, and with the mood Lotty was in, she'd be bound to screw up any embroidery I came up with.

Pockmark and Fatso gave way to some senior cops fairly early in the evening. It must have been around midnight when

143

Charles Nicholson came in from the D.A.'s office. I knew Charles. He was a figure in the Cook County court system. He liked to think he was an heir of Clarence Darrow, and resembled him superficially, at least as far as shaggy hair and a substantial stomach went. Charles was the kind of guy who liked to catch his subordinates making personal phone calls on county time. We'd never been what you might call close.

"Well, well, Warshawski. Feels like old times. You, me, a few differences, and a table between us."

"Hello, Charlie," I said calmly. "It does seem like old times. Even down to your shirt not quite meeting at the sixth button."

He looked down at his stomach and tried pulling the straining fabric together, then looked at me furiously. "Still your old flippant self, I see—even on a murder-one charge."

"If it's murder one, they changed the booking without telling me," I said irritably. "And that violates my Miranda rights. Better read the charge slip and double-check it."

"No, no," he said in his mayonnaise voice. "You're right—just a manner of speaking. Obstruction was and is the charge. Let's talk about what you were doing in the old man's apartment, Warshawski."

I shook my head. "Not until I have legal advice—in my opinion anything I say on that topic may incriminate me, and since I don't have specific knowledge of the crime, there isn't anything I can do to forward the police investigation." That was the last sentence I uttered for some time.

Charlie tried a lot of different tactics—insults, camaraderie, high-flown theories about the crime to invite my comments. I started doing some squad exercises—raise the right leg, hold for a count of five, lower, raise the left. Counting gave me a way to ignore Charlie, and the exercises rattled him. I'd gotten to seventy-five with each leg when he gave up.

Things changed at two-thirty when Bobby Mallory came in. "We're taking you downtown," he informed me. "I have had it up to here"—he indicated his neck—"with your smartass dancing around. Telling the truth when you feel like it. How dared you—how *dared* you give that acid story to Ryerson and not tell us this morning? We talked to your friend Ferrant a few hours ago. I'm not so dumb I didn't notice you cutting him off this morning when he started to ask if these were the same

144

people who threw something. Acid. You should be in Cook County Psychiatric. And before the night's over, you're either going to spill what you know or we're going to send you there and make it stick."

That was just talk, and Bobby knew it. Half of him was furious with me for concealing evidence, and half was plain mad because I was Tony's daughter and might have gotten myself killed or blinded.

I stood up. "Okay. You got it. Although Murray ran the acid story when it happened. Just get me out of the suburbs and away from Charlie and I'll talk."

"And the truth, Warshawski. You cover up anything, *anything*, and we'll have you in jail. I don't care if I run you in for dope possession."

"I don't do dope, Bobby. They find any in my place, it's planted. Anyway, I don't have a place."

His round face turned red. "I'm not taking it, Warshawski. You're two sentences away from Cook County. No smartassing, no lies. Got it?"

"Got it."

Bobby got the Skokie people to drop charges and took me away. Technically I wasn't under arrest and didn't have to go with him. I also wasn't under any illusions.

The driver was a likable young man who seemed willing to chat. I asked him whether he thought the Cubs were going to let Rick Sutcliffe go. One blistering remark from Bobby shut him up, however, so I discoursed alone on the topic. "My feeling is, Sutcliffe turned that team around after the All-Star break. So he wants five, six million. It's worth it for another crack at the World Series."

When we got to Eleventh Street, Bobby hustled me into an interrogation room. Detective Finchley, a young black cop who'd been in uniform when I first met him, joined us and took notes.

Bobby sent for coffee, shut the door, and sat behind his cluttered desk.

"No more about Sutcliffe and Gary Matthews. Just the facts."

I gave him the facts. I told him about Rosa and the securities, and the threatening phone calls. I told him about the attack in

145

the hallway and how Murray thought it might be Walter Novick. And I told him about the phone call this morning when I went back for my clothes. "No one is lucky forever."

"And what about Stefan Herschel? What were you doing there the day he was stabbed?"

"Just chance. Is he all right?"

"No way, Warshawski. I'm asking the questions tonight. What were you doing at his place?"

"He's an uncle of a friend of mine. You know Dr. Herschel . . . He's an interesting old man and he gets lonely; he wanted me to have tea with him."

"Tea? So you let yourself in?"

"The door was open when I got there—that worried me."

"I'll bet. The girl across the hall says the door was shut and that worried her."

"Not standing open—just not locked."

Bobby held up my collection of picklocks. "You wouldn't have used these, by any chance?"

I shook my head. "Don't know how to use them—they're a souvenir from one of my clients when I was a public defender."

"And you carry them around for sentiment after what— eight years as a P.I.? Come on, let's have it."

"You got it, Bobby. You got the acid, you got Novick, you got Rosa. Talk to Derek Hatfield, why don't you. I'd be real curious who was backing the FBI off those securities."

"I'm talking to you. And speaking of Hatfield, you wouldn't know why his name was on the register at the Stock Exchange, would you, the night someone broke into Tilford and Sutton's office?"

"You ask Hatfield what he was doing there?"

"He says he wasn't."

I shrugged. "The feds never tell you anything. You know that."

"Well, neither do you, and you've got less excuse to hold back. Why were you visiting Stefan Herschel?"

"He invited me."

"Yeah. Your apartment burned down last night, so today you've been feeling chipper, you'll just go to tea in Skokie. *Damn* it, Vicki, *level with me*." Mallory was truly upset. He doesn't hold with swearing around women. Finchley looked

146

worried. I was worried, too, but I just couldn't blow the whistle on Stefan Herschel. The old man had got himself killed, or close to it, on account of the forgery. I didn't want to get him arrested, too.

At five, Bobby charged me with concealing evidence of a crime. I was printed, photographed, and taken to the holding cells at Twenty-sixth and California with some rather disgruntled prostitutes. Most wore high-heeled boots and very short skirts—jail must at least have been a warmer place on a January night than Rush and Oak. There was a little hostility at first as they tried to make sure I wasn't working any of their territories.

"Sorry, ladies—I'm just here on a murder charge." Yeah, my old man, I explained. Yeah, the bastard beat me. But the last straw was when he tried to burn me. I showed them my arms where the fire had scorched the skin.

Lots of sympathetic clucking. "Oh, honey, you did right . . . Man touch me that way, I stick him." "Oh, yeah, 'member when Freddie tried to cut me, I throw boil' water on him."

They quickly forgot me as each tried to outdo the other with tales of male violence and bravado in handling it. The stories made my skin crawl. At eight though, when the Freddies and Slims and JJs showed up to collect them, they acted glad enough to see them. Home is where they have to take you in, I guess.

Freeman Carter came for me at nine. He's the partner in Crawford, Meade—my ex-husband's high-prestige firm—who does their criminal stuff. It's a constant thorn to Dick—my ex—that Freeman does my legal work. But not only is he good, in a smooth, WASPy way, he likes me.

"Hi, Freeman. The other pimps got their hookers out an hour ago. I guess I'm not very valuable merchandise."

"Hi, Vic. If you had a mirror you'd see why your street value has plummeted. You're going to have a hearing in Women's Court at eleven. Just a formality, and they'll release you on an I-bond." An I-bond, as in I-solemnly-swear-to-come-back-for-the-trial, is given to people the court knows as responsible citizens. Like me. Freeman lent me a comb and I made myself as presentable as possible.

We went down the hall to a small meeting room. Freeman

looked as elegant as ever, his pale blond hair cut close to his head, smooth-shaven, his perfectly tailored navy suit fitted to his lean body. If I looked only half as grubby as I felt, I must be pretty disgusting. Freeman glanced at his watch. "Want to talk? They booked you because they felt you were withholding on Stefan Herschel."

"I was," I admitted. "How is he?"

"I called the hospital on my way over here. He's in intensive care, but seems to have stabilized."

"I see." I felt a lot better already. "You know he had a forgery rap back in the fifties? Well, I'm afraid someone knifed him because he was playing boy detective on some stock forgeries. But I can't tell Bobby Mallory until I've talked to the old man. I just don't want to get him in trouble with the police and the feds."

Freeman made a sour face. "If I were your pimp, I'd beat you with a clothes hanger. Since I'm just your lawyer, could I urge you to tell Mallory all you know? He's a good cop. He's not going to railroad an eighty-year-old man."

"He might not, but Derek Hatfield would in thirty seconds. Less. And once the feds move in, there isn't shit Bobby or I— or even you—can do."

Freeman remained unconvinced as I told him about the forgeries and Uncle Stefan's role in them, but he swept me through the hearing with aplomb. He kissed me good-bye afterward when he dropped me at the Roosevelt Road L stop. "And that is proof of devotion, Vic. You are badly in need of a bath."

I rode the L to Howard street, caught the Skokie Swift, and walked the ten blocks from the station to my car. A bath, a nap, Roger, Lotty, and Uncle Stefan. Those were priorities in reverse order, but I needed to get clean before I could face talking to anyone else.

The priorities got reversed a bit—Roger was waiting for me when I got back to the Hancock. He was on the phone, apparently with Ajax. I sketched a wave and headed for the bathroom. He came in ten minutes later as I was lying in the tub. Trying to lie in the tub. It was one of those nasty modern affairs where your knees come up to your chin. My apartment had a wonderful thirties bath, long enough for a tall person to lie down in it.

Roger closed the toilet and sat on it. "The police woke me at one this morning to ask me about your acid burn. I told them everything I knew, which was damned little. I had no idea where you were, what you were doing, what danger you might be in. I begged you yesterday morning not to do anything stupid. But when I wake up at one in the morning and you're not here, no note—goddamn it, why did you do this?"

I sat up in the tub. "I had an eventful evening. Saved an old man's life, then spent five hours in a Skokie jail and four in a Chicago one. I got one phone call and I needed it for my lawyer. Since he wasn't home, only his kid, I couldn't send messages to my friends and relations."

"But damn it, Vic, you know I'm worried sick about you and this whole business"—he waved an arm, indicating frustration and incoherence. "Why the hell didn't you leave me a note?"

I shook my head. "I didn't think I was going to be gone long. Gosh, Roger, if I'd known what I was going to find, I would have written you a novel."

"That's not the point. You know it's not. We talked about this last night, or two nights ago, whenever the hell your place burned down. You can't just slide off and leave everyone else gasping for air."

I was starting to get angry, too. "You don't own me, Ferrant. And if my staying here makes you think you do, I'll leave at once. I'm a detective. I'm paid to detect things. If I told everyone and his dog Rover what I was up to, not only would my clients lose all confidence in me, I'd be sandbagged everywhere I went. You told the cops everything you knew. If you'd known everything I know, a poor old man would be under arrest right now as well as in intensive care."

Roger looked at me bleakly, his face pale. "Maybe you should leave, Vic. I don't have the stamina for any more nights like this. But let me tell you one thing, Wonder Woman: If you'd shared what you were doing with me, I wouldn't have had to tell the cops—I'd have known that you didn't need their particular help. I told them not to sandbag you but to protect you."

Anger was tightening my vocal cords. "No one protects me, Roger. I don't live in that kind of universe. I wouldn't screw around with some business deal you were cutting just because there are a lot of dangerous and unscrupulous people dealing in your world. You want to talk to me about your work, I'll listen and try to make suggestions if you want them. But I won't try to protect you." I got out of the tub. "Well, give me the same respect. Just because the people I deal with play with fire instead of money doesn't mean I need or want protection. If I did, how do you think I'd have survived all these years?"

I was clenching and unclenching my fists, trying to keep rage under control. Protection. The middle-class dream. My father protecting Gabriella in a Milwaukee Avenue bar. My mother giving him loyalty and channeling her fierce creative passions into a South Chicago tenement in gratitude.

Roger picked up a towel and began soberly drying my back. He wrapped it around my shoulders and gave me a hug. I tried to relax, but couldn't. "Vic. I have to go screw around in some business deals . . . You're right—I glory in knowing I can come out on top in a real scrum. If you sailed in and dislocated someone's thorax, or whatever you do, I'd be furious . . . I don't think I own you. But the remoter you get, the more I need something to grab hold of."

"I see." I turned around. "I still think it would be easier on both of us if I found another place to stay. But I'll—I'll try to keep in better touch." I stood on my toes and kissed him gently.

The phone rang. I went to the dryer where I'd left my clothes and pulled out fresh jeans and another shirt while Roger picked up the bathroom extension. "For you, Vic."

I took it in the bedroom. Roger said he was leaving and hung up. The caller was Phil Paciorek. "You still want your man with the non-accent? There's an archdiocesan dinner tonight at the Hanover House Hotel—Farber's giving a party for O'Faolin. Because Mother shells out a million or so to the Church every year, we're invited. Most of the people at the funeral will be there. Want to be my date?"

An archdiocesan dinner. Thrills. That meant a dress and nylons. Which meant a trip to the shops, as anything even

150

remotely suitable for the Hanover House was still lying smoke-filled in my suitcase. Since Phil wouldn't be able to leave the hospital until seven, he asked if I'd mind meeting him at the hotel—he'd be there as close to seven-thirty as possible. "And I've called the archdiocese—if I'm not there, just give your name to the woman at the reception desk."

After that I tried taking a nap, but I couldn't sleep. Lotty, Uncle Stefan, Don Pasquale were churning around in the foreground of my brain. Along with Rosa and Albert and Agnes.

At noon I gave up on rest and tried calling Lotty. Carol Alvarado, the nurse at Lotty's North Side clinic, answered the phone. She went to find the doctor, but came back with the message that she was too busy to talk to me right now.

I walked across the street to Water Tower and found a severely tailored crimson wool crepe dress on sale at Lord & Taylor. In front, it had a scalloped neck; in back the neckline dropped to a V closing just above my bra strap. I could wear my mother's diamond drops with it and be the belle of the ball.

Back at the Hancock I tried Lotty again. She was still too busy to talk. I got the morning paper and looked through the classifieds for furnished apartments. After an hour of calling, I found a place on Racine and Montrose that offered two-month leases. I packed the suitcase again, mushing laundered clothes together with the smoke-stained ones, then left a long note to Roger, explaining where I was moving and what I was doing for dinner and could we please stay in touch, and tried Lotty one last time. Still too busy.

The Bellerophon had seen better days, but it was well cared for. For two fifty a month, I had possession of a sitting room with a Murphy bed, a comfortable armchair, a small TV, and a respectable table. The kitchen included a minuscule refrigerator and two gas burners, no oven, while the bathroom had a real tub in it. Good enough. The room had phone jacks. If the neighborhood vandals hadn't walked off with my phones, I ought to be able to get service switched through. I gave Mrs. Climzak a check for the first month's rent and left.

My old apartment looked forlorn in the winter sunlight—Manderley burned out—broken glass in the windows, the Takamokus' print curtains sagging on their rods. I climbed past the debris on the stairs through the hole in the living-room wall. The piano was still there—too big to move—but the sofa and coffee table were gone. Charred copies of *Forbes* and *The Wall Street Journal* were scattered around the room. The living-room phone had been ripped out of the wall. In the dining room, someone had swiped all the liquor. Naturally. Most of the plates were gone. Thank God I'd never had enough money for Crown Derby.

My bedroom extension was still there, buried under a pile of loose plaster. I unplugged it from the wall and left. Stopped at the Lincoln Park Post Office to arrange forwarding for my mail and pick up what they'd held for me since the fire. Then, gritting my teeth, I drove north on Sheffield to Lotty's store-front clinic.

The waiting room was full of women and small children. A din combined of Spanish, Korean, and Lebanese shrieks made the small space seem even tinier. Babies crawled on the floor with sturdy wooden blocks in their fists.

Lotty's receptionist was a sixty-year-old woman who'd raised seven children of her own. Her chief skills were keeping order in the waiting room and making sure that people were seen in order either of appearance or emergency. She never lost her temper, but she knew her clientele like a good bartender and kept order the same way.

"Miss Warshawski. Nice to see you. We have a pretty full house today—lots of winters cold and flu. Is Dr. Herschel expecting you?"

Mrs. Coltrain would not call anyone by her first name. After years of coaxing, Lotty and I had given up. "No, Mrs. Coltrain. I stopped by to see how her uncle was doing, to find out if I can visit him."

Mrs. Coltrain disappeared into the back of the clinic. She came back with Carol Alvarado a few minutes later. Carol told me Lotty was with a patient but would see me for a few minutes if I'd go into her office.

Lotty's office, like the waiting room, was furnished to set worried mothers and frightened children at ease. She didn't need a desk, she said—after all, Mrs. Coltrain kept all the files in file cabinets. Instead, a few comfortable chairs, pictures, a thick carpet, and the ever-present building blocks made the room a cheerful place. Today I didn't find it relaxing.

Lotty made me wait half an hour. I thumbed through the *Journal of Surgical Obstetrics*. I drummed my fingers on the table next to my chair, did leg lifts and a few other stretches.

At four, Lotty came in quietly. Above her white lab coat her face was set in uncompromising lines. "I am almost too angry to speak to you, Vic. Fortunately, my uncle has survived. And I know he owes his life to you. But he almost owes his death to you, too."

I was too tired for another fight today. I ran my hands through my hair, trying to stimulate my brain. "Lotty, you don't have to work to make me feel guilty: I do. I should never have involved him in such a crazy, dangerous business. All I can say is, I've taken my share of the knocks. If I'd known what was coming, I would have done my utmost to keep him from being attacked." I laughed mirthlessly. "A few hours ago I had a blazing fight with Roger Ferrant—he wants to protect me from arsonists and suchlike. Now you're fighting me because I didn't protect your uncle."

Lotty didn't smile. "He wants to talk to you. I tried to forbid this—he doesn't need any more excitement or strain. But it seems to be more stress to keep him from you than otherwise. The police want to question him and he's refusing until he's seen you."

"Lotty, he's an old man, but he's a sane man. He makes his own choices. Don't you think some of your anger comes from that? And from helping me involve him? I do my best with my clients, but I know I can't help all of them, not a hundred percent."

"Dr. Metzinger is in charge of his case. I'll call and let him know you'll be out—when?"

I gave up the argument and looked at my watch. I could just make it and dress for dinner if I went now. "In half an hour."

She nodded and left.

XIX

Dinner Date

BEN GURION HOSPITAL lay close to the Edens. Visible from the expressway, it was easy to get to. It was barely five o'clock when I got out of the car in the hospital parking lot, even after stopping to buy a pea jacket at an Amvets Store. It's always struck me as the ultimate insult to pay to park at hospitals; they incarcerate your friends and relations in rooms that cost six or seven hundred dollars a day, then put a little sting in by charging a few extra bucks to visit them. I pocketed the lot ticket with ill humor and stomped into the lobby. A woman at the information desk called the evening nurse in Intensive Care, then told me I was expected, to go on up.

Five o'clock is a quiet time in a hospital. Surgery and therapies are over for the day; the evening visitors haven't started arriving yet. I followed red arrows painted on deserted hallways up two flights of stairs to the intensive-care unit.

A policeman sat outside the door to the unit. He was there to protect Uncle Stefan, the night nurse explained. Would I mind showing identification and letting him pat me down. I thoroughly approved the caution. At the back of my mind was the fear that whoever had stabbed the old man might return to finish the job.

The policeman satisfied, medical hygiene had to be accommodated. I put on a sterile mask and disposable gown. In the changing-room mirror I looked like a stranger: gray eyes heavy with fatigue, hair wind-tangled, the mask disguising my personality. I hoped it wouldn't terrify a weak old man.

When I came out, Dr. Metzinger was waiting for me. He was a balding man in his late forties. He wore Gucci loafers and had a heavy gold bracelet on his left wrist. Got to spend the money somehow, I guess.

"Mr. Herschel has insisted so hard on talking to you we thought it best for you to see him," he said in a low voice, as though Uncle Stefan might hear and be disturbed. "I want you to be very careful, though. He's lost a lot of blood, been through a very severe trauma. I don't want you to say anything that might cause a relapse."

I couldn't afford to antagonize anyone else today. I just nodded and told him I understood. He opened the door to the intensive-care unit and ushered me through. I felt as though I were being conducted into the presence of royalty. Uncle Stefan had been isolated from the rest of the unit in a private room. When I realized Metzinger was following me into it I stopped. "I have a feeling what Mr. Herschel has to say is confidential, Doctor. If you want to keep an eye on him, can you do it through the door?"

He didn't like that at all and insisted on coming in with me. Short of breaking his arm, which was a tempting idea, there wasn't much I could do to stop him.

The sight of Uncle Stefan lying small in a bed, attached to machines, to a couple of drips, to oxygen, made my stomach turn over. He was asleep; he looked closer to death than he had in the apartment last night.

Dr. Metzinger shook him lightly by the shoulder. He opened his guileless brown eyes, recognized me after a few bewildered seconds, and beamed feebly. "Miss Warshawski. My dear young lady. How I have been longing to see you. Lotty has told me how you saved my life. Come here, eh, and let me kiss you—never mind these terrible machines."

I knelt down next to the bed and hugged him. Metzinger told me sharply not to touch him—the whole point of the gown and gauze was to keep germs out. I got to my feet.

Uncle Stefan looked at the doctor. "So, Doctor. You are my good protector, eh? You keep the germs away and get me healthy quickly. Now, though, I have a few private words for Miss Warshawski only. So could I trouble you to leave?"

I studiously avoided Metzinger's face as he withdrew with a certain amount of ill grace. "You can have fifteen minutes. Remember, Miss Warshawski—you're not to touch the patient."

"No, Dr. Metzinger. I won't." When the doctor had closed the door with an offended snap I pulled a chair to the side of the bed.

"Uncle Stefan—I mean, Mr. Herschel—I'm so sorry I let

155

you get involved in this. Lotty is furious, and I don't blame her—it was thoughtless. I could beat myself."

The wicked grin that made him look like Lotty came. "Please—call me Uncle Stefan. I like it. And do not beat your beautiful body, my dear new niece—Victoria, is it not? I told you to begin with that I am not afraid of death. And so I am not. You gave me a beautiful adventure, which I do not at all regret. Do not be sad or angry. But be careful. That is why I had to see you. The man who attacked me is very, very dangerous."

"What happened? I didn't see your ad until yesterday afternoon—I've had sort of a wild week myself. But you made a stock certificate?"

He chuckled wearily. "Yes, a very fine one, if I say so. For IBM. A good, solid company. One hundred shares common stock. So. Last Wednesday I finished him, no them. Sorry, with this injury my English goes a bit." He stopped and breathed heavily for a minute. I wished I could hold his hand. Surely a little contact would do him more good than isolation and sterility.

His papery eyelids fluttered open again. "Then I call a man I know. Who it is, maybe best you do not hear, my dear niece. And he calls a man, and so on. And on Wednesday afternoon one week later, I get a call. Someone is interested. A buyer, and he will be there Thursday afternoon. I rush to get an ad in the paper.

"So, in the afternoon a man shows up. I know at once he is not a boss. The manner is that of an underling. Maybe you call him a legman."

"Legman. Yes. What did he look like?"

"A thug." Uncle Stefan produced the slang word proudly. "He is maybe forty. Heavy—not fat, you know. He looks Croatian, that thick jowl, thick eyebrows. He is as tall as you, but not as beautiful. Maybe a hundred pounds heavier."

He stopped again to breathe, and closed his eyes briefly. I glanced surreptitiously at my watch. Only five more minutes. I didn't try to hurry him; that would only make him lose his train of thought.

"Well, you were not there, and I, I had to play the clever detective. So I tell him I know about the priory forgeries, and I

156

want a piece of that particular business. But I have to know who pays. Who the boss is. So we get into a—a fight. He takes my IBM stock. He takes your Acorn stock. He says, 'You know too much for your own good, old man!' and pulls out the knife, which I see. I have acid at my side, acid for my etching, you understand. This I throw at him, so when he stabs me, his hand is not quite true."

I laughed. "Wonderful. When you've recovered maybe you'd like to join my detective agency. I've never wanted a partner before, but you'd bring class to the operation."

The mischievous smile appeared briefly, weakly; he shut his eyes again. "It's a deal, dear Victoria," he said. I had to strain to catch the words.

Dr. Metzinger bustled in. "You'll have to leave now, Miss Warshawski."

I got up. "When the police talk to you, give them a description of the man. Not anything else. Random burglar after your silver, perhaps. And put in a good word for me with Lotty—she's ready to flay me."

The lids fluttered open and his brown eyes twinkled weakly. "Lotty was always a headstrong, unmanageable child. When she was six—"

Dr. Metzinger interrupted him. "You're going to rest now. You can tell Miss Warshawski later."

"Oh, very well. Just ask her about her pony and the castle at Kleinsee," he called as Metzinger hustled me out of the room.

The policeman stopped me in the hallway. "I need a full report on your conversation."

"For what? Your memoirs?"

The policeman grabbed my arm. "My orders are, if anyone talks to him, I have to find out what he said."

I jerked my arm down and away. "Very well. He told me he was sitting home on Thursday afternoon when a man came up the stairs. He let him in. Mr. Herschel's an old man, lonely, wants visitors more than he wants to suspect people. He's got a lot of valuable stuff in that apartment and it probably isn't too much of a secret. Anyway, they got into a tussle of sorts— as much as a thug can be said to tussle with an eighty-year-old man. He had some jewelry cleaner in his desk, acid of some

157

kind, threw it at him and got a knife in his side. I think he can give you a description of sorts."

"Why did he want to see you?" Metzinger demanded.

I wanted to get home more than I wanted to fight. "I'm a friend of his niece, Dr. Herschel. He knows me through her, knows I'm a private detective. An old man like that would rather talk to someone he knows about his troubles than get caught in the impersonal police machinery."

The policeman insisted on my writing down what I had just told him and signing it before he let me go. "And your phone number. We need a number where we can reach you." That reminded me—I hadn't gotten to the phone company. I gave him my office number and left.

Traffic on the Edens was thick by the time I reached it. It would be a parking lot where it joined the Kennedy. I exited on Peterson and headed south on side streets to Montrose. It was six-fifteen when I got to the Bellerophon. Setting my alarm for seven, I pulled the Murphy bed out of the wall and fell across it into a dreamless sleep.

When the alarm rang, it took me a long time to wake up. At first I thought it was morning in my old place on Halsted. I switched off the ringing and started to go back to sleep. It dawned on me, however, that the bedside table was missing. I'd had to reach over the side of the bed to the floor to turn off the clock. This woke me enough to remember where I was and why I had to get up.

I staggered into the bathroom, took a cold shower, and dressed in the new crimson outfit with more haste than grace. I dumped makeup from my suitcase into my purse, pulled on nylons and boots, stuck my Magli pumps under my arm, and headed for the car. I had a choice of the navy pea jacket or something filled with smoke, and chose the pea jacket—I'd just be checking it, after all.

I was only twenty minutes late to the Hanover House, and happened to arrive at the same time as Phil. He was too well behaved to look askance at my outfit. Kissing me lightly on the cheek, he tucked my arm into his and escorted me into the hotel. He took boots and coat from me to check. The perfect gentleman.

I'd put my makeup on at traffic lights and run a comb

through my hair before leaving the car. Remembering the great Beau Brummell, who said that only the insecure primp once they've reached the party, I resisted the temptation to study myself in the floor-length mirrors covering the lobby walls.

Dinner was served in the Trident Salon on the fourth floor. Smaller than the Grand Ballroom, it seated two hundred people who had paid a hundred dollars each for the privilege of dining with the archbishop. A gaunt woman in black collected tickets at the entrance to the salon. She greeted Phil by name, her thin, sour face coming close to pleasure at seeing him.

"I guess it's Dr. Paciorek, now isn't it? I know how proud your parents must be of you. And is this the lucky young lady?"

Phil blushed, suddenly looking very young indeed. "No, no, Sonia . . . Which table for us?"

We were seated at table five, in the front of the room. Dr. and Mrs. Paciorek were at the head table, along with O'Faolin, Farber, and other well-to-do Catholics. Cecelia and her husband, Morris, were at our table. She was wearing a black evening gown that emphasized her twenty extra pounds and the soft flab in her triceps.

"Hello, Cecelia. Hi, Morris, good to see you," I said cheerfully. Cecelia looked at me coldly, but Morris stood up to shake hands with me. An innocuous metals broker, he didn't share the family feud against Agnes and her friends.

For a hundred dollars, we got a tomato-based seafood chowder. The others at our table had already started eating; waiters brought Phil and me servings while I studied the program next to my plate. Funds raised by the dinner would support the Vatican, whose assets had been depleted by the recent recessionary spiral and the fall of the lira. Archbishop O'Faolin, head of the Vatican Finance Committee, was here to thank us in person for our generosity. After dinner and speeches by Farber and O'Faolin, and by Mrs. Catherine Paciorek, who had graciously organized the dinner, there would be an informal reception with cash bar in the George IV Salon next to our dining room.

The overweight man on my left took a second roll from the

basket in front of him but forbore to offer me any: hoard the supplies. I asked him what kind of business he was in and he responded briefly, "Insurance," before popping half the roll into his mouth.

"Splendid," I said heartily. "Brokerage? Company?"

His wife, a thin, twittery woman with a wreath of diamonds around her neck, leaned across him. "Harold is head of Burhop and Calends' Chicago office."

"How fascinating!" I exclaimed. Burhop and Calends was a large national brokerage house, second in size behind Marsh and McLennan. "It so happens I'm working for Ajax Insurance right now. What do you think the impact would be on the industry if an outside interest acquired them?"

"Wouldn't affect the industry at all," he muttered, pouring a pint of Thousand Island dressing over the salad he'd just received.

Phil nudged my arm. "Vic you don't have to do a suburban Girl Scout impersonation just because I asked you to dinner. Tell me what you've been doing, instead."

I told him about my fire He grimaced. "I've been on call almost all week. Haven't seen a paper. I sometimes think the world could blow up and the only way I'd know would be by the casualties coming into ER."

"But you like what you do?"

His face lit up "I love it. Especially the research end. I've been working with epileptics during surgery to try to map neuron activity" He was still young enough to give an uneducated audience the full force of his technical knowledge. I followed as best I could, more entertained by his enthusiasm than by what he was actually saying. How you get a verbal response from people whose brains are being operated on carried us through some decent halibut steak, which Phil ignored as he drew a diagram in pen on his cloth napkin.

Cecelia tried to catch his eye several times; she felt tales of blood and surgery were not suited to the dinner table, although most of the guests were discussing their own operations, along with their children or what kind of snow-removal equipment they owned.

When the waiters removed the dessert plates, including Phil's uneaten profiteroles, the room quieted so that his was the

160

only voice that carried. "That's what they really mean by a physiological map," he said earnestly. A ripple of laughter made him blush and break off in midsentence. It also drew the head table's attention to him.

Mrs. Paciorek had been too busy entertaining Archbishop O'Faolin to look at her children during dinner. Since eating had been well under way when we arrived, she probably never noticed Phil and me at all. Now his exposition and the laughter made her turn slightly so that she could identify the source. She saw him, then me. She froze, her well-bred mask slipping slightly. She glanced sharply at Cecelia, who made a helpless gesture.

Mrs. Paciorek nudged Archbishop O'Faolin and whispered to him. He, too, turned to stare at our table, which was only fifteen feet or so away. Then he whispered back to Mrs. Paciorek, who nodded firmly. Instructions to get the Swiss Guard to throw me out?

Phil was furiously stirring cream into his coffee. He was also still young enough to mind very much being laughed at. Under the noise of scraping chairs, as people rose for Cardinal Farber's post-dinner benediction, I patted his arm comfortingly and said, "Remember: The only real social sin is to care what other people think of you."

Farber gave a brisk blessing for the meal we had just enjoyed, and went on to talk about how the Kingdom of Heaven could only be tended on earth with the help of earthly things, that God had given us an earthly creation to care for, and that the work of the temporal church could only be carried out with material goods. He felt especially blessed in being the archbishop of Chicago, not just the world's largest archdiocese but also the most generous and loving. He was gratified at the response Chicago had made to the urgent needs of the Vatican, and here to thank us in person was the Most Reverend Xavier O'Faolin, archbishop of Ciudad Isabella and head of the Vatican Finance Committee.

Well pleased with his praise, the crowd clapped enthusiastically. O'Faolin stepped to the podium at a raised stand in front of the room, commended his words to God in Latin, and began to speak. Once again the Spanish accent was so thick as

161

to be nearly incomprehensible. People strained to listen, then squirmed, and finally began murmured private conversations.

Phil shook his head. "I don't know what's wrong with him tonight," he said. "The old boy usually speaks perfect English. Mother must have knocked him off balance."

I wondered again at the whispered exchange between her and O'Faolin. Since it was impossible to follow the Panamanian archbishop I let my mind wander. Applause roused me from a doze, and I shook my head to try to wake up again completely.

Phil commented sarcastically on my sleeping, then said, "Now comes the fun part. You go around the reception detecting to see if you can find your mysterious caller, and I'll watch."

"Great. Maybe you can incorporate it into an article on search-and-sort routines in the brain."

As we got up to follow the throng into the George IV Salon, Mrs. Paciorek pushed herself against the tide of traffic and came up to us. "What are you doing here?" she demanded of me abruptly.

Phil pulled my hand through his arm. "She's my dinner date, Mother. I didn't think I could face the Plattens and Carutherses without some moral support."

She stood fulminating, her color changed dangerously, but she had the sense to know she couldn't order me out of the hotel. At last she turned to Cecelia and Morris. "Try to keep her away from Archbishop Farber. He doesn't need to be insulted," she tossed over her shoulder.

Phil made a sour face. "Sorry about that, V.I. Want me to stay at your side? I don't want anyone else to be rude to you."

I was amused and touched. "Not necessary, my friend. If they're too rude, I'll break their necks or something and you can patch them up and come out looking like a hero."

Phil went to get me a brandy, while I started counterclockwise around the room, stopping at small knots of people, introducing myself, chatting enough to get everyone to say a few words, and moving on. About halfway up the left side, I ran into Father Pelly with Cecelia and some strangers.

"Father Pelly! Nice to see you."

He smiled austerely. "Miss Warshawski. I hardly thought of you as a supporter of the archdiocese."

I grinned appreciatively. "You thought correctly. Young Phil Paciorek brought me. How about yourself? I hardly thought the priory could afford this type of entertainment."

"We can't. Xavier O'Faolin invited me—we used to work together, and I was his secretary when he was sent to the Vatican ten years ago."

"And you keep in close touch. That's nice. He visit the priory while he's in town?" I asked idly.

"Actually, he'll stay with us for three days before he flies back to Rome."

"That's nice," I repeated. Faced with Cecelia's withering glare, I moved on. Phil caught up with me as I was nearing the knot around O'Faolin.

"Nothing like an evening with the old gang to make you feel you're in kindergarten," he said. "Every third person remembers when I broke the windows at the church with my catapult."

He introduced me to various people as I slowly worked my way up to O'Faolin. Someone was shaking hands with him and leaving just as I reached the group, so Phil and I were able to slip in next to him.

"Archbishop, this is Ms. Warshawski. Perhaps you remember her from my sister's funeral."

The great man favored me with a stately nod. He wore his episcopal purple shirt under a black suit of exquisite wool. His eyes were green, from his Irish father. I hadn't noticed them before. "Perhaps the archbishop would prefer to converse in Italian," I said, addressing him formally in that language.

"You speak Italian?" Like his English, his Italian accent was tinged with Spanish, but not so distortingly. Something about his voice sounded familiar. I wondered if he'd been on television or radio while he was in Chicago and asked him that.

"NBC was good enough to do a small interview. People think of the Vatican as a very wealthy organization, so it is hard for us to bring our story of poverty and begging to the people. They were kind enough to help."

I nodded. Chicago's NBC station gave a lot of support to Catholic figures and causes. "Yes. The Vatican finances have been much in the papers here. Particularly after the unfortunate death of Signor Calvi last summer." Was it my imagination, or did he flinch a bit? "Has your work with the Vatican Finance Committee involved you at all with the Banco Ambrosiano?"

"Signor Calvi was a most loyal Catholic. Unfortunately, his ardor caused him to overstep the bounds of propriety." He had switched back to his heavily accented English. Although I made one or two more attempts at conversation, the interview was clearly over.

Phil and I moved off to sit on a small couch. I needed to rest my feet before tackling the other side of the room. "What was that about Calvi and the Banco Ambrosiano?" he asked. "My Spanish is just good enough that I could follow some of the Italian . . . . You must have miffed him, though, for his English to go bad again like that."

"Possibly. He certainly didn't want to talk about Ambrosiano."

We sat in silence for a few minutes. I gathered my wits for an assault on the rest of the party. Suddenly, behind me, I heard the Voice again. "Thank you so much, Mrs. Addington. His Holiness will be joining me in prayer for all of you generous Chicago Catholics."

I leaped to my feet, spilling brandy down the front of the new crimson dress.

Phil stood up in alarm. "What is it, Vic?"

"That's the man who's been calling me. Who is that?"

"Who?"

"Didn't you hear someone just promising the pope's prayers? Who said that?"

Phil was bewildered. "That was Archbishop O'Faolin. Has he been calling you?"

"Never mind. No wonder you were so surprised by his accent, though." The voice of a man whose English has been carefully taught to avoid an accent. Irish or Spanish or both. I rejoined the group around the archbishop.

He stopped in midsentence when he saw me.

"Never mind," I said. "You don't have to put the thick Spanish back on again. I know who you are. What I don't understand is your connection with the Mafia."

I found I was shaking so badly I could hardly stand. This was the man who wanted to blind me. I had just enough control not to jump him on the spot.

"You're confusing me with someone else, young woman." O'Faolin spoke coldly, but in his normal voice. The rest of the group around him stood like Stonehenge. Mrs. Paciorek swooped up from nowhere.

"Dear Archbishop," she said. "Cardinal Farber is ready to leave."

"Ah, yes. I'll come at once. I must thank him for his most generous hospitality."

As he got ready to leave I said coldly, "Just remember, Archbishop: No one is lucky forever."

Phil helped me back to the couch. "Vic, what's wrong? What has O'Faolin done to you? Surely you don't know him?"

I shook my head. "I thought I did. He's probably right, though. I must be confusing him with someone else." I knew I wasn't, though. You do not forget the voice of someone who wants to pour acid in your eyes.

Phil offered to drive me home, to get more brandy, to do anything and everything. I smiled at him gratefully. "I'm okay. Just, with the fire at my place and everything, I haven't had much sleep. I'll sit here for a while and then drive back to my apartment." Or whatever the Bellerophon was.

Phil sat next to me. He held my hand and talked about general things. He was a very likable young man. I pondered again how Mrs. Paciorek could have produced three such attractive children as Agnes, Phil, and Barbara. "Cecelia's your mother's only success," I said abruptly.

He smiled. "You only see Mother at her worst. She's a fine person in a lot of ways. All the good she does, for example. She inherited that huge Savage fortune, and instead of turning into a Gloria Vanderbilt or Barbara Post, she's used it almost exclusively for charity. She set up trusts for us kids, enough to keep us from want—mine paid my medical-school tuition, for example. But most of it goes to different charities. Especially to the Church."

"Corpus Christi, perhaps?"

He looked at me sharply. "How do you know about that?"

"Oh," I said vaguely. "Even members of secret societies talk. Your mother must be pretty active in it."

He shook his head. "We're not supposed to talk about it. She explained it to each of us when we turned twenty-one, so

165

we'd know why there wasn't going to be much of an estate to inherit. Barbara doesn't know yet. We don't even discuss it among ourselves, although Cecelia's a member."

"But you're not?"

He smiled ruefully. "I'm not like Agnes—haven't lost my faith and turned my back on the Church. It's just, with Mother so active, I've had too much opportunity to see the venality of the organization. It doesn't surprise me—after all, priests and bishops are human, and they get their share of temptation. But I don't want them managing my money for me."

"Yes, I can see that. Someone like O'Faolin, for example, getting a chance to play ducks and drakes with the faithful's money. Is he part of Corpus Christi?"

Phil shrugged.

"But Father Pelly is," I said with calm certainty.

"Yeah, Pelly's a good guy. He's hot-tempered, but he's a fanatic like Mother. I don't think anyone could accuse him of working for his own self-interest."

The room was starting to shimmer in front of me. Too much knowledge, rage, and fatigue made me feel as if I might faint.

With Farber's and O'Faolin's departure the room was thinning rapidly of people. I got up. "I need to get home."

Phil reiterated his willingness to drive me. "You don't look in any shape to be on the road, Vic . . . I see too many head and neck injuries in the Emergency Room—let me drive you."

I declined firmly. "The air will wake me up. I always wear my seat belt, and I'm a careful driver." I had too much to sort out. I needed to be alone.

Phil retrieved my boots and coat for me and helped me into them with anxious courtesy. He walked me to the entrance of the lot where I was parked and insisted on paying the ticket. I was touched by his good manners and didn't try to override him. "Do me a favor," he said, as I turned to go into the garage. "Call me when you get in. I'm catching a train to the South Side—should be at my place in an hour. I'd just like to know you got home safely."

"Sure, Phil," I called, and turned in to the garage.

The Omega was parked on the third level. I rode the elevator up, keeping a cautious eye out for prowlers. Elevators are nasty places at night.

As I bent to unlock the car door, someone grabbed my arm. I whirled and kicked as hard as I could. My booted foot rammed his shin and he gave a yelp of pain and fell back.

"You're covered, Warshawski. Don't try to fight." The voice came from the shadows beyond my car. Light glinted on metal. I remembered in dismay that the farts in the Skokie police had my gun. But a fight is no time for regrets.

"Okay, I'm covered," I agreed levelly. I let my Magli pumps slide to the ground and judged distances. He'd have a hard time killing me in the dark, but he could probably hit me.

"I could have killed you as you unlocked your car," the man with the gun pointed out, as if reading my thoughts. He had a heavy, gravelly voice. "I'm not here to shoot you. Don Pasquale wants to talk to you. My partner will forgive you for kicking him—he shouldn't have tried to grab you. We were told you were a good street fighter."

"Thank you," I said gravely. "My car or yours?"

"Ours. We're going to blindfold you for the drive."

I picked up my shoes and let the man take me to a Cadillac limousine waiting on the far side of the floor with its motor running. There was no point in fighting. They wrapped a large black silk scarf around my eyes. I felt like Julius Schmeese waiting for the firing squad.

Gravel Voice sat in the back with me, his gun held lightly against my side. "You can put that away," I told him tiredly. "I'm not going to jump you."

The metal withdrew. I leaned back in the well-sprung plush seat and dozed. I must have fallen asleep in earnest; Gravel Voice had to shake me awake when the car stopped. "We take the blindfold off when you're inside." He guided me quickly but not roughly along a stone path and up a flight of stairs, exchanged greetings with a guard at the entrance, and led me down a carpeted hallway. Gravel knocked at a door. A faint voice told him to come in.

"Wait here," he ordered.

I leaned against the wall and waited. In a few moments the door opened. "Come in," Gravel told me.

I followed his voice and smelled cigar smoke and a fire. Gravel untied the scarf. I blinked a few times, adjusting to the light. I was in a large room, decorated in crimson—carpet,

167

drapes, and chairs all done in matching velvets and wools. The effect was opulent, but not unbearable.

In an armchair by a large fireplace sat Don Pasquale. I recognized him at once from his courtroom appearances, although he appeared older and frailer now. He might be seventy or more. He was thin, with gray hair and a pair of horn-rimmed glasses. He wore a red-velvet smoking jacket and held an enormous cigar in his left hand.

"So, Miss Warshawski, you want to speak to me."

I stepped up to the fire and took an armchair facing his. I felt a bit like Dorothy in Oz, finally getting to meet the talking head.

"You are a very courageous young lady, Miss Warshawski." The voice was old, but heavy, like parchment. "No man has ever fallen asleep while being driven to see me."

"You've worn me out, Don Pasquale. Your people burned down my apartment. Walter Novick tried to blind me. Someone stabbed poor Mr. Herschel. I'm short on sleep now, and I take it where I can."

He nodded. "Very sensible . . . Someone told me you speak Italian. Can we converse in that language, please."

"*Certo*," I said. "I have an aunt, an old woman. Rosa Vignelli. Two weeks ago she phoned me in deep distress. The safe at the Priory of Albertus Magnus, for which she was responsible, was found to contain forged stock certificates." I'd learned most of my Italian before I was fifteen, when Gabriella died. I had to scramble for some of the words, particularly a way to describe forgery. Don Pasquale provided a phrase.

"Thank you, Don Pasquale. Now owing to the Fascists and their friends the Nazis, my aunt has very little family left. In fact, only her son and I remain. So she turned to me for help. Naturally."

Don Pasquale nodded gravely. In an Italian family, you turn first to one another for help. Even if the family is Rosa and me.

"Soon after that, someone telephoned me. He threatened me with acid, and told me to stay away from the priory. And eventually, in fact, someone did throw acid on me. Walter Novick."

I picked my next words with utmost care. "Now naturally, I

am curious about those forged securities. But to be truthful, if they are going to be investigated and the facts about them discovered, it will be the FBI that does it. I don't have the money or the staff to do that kind of work." I watched Pasquale's face. Its expression of polite attention didn't change.

"My main concern is for my aunt, even though she is a disagreeable old woman. I made a promise to my mother, you see, a promise as she was dying. But when someone attacks me, then my honor is involved, too." I hoped I wasn't overdoing it.

Don Pasquale looked at his cigar, measuring the ash. He puffed on it a few times and carefully knocked the ash into a bronze cube at his left hand. "Yes, Miss Warshawski. I sympathize with your tale. But still—how does it involve me?"

"Walter Novick has . . . boasted . . . of being under your protection. Now I am not certain, but I believe it was he who tried to stab Stefan Herschel two days ago. Because this man is old, and because he was helping me, I am obligated to seek out his assassin. That is two counts against Walter Novick.

"If it were clear to everyone that he is not under your protection, I could deal with him with a clear conscience just on the grounds of his stabbing Mr. Herschel. I would forget the attack on me. And I would lose all interest in the securities—unless my aunt's name became involved in them again."

Pasquale gave a little smile. "You are one woman working alone. You are very brave, but you are still alone. With what do you propose to bargain?"

"The FBI has lost interest in the case. But if it knew in which direction to look, its interest might be aroused again."

"If you never left this house, the FBI would never know." The parchment voice was gentle, but I felt the hairs prickle along the back of my neck.

I looked at my hands. They appeared remarkably small and fragile. "It's a gamble, Don Pasquale," I finally said. "I know now who called to threaten me. If your interests are tied to his, then it's hopeless. One of these times, someone will kill me. I won't always make it out of the burning apartment, or be able to break my attacker's jaw. I will fight to the end, but the end will be clearly discernible to everyone.

"But if you and my caller are—business acquaintances only—then the story is a little altered. You're right—I have

169

nothing to bargain with. The *Herald-Star*, the Chicago police, even the FBI, all these would vigorously investigate my death. Or even a tale of forgery if I told it. But how many indictments have you avoided in the past?" I shrugged.

"I appeal only to your sense of honor, your sense of family, to understand why I've done what I've done, and why I want what I want." To the myth of the Mafia, I thought. To the myth of honor. But many of them liked to believe it. My only hope was that Pasquale's view of himself mattered to him.

The ash on the cigar grew long again before he spoke. "Ernesto will drive you home now, Miss Warshawski. You will hear from me in a few days."

Gravel Voice, or Ernesto, had stood silently by the door while we talked. Now he came to me with the blindfold. "Unnecessary, Ernesto," Pasquale said. "If Miss Warshawski decides to tell all she knows, she will be unable to say it."

Once again the goosepimples stood out on my neck. I curled my toes inside my boots to control the shaking in my legs. Trying hard to keep my voice level, I bade the don good-night.

I told Ernesto to take me to the Bellerophon. By now Phil Paciorek was right. I was in no condition to drive a car. The strain of talking to Pasquale, on top of the other stresses of the day, had pushed me over the edge of fatigue. So what if driving me home showed Ernesto where I lived. If Pasquale wanted to find me, this would only cut a day or two off his time.

I slept all the way back. When I got to the Bellerophon, I staggered up the stairs to the fourth floor, kicked off my boots, dropped the new dress on the floor, and fell into bed.

XX

Going to the Cleaners

IT WAS PAST eleven when I woke up again. I lay in bed for a while, reveling in the sense of rest, trying to reconstruct a dream I'd had in the middle of my sleep. Gabriella had come to me, not wasted as in the final days of her illness, but full of life. She knew I was in danger and wanted to wrap me in a white sheet to save me.

I had an urgent feeling that the dream held a clue to my problem or how to solve it, but I couldn't grab hold of it. I had very little time, and needed whatever prodding my subconscious could give me. Don Pasquale had said I would hear from him in a few days. That meant I might have forty-eight hours to straighten matters out to the point that any action of his against me would be superfluous.

I got out of bed and took a quick shower. The burns on my arms were healing well. Physically I was in condition to run again, but I couldn't bring myself to put on my sweats and go into the cold. The fire in my apartment had upset me more than I would admit to Roger. I wanted some security, and running through winter streets didn't feel like a way to get it.

I pulled the clothes out of my suitcase. The laundered ones still smelled of smoke. I put them away in the closet that housed the Murphy bed. My mother's wineglasses I set on the little dining table. That done, I'd moved in.

I bundled up the remaining clothes to take to a dry cleaner and went downstairs. Mrs. Climzak, the manager, saw me and called to me as I was walking out the door. She was a thin, anxious woman who always seemed to be gulping for air.

She came out from behind the lobby counter and hurried over to me with a brown paper bag. "Someone left these for you this morning," she gasped.

I took the bag dubiously, fearing the worst. Inside were my red Magli pumps, forgotten in Don Pasquale's limousine last night. No message. But at least it was a friendly gesture.

After so much breathless protesting that I could have walked the four flights up to my room and back, Mrs. Climzak agreed to keep them downstairs for me until I returned. She came running up behind me as I was going to the door to add, "And if you're taking those to a dry cleaner, there's a good one around the corner on Racine."

The woman at the cleaners informed me triumphantly that it would cost me extra to get the smoke out. She made a great show of inspecting each garment, clucking her teeth over it, and writing it down on a slip with the laboriousness of a traffic cop writing a ticket. At last, impatient, I grabbed up the clothes and left.

A second cleaner, sharing a dingy storefront with a tailor

171

several blocks down, was more obliging. The woman at the counter accepted the smoky clothes without comment and wrote up the ticket quickly. She directed me to a lunch counter that served homemade soup and stuffed cabbage. Not the ideal choice for the day's first meal, but the piping hot, fresh barley soup was delicious.

Using their pay phone to check in with my answering service, I learned Phil Paciorek had called several times. I'd forgotten all about him. Murray Ryerson. Detective Finchley.

I called Illinois Bell and explained my situation. They agreed to switch my number over to the Bellerophon. Also to charge me for the stolen phone. I called Freeman Carter and said I'd seen Uncle Stefan and would make a statement to the police if they would drop charges. He agreed to look into it. I called Phil and left a message with the hospital that I would get back to him. I saved Murray and the police for later.

Once downtown I retrieved my car and headed for the Pulteney Building. The mail piled in front of my office door was horrendous. Sorting through it quickly for checks and letters, I tossed the rest. No bills until my life had stabilized a bit. I looked around me affectionately. Bare, but mine. Maybe I could move in a mattress and a little sink and stove and live here for a while.

The desk top was covered with a film of grime. Whatever pollution the L exudes had filtered under the window. I filled an old coffee cup at the hall drinking fountain and scrubbed the desk with some Kleenex. Good enough.

Using one of the envelopes I'd just pitched, I made out a "To Do" list:

1. Inspect Mrs. Paciorek's private finances & papers
2. Ditto for O'Faolin
3. Ditto for Pelly
4. Find out if Walter Novick had stabbed Uncle Stefan
5. If yes, bag him

I couldn't figure out what to do with the first three items. But it should be easy enough to take care of four. Five might follow. I called Murray at the *Herald-Star*.

"V.I.—you ain't dead yet," he greeted me.

"Not for lack of trying," I answered. "I need some photographs."

"Wonderful. The Art Institute has some on sale. I tried calling you last night. We'd like to do a story about Stefan Herschel and your arrest."

"Why talk to me? Just make it up. Like your story of a couple of days ago."

"Trade you photographs for a story. Who do you want?"

"Walter Novick."

"You figure he stabbed Herschel?"

"I just want to know what he looks like in case he comes after me again."

"All right, all right. I'll have your pictures at the Golden Glow around four. And you give me half an hour."

"Just remember you're not Bobby Mallory," I said irritably. "I don't have to tell you anything."

"What I hear, you don't tell Mallory much either." He hung up.

I looked at my watch. Two o'clock. Time enough to think of a way to get at the papers I wanted to see. I could disguise myself as an itinerant member of Corpus Christi and go knocking on Mrs. Paciorek's door. Then, while she was praying intensely, I could find her safe, crack the combination and . . .

And . . . *I could disguise myself*. Not for Mrs. Paciorek, but for the priory. If O'Faolin was out there, I could take care of him and Pelly in one trip. If the disguise worked. It sounded like a lunatic idea. But I couldn't think of anything better.

As you go along Jackson Street to the river, you pass a number of fabric shops. At Hofmanstahls, on the corner of Jackson and Wells, I found a bolt of soft white wool. When they asked how much I needed I had no idea. I sketched the garment and we settled on ten yards. At eight dollars a yard, not exactly a bargain. They didn't have belts and it took close to an hour of wandering around leather stores and men's shops to find the heavy black strap I needed. A religious-goods store near Union Station provided the other accessories.

As I walked back across the slushy streets toward the Golden Glow, I passed a seedy print shop. On an impulse I went in. They had some photographs of old Chicago gangsters. I took a

173

collection of six to mix in with the shots of Novick that Murray was bringing me.

It was almost four—there wasn't time to get to the little tailor on Montrose before meeting Murray. But if I didn't make it there today, it would have to wait till Monday and that was too late. Murray would have to come with me and talk in the car.

He obliged with ill grace. When I came in he was happily absorbed in his second beer, had taken off his boots, and was warming his socks on a small fender next to the horseshoe mahogany bar. While he bitterly pulled on his wet boots I picked up a manila folder from the bar in front of him. In it were two shots of Novick, neither in sharp focus, but clear enough to identify him. Both were courtroom shots taken when Novick had been arrested for attempted manslaughter and armed robbery. He'd never been convicted. Pasquale's friends seldom were.

I was relieved at not recognizing Novick's face. I'd been half afraid that he might have been the man I'd kicked last night—if he was that close to Pasquale there was no chance the don would turn him loose.

I led Murray down the street to my car at a good clip.

"Damn it, V.I., slow down. I've been working all day and just drank a beer."

"You want your story, come and get it, Ryerson."

He climbed into the passenger seat, grumbling that the car was too small for him. I put the Omega in gear and headed for Lake Shore Drive.

"So how come you were visiting Stefan Herschel the day he got knifed?"

"What's he say about it?"

"Damned hospital won't let us in to talk to him. That's why I'm stuck asking you, and I know what that means—half a story. My gofer at the police station told me you'd been booked. For concealing evidence of a crime. What crime?"

"That's just Lieutenant Mallory's flamboyant imagination. He didn't like my being at Mr. Herschel's apartment and saving his life. He had to charge me with something."

Murray demanded to know what I was doing there. I gave him my standard story—about Uncle Stefan being a lonely old

174

man and my just happening to drop in. "Now when I saw him at the hospital—"

"You've talked to him!" Murray's shout made the little car's windows rattle. "What did he say? Are you going there now? Did Novick stab him?"

"No, I'm not going there now. I don't know if Novick stabbed him. The police story right now is that this was random housebreaking. Since Novick runs with the mob I don't see him as a housebreaker unless he does his own thing on the side. I don't know." I explained about the silver collection, and how eager Uncle Stefan was to shower people with tortes and hot chocolate. "If someone rang the bell, he'd just assume it was the neighborhood kids and let them in. Maybe it was the neighborhood kids. Poor old goon." I had an inspiration. "You know, you should talk to his neighbor—Mrs. Silverstein. She saw a lot of him. I bet she could give you some good tips."

Murray made a few notes. "Still, I don't trust you, V.I. It's just too damned pat, you being there."

I shrugged and pulled up in front of the cleaners. "That's the story. Take it or leave it."

"We had to drive all this way so you could get to the cleaners? That's your emergency? You'd better be planning on getting me back to the Loop."

"Some emergencies are more obscure than others."

I took my parcel of fabric and went into the little store. The tailoring part of the shop was a jumbled array of old spools of thread, a Singer that must have dated to the turn of the century, and scraps and snippets of cloth. The man huddled crosslegged on a chair in the corner, hunched over a length of brown suiting, might have gone back to 1900 as well.

Although he jerked a sideways glance at me, he continued to sew. When he'd finished whatever he was doing, he folded the fabric tidily, put it on a heaped table to his left, and looked at me. "Yes?" He spoke with a heavy accent.

"Could you sew something for me without a pattern?"

"Oh, yes, young lady. No question about it. When I was a young man, I cut for Marshall Field, for Charles Stevens. Those were the days before you were born, when they made clothes right there in the store. I cut all day long, and made, with no patterns. What is it you want?"

I showed him my sketch and pulled the wool from its brown wrapping. He studied the picture for a moment, and then me. "Oh, that would be no problem. No problem at all."

"And—could I have it by Monday?"

"Monday? Oh, the young lady is in a hurry." He waved an arm in the direction of several heaps of cloth. "Look at all these orders. They thought in advance. They bring their work in many weeks ahead of you. *Monday*, my dear young lady!"

I sat down on a footstool and negotiated in earnest. At last he agreed to do it for double his normal fee, payable in advance. "Forty dollars. I cannot do it for a penny less."

I tried to appear incredulous, as if I thought I was being gouged. The fabric alone had cost double that. Finally I pulled two twenties from my wallet. He told me to stop in at noon on Monday. "But next time, no rushes."

Murray had left a note under my windshield wiper, informing me that he'd caught a cab downtown and that I owed him sixteen dollars. I tossed the paper in the trashcan and headed for Skokie.

Uncle Stefan had been moved to a regular room that afternoon. That meant I didn't have to go through a routine with nurses and Metzinger just to see him. However, the police guard had also been removed—if his attackers were ordinary B & E men, he wasn't in any danger, according to the cops. I bit my lip. Caught by my own story, damn it. Unless I told the truth about the forgeries and the Mob, there was no way to convince the police that Uncle Stefan needed protection.

The old man was delighted to see me. Lotty had been by in the morning, but no one else was visiting him. I pulled out the photographs and showed them to him. He nodded calmly, "Just like *Hill Street Blues*. Do I recognize the mug shots?"

He selected Novick from the pile without hesitation.

"Oh, yes. That face is not easy to forget. Even though this picture is not totally clear, I have no doubt, no question. That is the man with the knife."

I stayed and talked with him for a while, turning over in the back of my mind various possibilities for his protection. If I just gave Novick's picture to the police . . . but if Pasquale wasn't willing to let him go, then he'd get both me and Uncle Stefan without any compunction or difficulty.

I abruptly interrupted a reminiscence of Fort Leavenworth. "Excuse me. I can't leave you here without a guard. And while I can stay until the end of visiting hours tonight, it's just too easy for someone to get in and out of a hospital. If I call a security service I trust and get someone over here, will you tell Dr. Metzinger it's your idea? He may think you're a paranoid old man, but he won't turn your guard out the way he will if I put it to him."

Uncle Stefan was disposed to be heroic and fought the idea, until I told him the same hoods were gunning for me: "If they kill me, and you're dead, there isn't a soul on earth who can go to the police for me. And our detective agency will vanish." Put as an appeal to his chivalry, the idea was palatable.

The service I used was called All Night—All Right. In a way, its employees were as amateurish as their name. Three enormous brothers and two of their friends made up the entire staff, and they only took jobs that appealed to them. No North Shore weddings, for example. I'd used them once when I had a load of rare coins I was returning to an Afghani refugee.

Jim Streeter answered the phone. When I explained the situation to him, he agreed to send someone up in a couple of hours. "The boys are out moving someone's furniture"—one of their sidelines. "When they get back I'll send Tom up."

Uncle Stefan obediently rang for the night nurse and explained his fears to her. She was inclined to be sarcastic, but I murmured a few words about hospital safety and malpractice suits and she said she would tell "Doctor."

Uncle Stefan nodded approvingly at me. "You are a very tough young lady. Ah, if only I had known you thirty years ago, the FBI never would have caught me."

A gift shop in the lobby yielded a pack of cards. We played gin until Tom Streeter showed up at eight-thirty. He was a big, quiet, gentle man. Seeing him, I knew I'd stopped one hole. At least temporarily.

I kissed Uncle Stefan good-night and left the hospital, checking carefully at each doorway, mixing with a large family group leaving the building. I inspected my car before opening the door. As near as I could tell, no one had wired it with dynamite.

Driving down the Edens, what puzzled me was the connection between O'Faolin and the forgeries. He hires Novick from Pasquale. How does he know Pasquale? How would a Panamanian archbishop know a Chicago mobster? Anyway, he hires Novick from Pasquale to back me off the forgeries. But why? The only connection I could think of was his longterm friendship with Pelly. But that made Pelly responsible for the forgeries and that still didn't make sense. The answer had to be at the friary and I had to get through Sunday somehow before I could find it.

Back at the Bellerophon, I plugged my phone into the wall. It seemed to work. My answering service told me Ferrant had tried phoning me as well as Detective Finchley.

I tried Roger first. He sounded subdued. "There's been a disturbing development in this takeover attempt. Or maybe it's a relief. Someone has stepped forward and filed five percent ownership with the SEC." He'd been closeted with the Ajax board all day discussing it. One of the other managing partners from Scupperfield, Plouder would be flying in tomorrow. Roger wanted to have dinner with me and get my ideas, if any.

I agreed to meet him. If nothing else, it would give me something to think about until Monday.

While I ran water in the bathtub I made my other call. Detective Finchley had left for the day, but Mallory was still at work. "Your lawyer says you're ready to make a statement about Stefan Herschel," he growled.

I offered to see him first thing Monday morning. "What did Detective Finchley want?"

I could get my gun back, Bobby said grudgingly. They'd gotten the Skokie police to send it down to them. They were confiscating the picklocks, though. It hurt Bobby physically to tell me about the gun. He didn't want me carrying it, he didn't want me in the detective business, he wanted me in Bridgeport or Melrose Park with six children and, presumably, a husband.

XXI

Deadline

ROGER POKED MOODILY at his steak. "By the way, thanks for the note you left yesterday. How was the archbishop?"

"There were two. One was fulsome, the other ugly. Tell me about this filing."

I had met him at the Filigree and been moved by his total exhaustion. We had drinks in the bar before dinner, Roger so worn that he hadn't felt like talking. Now he rubbed his forehead tiredly.

"I am baffled. Totally and utterly baffled. I've been dealing with it all day, and I still can't understand it. . . . It's like this. If you own five percent or more of a company's stock, you have to file with the SEC and tell them what you mean to do with your holding. You know you asked me a week or so ago about a Wood-Sage company? Well, they're the ones who made the filing.

"Now they did it late yesterday, just so they wouldn't have to answer a lot of questions or be in the *Journal* or anything. But of course, our lawyers got all the material. Such as it was. Wood-Sage isn't a corporation that *does* anything apparently. They're just a group of people who buy and sell stocks for their mutual benefit, figuring if they pool their investments they can do better than they would alone. It's not that unusual. And they're claiming they only bought so many Ajax shares because they think the company's a good buy. The trouble is, we can't get any kind of line on who owns Wood-Sage." He ran his fingers through his long hair and pushed his plate away, much of the steak uneaten.

"The disclosure to the SEC should include the owners, shouldn't it?" I asked.

He shrugged. "The owners are the shareholders. There is a board of directors, but it seems to be made up of brokers, including Tilford and Sutton."

"The buyers must include their customers, then." I thought back to my burglary of their offices. "I don't have a list of all their customers. And I don't know what it would tell you, anyway. The one strange thing about them is they do business for Corpus Christi. Corpus Christi bought several million dollars of stock last fall. It might have given them to Wood-Sage."

Roger had never heard of Corpus Christi.

"Not surprising—it's a group that tries to stay secret." I told him what I'd read about them in the *Journal*. "Because they do everything in secret, maybe they don't publicize their ownership of a company like Wood-Sage. . . . Catherine Paciorek is a member—her son let that fall inadvertently. . . ."

Roger fiddled with the stem of his wineglass. "There's something I want to ask you," he finally said abruptly. "It's hard for me, because we've gotten into difficulties about your detective work and my reaction to it. But I'd like to hire you, for Scupperfield, Plouder. I'd like you to try to find out who's behind Wood-Sage. Now this business with Corpus Christi and Mrs. Paciorek—it gives you an inside edge on the investigation."

"Roger, the SEC and the FBI have the kind of resources you need for that sort of investigation. I don't. By Tuesday or Wednesday they'll have the information. It'll be in the public domain."

"Maybe. But that may be too late. We're doing what we can—sending mailings to shareholders urging them to support current management. Our lawyers are working madly. But no one's getting results." He leaned across the table earnestly and took my hand. "Look. It's a lot to ask. I realize that. But you know Mrs. Paciorek. Can't you talk to her—find out if Corpus Christi is involved in this Wood-Sage thing at all?"

"Roger, the lady doesn't talk to me. I don't even know what I could do to get her to see me."

He looked at me soberly. "I'm not asking you to do me a favor. I'll hire you. Whatever your normal fee is, Scupperfield, Plouder will double it. I just cannot run the risk of omitting a course of action that might help. If we knew who the owners were, if we knew why they were trying to buy the company, it could make a big difference to our being able to hold on to Ajax."

I thought of the three dollars in my wallet, the new furniture I was going to have to buy, the fee to the Streeter brothers for protecting Uncle Stefan. And then my shoulders sank. It was my fault Uncle Stefan was lying in the hospital needing protection. After a couple of weeks of working on the forgeries, I had done nothing but lose my apartment and my life's possessions. Lotty, my refuge, wouldn't speak to me. I had never felt so discouraged or incapable in all my years as an investigator. I tried, awkwardly, to explain some of my feelings.

Roger squeezed my hand. "I understand how you feel." He grinned briefly. "I was the young hotshot coming over to manage the Ajax operation, show them how to do the job. Now our management are fighting for our lives. I know it's not my fault—but I feel futile and embarrassed that I can't do anything about it."

I made a wry face, but returned his handshake. "So we'll bolster each other's failing vanity? I suppose . . . But next week you've got to go to the FBI and the SEC. Set up a meeting for me with them. They won't talk to me otherwise. Just as long as you know it's a most unlikely project, I'll try to think of a way to get Catherine Paciorek to talk to me."

He smiled gratefully. "You don't know what a relief this is to me, Vic. Just the idea that someone I can trust absolutely will be involved. Can you come in Monday and meet the board? The lawyers can give you a full picture on what they know—three hours to say nothing, maybe."

"Monday's full. Tuesday?" He agreed. Eight A.M. I blenched slightly but wrote the time into my date book.

We left the Filigree at nine and went to a movie. I called the hospital from the theater to check on Uncle Stefan. All was well there. I wished someone cared enough for my safety to hire some huge bodyguards to protect me. Of course, a hard-boiled detective is never scared. So what I was feeling couldn't be fear. Perhaps nervous excitement at the treats in store for me. Even so, when Roger asked me, tentatively, if I wanted to go back to the Hancock with him, I assented without hesitation.

By morning the *Herald-Star* and the *Tribune* had both picked up the Wood-Sage story in their Sunday business sections. No one on the Ajax board had been available for comment. Pat Kollar, the *Herald-Star*'s financial analyst, explained why someone would want to acquire an insurance company. There wasn't much else to say about Wood-Sage.

181

Roger read the papers gloomily. He left at two to meet his partner's plane. "He'll have the *Financial Times* and the *Guardian* with him and I'll get *The New York Times* on my way to the car. That way we can have a real wake surrounded by all the bad news at once . . . Want to stay to meet him?"

I shook my head. Godfrey Anstey would be sleeping in the apartment's second bedroom. Two's company but three's embarrassing.

After Roger left, I stayed for a few minutes to call my answering service. Phyllis Lording had phoned several times around noon. Somewhat surprised, I dialed the Chestnut Street apartment.

Phyllis's high, rather squeaky voice sounded more flustered than usual. "Oh, hi, Vic. Is that you? Do you have any time this afternoon, by any chance?"

"What's up?"

She gave a nervous laugh. "Probably nothing. Only it's hard to explain over the phone."

I shrugged and agreed to walk over. When she met me at the door, she appeared thinner than ever. Her chestnut hair was pulled carelessly from her face, pinned on her head. Her swanlike neck seemed pitifully slender beneath the mass of hair, the fine planes in her face standing out sharply. In an oversize shirt and tight jeans she looked unbearably fragile.

She led me into the living room where the day's papers were spread out on the floor. Like Agnes, she was a heavy smoker, and a blue haze hung in the air. I sneezed involuntarily.

She offered me coffee from an electric percolator sitting on the floor near the overflowing ashtray. When I saw how brackish it was I asked for milk.

"You can check in the refrigerator," she said doubtfully, "but I don't think I have any."

The huge refrigerator held nothing except a few condiments and a bottle of beer. I went back to the living room. "Phyllis! What are you eating?"

She lit a cigarette. "I'm just not hungry, Vic. At first I kept trying to make myself meals, but I'd get sick if I ate anything. Now I'm just not hungry."

I squatted down on the floor next to her and put a hand on

her arm. "Not good, Phyl. It's not a way to memorialize Agnes."

She blinked a few times through the smoke. "I just feel so alone, Vic. Agnes and I didn't have many friends in common—the people I know are all at the university and her friends were brokers and investors. Her family won't talk to me . . ." Her voice trailed off and she hunched her thin shoulders.

"Agnes's youngest sister would like very much to talk to you. Why don't you give her a call? She was twenty years younger than Agnes and didn't know her too well, but she liked and admired her. She's too young to know how to phone you without embarrassment after the way her mother's acted."

She didn't say anything for a few minutes. Then she gave her intense smile and a brief nod. "Okay. I'll call her."

"And start eating something?"

She nodded again. "I'll try, Vic."

We talked about her courses for a bit. I wondered if she could get someone to take them for her a week while she went south for some sunshine; she said she'd think about it. After a while, she got around to the reason behind her phone call.

"Agnes and I shared a subscription to *The New York Times*." She smiled painfully and lit another cigarette—her fifth since I'd arrived forty minutes earlier. "She always went straight to the business section while I hit the book reviews. She . . . she teased me about it. I don't have much of a sense of humor; Agnes did, and it always got under my skin a bit . . . Since she died, I've, I've"—she bit her lips and looked away, trying to hide tears trickling down the inner corners of her face—"I've started reading the business section. It's . . . it's a way to feel I'm still in touch with her."

The last sentence came out in a whisper and I had to strain to hear her. "I don't think that's foolish, Phyl. I have a feeling if it had been you who died, Agnes would plunge into Proust with the same spirit."

She turned to look at me again. "You were closer to Agnes in some ways than I could ever be. You and she are a lot alike. It's funny. I loved her, desperately, but I didn't understand her very well. . . . I was always a little jealous of you because you understood her."

I nodded. "Agnes and I were good friends for a long time. I've had times when I was jealous of your closeness with her."

She put her cigarette out and seemed to relax; her shoulders fell back from their hunched position. "That's very generous of you, Vic. Thanks . . . Anyway, in the *Times* this morning I saw a story about a takeover bid for Ajax. You know, the big insurance company downtown."

"I know. Agnes was looking at that before she died and I've been scratching around at it, too."

"Alicia Vargas—Agnes's secretary—sent me all her personal papers. Things she'd kept notes on, anything that was handwritten and didn't relate to company business. I went through them all. Her latest notebook especially. She kept them—like Jonathan Edwards—or Proust."

She stood up and went to the coffee table where I could see some spiral college notebooks among stacks of *Harper's* and *The New York Review of Books*. I'd assumed they belonged to Phyllis.

She took the top one and riffled through it quickly, then folded it back to show me the page. Agnes's sprawling hand was difficult to read. She'd written in "1/12," followed by "R.F., Ajax." That wasn't too difficult to follow—she'd first talked to Ferrant about Ajax on January 12. Other cryptic entries that week apparently referred to various things she was thinking about or working on. One was a note to go to Phyllis's poetry reading, for example. Then, on the eighteenth, the day she died, was a heavily scored entry: "$12 million, C-C for Wood-Sage."

Phyllis was looking at me intently. "You see, Wood-Sage didn't mean anything to me by itself. But after I read the paper this morning. . . . And the C-C. Agnes told me about Corpus Christi. I couldn't help but think . . ."

"Neither can I. Where the hell did she get that information?"

Phyllis shrugged. "She knew a lot of brokers and lawyers."

"Can I use your phone?" I asked Phyllis abruptly.

She led me to a porcelain-gold replica of the early telephones; I dialed the Paciorek number. Barbara answered. She was glad to talk to me; she'd be really happy to hear from Phyllis; and yes, her mother was home. She came back a few minutes later to say in considerable confusion that Mrs. Paciorek refused to talk to me.

"Tell her I just called to let her know that Corpus Christi's ownership of Wood-Sage will be in the *Herald-Star* next week."

"Corpus Christi?" she repeated doubtfully.

"You got it."

Five minutes passed. I read the *Times* story on Ajax—more words to say less than had been in the Chicago papers. I scanned more verbiage on the AT&T divestiture. I looked at help wanted ads. Maybe I could find a better line of work. "Seasoned professional not afraid of challenges." That meant someone to work hard for low pay. What do you season professionals with, anyway?

Finally Mrs. Paciorek came on the line. "Barbara gave me some garbled message." Her voice was tight.

"It's like this, Mrs. Paciorek: The SEC knows, of course, that Wood-Sage has bought a five-percent position in Ajax. What they don't know is that most of the money was put up by Corpus Christi. And that most of Corpus Christi's money comes from you, the Savage fortune you turned over to them. Securities law is not my specialty, but if Corpus Christi is putting up the money for Wood-Sage to buy Ajax stock, the SEC is not going to be happy that it wasn't mentioned in your filing."

"I don't know what you're talking about."

"You've got to work on your answers. When the papers get hold of you, they're not going to believe that for one minute."

"If something called Corpus Christi is buying Ajax stock, I know nothing about it."

"That's marginally better," I conceded. "The problem is, when Agnes—your daughter, you know—died, she left behind some notes showing a connection between Corpus Christi and Wood-Sage. If I turn the FBI's attention to your lawyers, I'm sure it would be able to get the name of the broker who handles the Corpus Christi portfolio. That is presumably where Agnes got her information. In addition, on a smaller scale, it will be interested in the block transfers Preston Tilford handled."

There was silence at the other end while Mrs. Paciorek marshaled her defenses. I shouldn't have expected to force such a controlled woman into blurting out anything indiscreet. At last she said, "My attorneys will doubtless know how to handle any investigation, however harassing. That isn't my concern."

"We'll see about that. But the police may want to ask you some questions, too. They may want to know to what lengths you would go to keep Agnes from publishing Corpus Christi's attempted takeover of Ajax."

After a long pause, she replied, "Victoria, you are obviously hysterical. If you think you know something about the death of my daughter, perhaps I will see you."

I started to say something, then thought better of it. The woman was going to talk to me—what more did I need right now? She wasn't free today, but she could see me at her home tomorrow night at eight.

With my nerves in their current jangled state, I didn't feel like going back to the Bellerophon. I explained the fire and my predicament to Phyllis, who instantly offered me her spare bedroom. She drove with me to visit Uncle Stefan, now feeling well enough to be bored in the hospital. To my relief, the doctors wanted to hold him a few more days—once he got home he would be impossible to keep an eye on.

Robert Streeter, the youngest brother, was with him when we arrived. Apparently someone had tried to get into the room around midnight. Jim, then on duty, sensibly didn't try to chase him since that would have left the room unguarded. By the time he'd roused hospital security, the intruder was long gone.

I shook my head helplessly. One more problem I couldn't handle. Lotty arrived as we were leaving. At the sight of Phyllis, her heavy black brows went up. "So! Vic is roping you into her masquerade as well?"

"Lotty! You and I need to talk," I said sharply.

She gave me a measuring look. "Yes. I think that would be a good thing. . . . Are these thugs with Stefan your idea or his?"

"Call me when you've climbed off your cross!" I snapped and walked away.

Phyllis was too polite to ask about the incident. We didn't

speak much, but had a pleasant meal at a little restaurant on Irving Park Road before heading back to Chestnut Street.

Cigarette smoke had permeated the bedclothes in the guest room. The smell, combined with my nervous tension, made sleep difficult. At three, I got up to read, and found Phyllis sitting in the living room with a biography of Margaret Fuller. We talked companionably for several hours. After that I slept until Phyllis stopped in to say good-bye before going to her eight-thirty class. She invited me to come back at night. Despite the stale air, I accepted gratefully.

I thought I might be safer with a rental car than my own, which was by now well known to any hoodlum in Chicago trying to find me. On my way over to the police station I stopped at a rental agency and got a Toyota whose steering must have been used by the U.S. weightlifting team while they trained for the Olympics. They told me they didn't have anything else that size and to take it or leave it. Snarling, I took it—I didn't have time to shop for cars.

Lieutenant Mallory wasn't in when I got to Roosevelt Road. I gave my statement to Detective Finchley. Not having Bobby's history with me, he accepted what I had to say and returned the Smith & Wesson. Freeman Carter, who accompanied me, told me we'd have a formal hearing in the morning, but that my character was once more unblemished—not even a moving violation in the last three years.

It was afternoon when I reached my ancient tailor on Montrose. He had finished the robe for me; it fit perfectly, right hem length, right sleeve length. I thanked him profusely, but he responded with more harsh words on young ladies who couldn't plan ahead—he'd had to work all day Sunday for me.

I had to make a stop at the Bellerophon to pick up the rest of my disguise. Mrs. Climzak came out breathlessly from behind the counter with my shoes. She'd never have taken them if she'd known she'd have to be responsible for them for two days. If I was going to turn out to be the thoughtless type of tenant, she didn't know if they could keep me. And certainly not if I entertained men in the middle of the night.

I was turning to go upstairs, but this seemed like a specific, not a generic accusation. "What men in the middle of the night?"

"Oh, don't try to act so innocent, Miss Warshawski. The neighbors heard him and called the night clerk. He got the police and your friend left. Don't pretend you don't remember that."

I left her midsentence and galloped up the stairs to the fourth floor. I hadn't had time to make a mess of my shabby little room. Someone else had done it for me. Fortunately, there wasn't too much to toss around—no books, except a Gideon Bible. No food. Just my clothes, the Murphy bed mattress, and the pots and pans in the kitchen. I held my breath while I inspected the Venetian glasses. Whoever had been here wasn't totally vindictive: They stood unharmed on the little card table.

"Oh, *damn*!" I shouted. "Leave me alone!" I shuffled things together as best I could, but didn't really have time to clean up. Didn't feel like cleaning up, come to that. What I felt like was taking to my bed for a week. Except I didn't have a bed anymore, not my own anyway.

I lugged the heavy mattress back onto the bed and lay on it. The cracks in the ceiling made a fine mesh. They resembled my own incoherent thoughts. I stared at them morosely for a quarter of an hour before forcing myself to abandon self-pity and start thinking. The likeliest reason someone was searching my room was to find the evidence I'd told Catherine Paciorek about yesterday. No wonder she hadn't wanted to see me last night. She was getting someone to find me and find whatever document Agnes had left behind. Very well. That would make it easier to get her to talk when I saw her tonight.

I put Catherine and the ransacking to one side. Now that I was thinking again, I could cope. Changing into jeans and boots, I put the robe into a paper bag with the rest of my disguise, digging the component pieces out of the mess in the room.

My shoulder holster was wedged under the chest of drawers in the closet. It took close to half an hour to find. I looked nervously at my watch, not sure what my deadline was, but fearing that time was running very short indeed. I still had to stop for some bullets, but that delay was essential. I wasn't going to the bathroom unarmed until this mess was straightened out.

XXII

Wandering Friar

A STORE IN Lincolnwood sold me three dozen bullets for twenty-five dollars. Despite what the gun haters may think, it isn't cheap killing people. Not only is it not cheap, it's time-consuming. It was nearly three. I didn't have time for lunch if I wanted to get to the priory on schedule. Stopping at a corner grocery I picked up an apple and ate it as I drove.

A bright winter sun reflected against the snow, breaking into diamonds of glinting, blinding color. My dark glasses, I suddenly remembered, had been in a dresser drawer in the old apartment. No doubt they were a lump of plastic now. I shielded my eyes as best I could with the visor and my left hand.

Once in Melrose Park, I toured the streets looking for a park. Pulling in from the roadway, I took off my pea jacket and pulled the white wool robe on over jeans and shirt. The black leather belt tightened the gown at the middle. The rosary I attached to the right side of the belt. It wasn't exactly the real thing, but in dim light I ought to be able to pass for a Dominican friar.

By the time I got back to the priory and parked behind the main building it was almost four-thirty, time for evening prayers and mass. I waited until four-thirty-five, and went into the main hallway.

The ascetic youth sat hunched over a devotional work. He glanced up at me briefly. When I headed for the stairs instead of the chapel, he said, "You're late for vespers, Brother," but went back to his reading.

My heart was pounding as I reached the wide landing where the marble staircase turned back on itself up into the private upper reaches of the friary. The area was cloistered, not open to the public, male or female, and I couldn't suppress a feeling of dread, as though I were committing some kind of sacrilege.

I'd been expecting a long, open ward like a nineteenth-century hospital. Instead, I came on a quiet corridor with doors opening onto it, rather like a hotel. The doors were shut, but not locked. Next to each, making my task infinitely easier, were little placards with the monks' names printed in a neat scroll. Each man had a room to himself.

I squinted at each in turn until I came to one that had no name on it. Cautiously, I knocked, then opened the door. The room contained only a bare single bed and a crucifix. At the far end of the hall, I came to a second nameless room, which I opened in turn. This was O'Faolin's temporary quarters.

Besides the bed and crucifix, the room held a small dresser and a little table with a drawer in the middle. O'Faolin's Panamanian passport and his airline ticket were in the drawer. He was on a ten P.M. Alitalia flight on Wednesday. Forty-eight hours to—to what?

The dresser was filled with stacks of beautiful linen, hand-tailored shirts, and a fine collection of silk socks. The Vatican's poverty didn't force her employees to live in squalor.

Finally, under the bed, I found a locked attaché case. I mourned my picklocks. Using the barrel of the Smith & Wesson, I smashed the hinges. I hated doing anything so blatant, but time was short.

The case was stacked with papers, most in Italian, some in Spanish. I looked at my watch. Five o'clock. Thirty minutes more. I shuffled through the stack. A number of papers with the Vatican seal—the keys to the kingdom—dealt with O'Faolin's fund-raising tour of the States. However, Ajax's name caught my eye and I looked slowly through the papers until I found three or four referring to the insurance company. I don't read Italian as fast as I do English, but these seemed to be technical documents from a financial house, detailing the assets, outstanding debt, number of shares of common stock, and names and expiration dates of the terms of the current board of directors.

The most interesting document in the collection was clipped to the inside cover of Ajax's 1983 annual report. It was a letter, in Spanish, to O'Faolin from someone named Raúl Díaz Figueredo. The letterhead, embossed with an intricate logo, and Figueredo's name as *Presidente*, was for the Italo-Panama Import-Export Company. Spanish is enough like Italian that I could work out the gist: After reviewing many U.S. financial institutions, Figueredo wished to bring Ajax to O'Faolin's attention, the easiest object—target?—for a plan of acquisition. The Banco Ambrosiano assets resided happily—no, safely—in Panamanian and Bahamian banks. Yet for these assets to be—fecund? no, productive—as His Excellency wisely understands, they must be usable in public works.

I sat back on my heels and looked soberly at the document. Here was evidence of what lay behind the Ajax takeover. And the connection with Wood-Sage and Corpus Christi? I looked nervously at my watch. Time enough to sort that out later. I slipped the letter from the paper clip, folded it, and put it in my jeans pocket under the robe. Stacking the papers together as neatly as I could, I put them back in the attaché case and slid the case under the bed.

The hallway was still deserted. I had one more stop. Given the Figueredo letter, it was worth the significant risk of being caught.

Father Pelly's room was at the other end of the hall, near the stairs. I cocked an ear. No voices below. The service must still be in progress. I pushed open his door.

As spartan as the other rooms, Pelly's nonetheless had the personal stamp of a place that's been inhabited for a long time by one person. Some family photographs stood on the little deal table, and a bookcase was filled several layers deep.

I found what I was looking for in the bottom drawer of the dresser. A list of Chicago area members of Corpus Christi with their addresses and phone numbers. I went through it quickly, keeping one nervous ear strained for voices. If worse came to worst, I might be able to leave from the window. It was narrow, but we were only on the second floor and I thought I could squeeze through.

Cecelia Paciorek Gleason was listed, and Catherine Paciorek of course. And near the bottom of the list, Rosa Vignelli. Don Pasquale was not a member. One secret society was enough for the man, I supposed.

As I stuck the list in the drawer and got up to leave, I heard voices in the hallway outside, and then a hand on the door. It was too late to try the window. I looked around desperately and slid under the bed, the rosary making a faint clicking noise as I pulled my robes in around me.

My heart was pounding so hard that my body vibrated. I

took deep, silent breaths, trying to still the movement. Black shoes appeared near my left eye. Then Pelly kicked them off and climbed onto the bed. The mattress and springs were old and not in the best of shape. The springs sagging under his weight almost touched my nose.

We lay like that for a good quarter of an hour, me stifling a sneeze prompted by the cold steel, Pelly breathing gently. Someone knocked at the door. Pelly sat up. "Come in."

"Gus. Someone's been in my room and broken into my attaché case."

O'Faolin. I'd know his voice anywhere for the rest of my life. Silence. Then Pelly: "When did you last look at it?"

"This morning. I needed to write a letter to an address I had in there. It's hard to believe one of your brothers would do a thing like this. But who? It couldn't possibly be Warshawski."

No indeed.

Pelly asked him sharply if anything was missing.

"Not as far as I can tell. And there wasn't anything that would prove anything, anyway ... Except for a letter Figueredo wrote me."

"If Warshawski broke in—" Pelly began.

"If Warshawski broke in, it doesn't really matter," O'Faolin interrupted. "She isn't going to be a problem after tonight. But if she shows the letter to someone in the meantime, I'll have to start all over again. I should never have left you on your own to handle this business. Forging those securities was a lunatic idea, and now ..." He broke off. "No point rehashing all that. Let's just see if the letter's missing."

He turned abruptly and left. Pelly pulled his shoes back on and followed him. I got up quickly. Pulled the hood well around my face and cracked the door to watch Pelly disappear into O'Faolin's room. Then, trying to remain calm, I went down the stairs with my head tucked into my chin. A couple of brothers greeted me en route, and I mumbled in response. At the bottom, Carroll said good evening. I mumbled and took off for the front door. Carroll said sharply, "Brother!" Then to someone else, "Who is that? I don't recognize him."

Outside, I hitched up my habit and ran to the back of the building, started the Toyota, and drove it bumpily down the drive back to Melrose Park. There I quickly divested myself of the robe at a dry cleaner, telling them it was for Augustine Pelly.

In the car I sat laughing for a few minutes, then soberly considered what I'd found and what it meant. The letter from Figueredo seemed to imply that they wanted to acquire Ajax in order to launder Banco Ambrosiano money. Bizarre. Or maybe not. A bank, or an insurance company, made a highly respectable cover for moving questionable capital into circulation. If you could do it so the multitude of auditors didn't notice. . . . I thought of Michael Sindona and the Franklin National Bank. Some people thought the Vatican had been involved in that escapade. With the Banco Ambrosiano, the connection was documented, if not understood: The Vatican was part owner of Ambrosiano's Panamanian subsidiaries. So was it strange that the head of the Vatican's finance committee would take an interest in the disposition of the Ambrosiano assets?

O'Faolin was an old friend of Kitty Paciorek. Mrs. Paciorek's sizable fortune was tied up with Corpus Christi. Ergo . . . She was expecting me in a couple of hours. I had some evidence, evidence she wanted badly enough to get someone to search the Bellerophon. But did it link her to the Wood-Sage/Corpus Christi connection strongly enough to make her talk? I didn't think so.

Thoughts of Mrs. Paciorek reminded me of O'Faolin's last remark: I wasn't going to be a problem after tonight. The queasiness, which seemed to be more and more a permanent resident, returned to my stomach. He might have meant they'd have Ajax sewn up by tonight. But I didn't think so. It seemed more likely that Walter Novick would be waiting for me in Lake Forest. Mrs. Paciorek presumably had no scruples about doing such a favor for her old friend, although she probably wouldn't have me killed while her husband and Barbara were watching. What would she try? An ambush on the grounds?

Between Melrose and Elmwood Park, North Avenue forms a continuous strip of fast-food restaurants, factories, used-car lots, and cheap, small shopping malls. I selected one of these at random and found a public phone. Mrs. Paciorek answered. Using the nasal twang of the South Side, I asked for Barbara. She was spending the night with friends, Mrs. Paciorek said, demanding in a sharp voice to know who was calling. "Lucy van Pelt," I answered, hanging up. I couldn't think of a way to find out where the doctor and the servants were.

A Jewel/Osco had a public photocopier, which yielded a greasy gray copy of Figueredo's letter to O'Faolin. I bought a packet of cheap envelopes and a stamp from a stamp machine and mailed the original to my office. I thought for a minute, then scribbled a note to Murray on one of the envelopes, telling him to look at my office mail if I turned into a Chicago floatfish. Folded in three, it fit into another envelope, which I mailed to the *Herald-Star*. As for Lotty and Roger, what I wanted to tell them was too complicated to fit onto an envelope.

By now it was close to seven, too late for me to have a proper sit-down meal. The apple I'd had at three had been my only meal since breakfast, though, and I needed something to brace me for a possible fight at Mrs. Paciorek's. I bought a large Hershey bar with almonds at the Jewel and stopped at Wendy's for a taco salad. Not the ideal thing to eat in a moving car, I realized as I joined the traffic on the tollway, and the salad dribbled down the front of my shirt. If Mrs. Paciorek was planning to sic German shepherds on me they'd know where I was by the chili.

As I exited onto Half Day Road, I went over what I knew of the Paciorek estate. If an ambush was attempted, it would be laid either by the front door or at the garage entrance. In back of the house were the remains of a wood. Agnes and I had sometimes taken sandwiches out there to eat sitting on logs by a stream feeding Lake Michigan.

The property ended a half mile or so back of the house at a bluff overlooking the lake. In the summer, in broad daylight, it might be possible to climb that bluff, but not on a winter's night with waves roaring underneath. I'd have to come at the house from the side, across neighboring lots, and hope for the best.

I left the Toyota on a side street next to Arbor Road. Lake Forest was dark. There were no street lights, and I had no flashlight. Fortunately the night was relatively clear—a snowstorm would have made the job impossible.

Hunching down in my navy-surplus pea jacket, I made my way quietly past the house on the corner. Once in the backyard, the snow muffled any sound of my feet; it also made walking laborious. As I reached the fence dividing the yard from its neighbor, a dog started barking to my left. Soon it sounded as though all the dogs in suburbia were yapping at me. I climbed over the fence and moved east, away from the baying, hoping to get deep enough to hit the Paciorek house from behind.

The third lot was comparable in size to the Paciorek's. As I moved into the wooded area, the dogs finally quieted down. Now I could hear the sullen roar of Lake Michigan in front of me. The regular, angry slapping of wave against cliff made me shiver violently with a cold deeper than that of freezing toes and ears.

Totally disoriented in the dark, I kept bumping into trees, stumbling over rotting logs, falling into unexpected holes. Suddenly I skidded down a small bank and landed with a jolt on my butt on some rocky ice. After picking myself up and slipping again, I realized I must be at the stream. If I walked away from the roaring lake, I should, with luck, be at the back of the Paciorek house.

In a few minutes I had fought my way clear of the trees. The house loomed as a blacker hole in the dark in front of me. Agnes and I had usually come out through the kitchen, which was on the far left along with rooms for the servants. No lights shone there now. If the servants were in, they were not giving any sign of it. In front of me were French windows leading into the conservatory-library-organ room.

My fingers were thick with cold. It took agonizing minutes to unbutton the pea jacket and take it off. I held it over the glass next to the window latch. With a numb hand, I pulled the Smith & Wesson clumsily from its holster, tapped the jacket lightly but firmly with the butt, and felt the glass give underneath. I paused for a minute. No alarms sounded. Holding my breath, I gently knocked glass away from the frame, stuck an arm through the opening, and unlatched the window.

Once inside the house I found a radiator. Pulling off boots and gloves, I warmed my frozen extremities. Ate the rest of the Hershey bar. Squinted at phosphorescent hands on my watch—past nine o'clock. Mrs. Paciorek must be getting impatient.

After a quarter of an hour, I felt recovered enough to meet

195

my hostess. Pulling the damp boots back on my toes was unpleasant, but the cold revived my mind, slightly torpid from the hike and the warmth.

Once outside the conservatory I could see lights coming from the front of the house. I followed them through long marble passages until I came to the family room where I'd talked to Mrs. Paciorek a couple of weeks ago. As I'd hoped, she was sitting there in front of the fire, the needlepoint project in her lap but her hands still. Standing at an angle in the hall, I watched her. Her handsome angry face was strained. She was waiting for the sound that would tell her I had been shot.

XXIII

Lake Forest Party

I'D BEEN HOLDING the Smith & Wesson in one hand, but she was clearly alone. I put the gun back in the holster and walked into the room.

"Good evening, Catherine. None of the servants seemed to be here, so I let myself in."

She stared at me, frozen. For a moment I wondered if she really were having a stroke. Then she found her voice. "What are you doing here?"

I sat down facing her in front of the fire. "You invited me, remember? I tried getting here at eight, but I got lost in the dark—sorry to be so late."

"Who?—how?—" she broke off and looked suspiciously at the hallway.

"Let me help you out," I said kindly. "You want to know how I got past Walter Novick—or whoever you have waiting for me out front, don't you?"

"I don't know what you're talking about," she said fiercely.

"Then we'll go and find out!" I stood up again. Walking behind her, I grabbed her under the armpits and pulled her to her feet. She wasn't much heavier than I and had no fighting skills whatsoever. She tried struggling with me, but it wasn't an equal contest. I frog-marched her to the front door.

"Now. You are going to call whoever is out there to come

in. My right hand is now holding my Smith and Wesson revolver, which is loaded and ready to shoot."

She opened the door angrily. Casting me a look of loathing, she went to the shallow porch. Two figures broke away from the shadows near the driveway and came toward her. "Leave!" she yelled. "Leave! She came in through the back."

The two men stood still for a minute. I aimed the gun at the one nearer my right hand. "Drop your weapons," I shouted. "Drop your weapons and come into the light."

At my voice they both shot at us. I pushed Mrs. Paciorek into the snow and fired. The man on the right staggered, tripped, sprawled in the snow. The other fled. I heard a car door slam and the sound of tires trying to grab hold.

"You'd better come with me, Catherine, while we see what kind of shape he's in. I don't trust you alone in there with a phone."

She didn't say anything as I dragged her pump-clad feet through the snow. When we came to the sprawled figure, he pointed a gun at us. "Don't shoot again, you lunatic," I cried. "You'll hit your employer!"

When he didn't put the gun down, I let go of Mrs. Paciorek and jumped on his arm. The gun went off, but the bullet sailed harmlessly into the night. I kicked the weapon from his hand and knelt to look at him.

In the lights marking the driveway I made out his heavy Slavic jawline. "Walter Novick!" I hissed. I couldn't keep my voice quite steady. "We can't keep meeting in the dark like this."

As nearly as I could tell, I'd hit his right leg just above the knee. It should have been a bad enough wound to keep him from moving, but he was strong and he was scared. He tried scrabbling away from me in the snow. I grabbed his right arm and yanked it up behind him.

Mrs. Paciorek turned on her heel and headed for the front door. "Catherine!" I yelled. "Better call an ambulance for your friend. I'm not sure O'Faolin can get reinforcements out here in time to shoot me if you phone him first anyway."

She must have heard me, but gave no sign. A few seconds later the front door slammed shut behind her. Novick was cursing loudly if unimaginatively, his voice slightly muffled by

197

the wiring holding his jaw together. I didn't want to leave him, but I didn't want Mrs. Paciorek summoning help, either. Gathering the hit man by the armpits, I started dragging him toward the house. He screamed with pain as his right leg bumped along the ground.

I dropped him and knelt again, this time looking him in the face. "We need to talk, Walter," I panted. "I'm not leaving you here on the chance you can make it to the road for your buddy to find you. Not that he's likely to—he's probably in DuPage County by now."

He tried to hit me, but the cold and blood loss were getting to him. The blow landed ineffectually on my shoulder.

"Your working days are over, Walter. Even if they patch that leg up, you're going to spend a long, long time in Joliet. So we'll talk. When you feel at a loss for words, I'll help you out."

"I don't have anything to say," he gasped hoarsely. "They haven't made—a—charge stick yet. They won't—won't do it now."

"Wrong, Walter. Stefan Herschel is going to be your downfall. You're slipping. You didn't kill him. He's alive. He's already ID'd you from your photo."

He managed a contemptuous shrug. "My—my friends—will prove—he's wrong."

Fury, compounded of fatigue, of Lotty's accusations, of the attempt on my eyes, rose in me. I shook him, enough to jar the injured leg, and was glad when he yelped.

"Your friends!" I shouted at him. "Don Pasquale, you mean. The don didn't send you here, did he? Did he?" When Novick didn't say anything, I picked him up by the shoulders and started dragging him toward the house again.

"Stop!" he yelled. "No. No, it wasn't the don. It—it was someone else."

I leaned over him in the snow. "Who, Novick?"

"I don't know."

I grabbed his armpits. "All right!" he screamed. "Put me down. I don't know his name. He's—he's someone who called me."

"Have you ever met him in person?"

In the floodlights, I saw him nod weakly. A middle-aged

198

man. He had met him once. The day he stabbed Uncle Stefan. This man had come with him to the apartment. No, Uncle Stefan might not have seen him—he'd waited in the hall until after the stabbing. Then gone in to collect the forged stocks. He was fifty-five or sixty. Green eyes. Gray hair. But the voice Novick especially remembered—a voice you'd recognize in hell, he called it.

O'Faolin. I sat back on my heels and looked at the hit man. Sour bile filled my mouth. I swallowed a handful of snow, gagged, swallowed again, trying to force down the desire to kill Novick where he lay.

"Walter, you're a lucky man. Pasquale doesn't give a damn whether you live or die. Neither do I. But you're going to live. Isn't that nice? And if you swear in court that the man who ordered you out here tonight was behind the stabbing of Stefan Herschel, I'll see you get a good plea bargain. We'll forget the acid. We'll even forget the fire. How about it?"

"The don won't forget me." This was in a thread of a voice. I had to stick my ear close to his revolting face to hear it.

"Yes, he will, Walter. He can't afford to be tied to the forgeries. He can't afford the FBI and the SEC subpoenaing his accounts. He isn't going to know you."

He still didn't say anything. I pulled the Smith & Wesson from my jeans belt. "If I shoot your left kneecap, you'll never be able to prove it didn't happen when you attacked me at the door."

"You wouldn't," he gasped.

He was probably right; my stomach was churning as it was. What kind of person kneels in the snow threatening to destroy the leg of an injured man? Not anyone I wanted to know. I pulled the hammer back with a loud click and pointed the gun at his left leg.

"No," he cried. "No, don't. I'll do it. Whatever you say. But you get me a doctor. Get me a doctor." He was sobbing pitifully. Toughest man in the Mafia.

I put the gun away. "Good boy, Walter. You won't regret it. Now, just a few more questions and we'll get you an ambulance—Kitty Paciorek seems to have forgotten you."

Novick eagerly told the little he knew. He'd never seen Mrs. Paciorek before. The Man with the Voice had called yesterday and told him to get out here at seven tonight, to make sure no one saw him, to shoot me as I walked up to the house from my car. Yes, it was the Man with the Voice who hired him to throw acid at me.

"How did he know you, Walter? How did he know to get in touch with you?"

He didn't know. "The don must have given him my number. That's all I can figure. He told the don he needed a good man and the don gave him my number."

"You are a good man, Walter. Pasquale must be proud of you. You came for me three times and all you got out of it was a broken jaw and a smashed up leg. . . . I'm going to get you an ambulance. You'd best be praying your godfather forgets all about you, because from what I hear he doesn't like failures too much."

I covered him with my coat and headed for the front door. As I reached the steps a car pulled into the driveway. Not an ambulance. I froze, then jumped from the shallow porch to shelter in some evergreens running from the house to the garage. The same place, I saw from the trampled snow, where Novick had waited for me.

The garage doors opened electronically; the car pulled in and stopped. I peered around the edge of a tree. A dark blue Mercedes. Dr. Paciorek. How much did he know about tonight's escapade? Now was as good a time as any to find out. I stepped into the garage.

He looked up in surprise as he locked the car door. "Victoria! What are you doing here?"

"I came out to see your wife—I had some papers of Agnes's she wanted to see. Someone was lying in wait out front here and took a shot at her. I've hit him in the leg and I need to get an ambulance for him."

He looked at me suspiciously. "Victoria. This isn't your idea of a joke, is it?"

"Come and see for yourself." He followed me to the front. Novick was dragging himself toward the road as fast as he could, a feeble activity that had moved him ten feet or so. "You!" Paciorek yelled. "Stop!"

Novick continued to move. We trotted over to him. Dr. Paciorek handed me the briefcase he was carrying and knelt to look at the hit man. Novick tried to fight with him, but Paciorek didn't need my help to hold him down. After a few minutes' feeling of the leg, during which Novick cursed more loudly than ever, Paciorek said briefly, "The bone is broken but there isn't much else the matter except cold. I'll get an ambulance and call the police. You don't mind staying with him, do you?"

I was starting to shiver. "I guess not. Can you lend me your coat? I gave him mine."

He gave me a surprised glance, then took off his cashmere coat and draped it around my shoulders. After the doctor's bulky body vanished into the house, I squatted down next to Novick. "Before you pass out, let's get our stories straight." By the time the Lake Forest police arrived, we had agreed that he'd gotten lost and come to the door looking for help. Mrs. Paciorek, terrified, had screamed. That brought me to the scene with my gun out. Walter had taken fright at that and fired at me. I shot him. Not very believable, but I was damned sure Mrs. Paciorek wouldn't contradict it.

The sirens sounded in the distance. Novick had fainted finally, and I stood back to let the officials take over. I was dizzy and close to fainting myself. Fatigue. Nausea at the depths of my own rage. How like a mobster I had behaved— torture, threats. I don't believe the end justifies the means. I'd just been plain raving angry.

As wave on wave of policemen interviewed me, I kept dozing off, waking up, keeping my wits together enough to tell the same story each time, then dozing again. It was one o'clock when they finished and left.

Dr. Paciorek had refused to let his wife talk. I don't know what she told him, but he sent her to bed; the locals didn't argue that decision. Not with that much money behind it.

Dr. Paciorek had let the police use his study as an interrogation room. After they left, he came in and sat in the leather swivel chair behind his desk. I was sprawled in a leather armchair, three parts asleep.

"Would you like a drink?"

I rubbed my eyes and sat up a little straighter. "Brandy would be nice."

He reached into a cabinet behind the desk for a bottle of Cordon Bleu and poured two hefty servings.

"What were you doing here tonight?" he asked abruptly.

"Mrs. Paciorek wanted to see me. She asked me to come out around eight."

"She says you showed up unexpectedly." His tone wasn't accusatory. "Monday nights are when the Lake County Medical Society gets together. I usually don't go. Catherine asked me to leave her alone tonight because she was having a meeting with a religious group she belongs to; she knows that isn't of much interest to me. She says you showed up threatening her and brought that man along with you; that she was struggling with you when your gun went off and hit him."

"Where did her religious friends go?"

"She says they had left before you showed up."

"Do you know much about this Corpus Christi outfit she belongs to?"

He stared at his brandy for a while, then finished it with one swallow and poured himself another shot. I held out my snifter; he filled it recklessly.

"Corpus Christi?" he finally said. "When I married Catherine, her family accused me of being a fortune hunter. She was an only child and that estate was worth close to fifty million. I didn't care much about the money. Some, but not much. I met her in Panama—her father was the ambassador; I was working off my loan from Uncle Sam. She was very idealistic, was doing a lot of work in the poor community there. Xavier O'Faolin was a priest in one of those shantytowns. He interested her in Corpus Christi. I met her because I was trying to keep dysentery and a lot of other unpleasant stuff under control in that shantytown. A hopeless battle, really."

He swallowed some more brandy. "Then we came back to Chicago. Her father built this house. When he died we moved in. Catherine turned most of the Savage fortune over to Corpus Christi. I started becoming successful as a heart surgeon. O'Faolin moved on to the Vatican.

"Catherine was genuinely idealistic, but O'Faolin is a charlatan. He knew how to look good and do well at the same time. It was John the Twenty-third who brought him to the Vatican—

thought of him as a real people's priest. After John died, O'Faolin headed quickly to where the money and power were."

We drank quietly for several minutes. Few things go down as easily as Cordon Bleu.

"I should have spent more time at home." He gave a mirthless smile. "The plaint of the suburban father. At first Catherine was pleased to see me at the hospital twenty hours a day—after all, it proved I shared her lofty ideals. But after a while, she burned out on suburban living. She should have had her own career. But it didn't go with her ideals of Catholic motherhood. By the time I saw how angry she'd become, Agnes was in college and it was too late for me to do anything. I spent the time with Phil and Barbara I should have spent with Agnes and Cecelia, but I couldn't help Catherine."

He held the bottle up to his desk lamp. "Enough for two more." He divided it between us and tossed the bottle into a leather wastebasket at his feet.

"I know she blamed you for Agnes's—life-style. I need to know. Was she so angry with you that she'd try to get someone to shoot you?"

It had taken him a quarter bottle of good brandy to get that out. "No," I said. "Not that simple, I'm afraid. I have some evidence showing that Corpus Christi is trying to take over a local insurance company. Mrs. Paciorek is most anxious that that information not become public. I'm afraid I had reasons for thinking someone might be waiting for me out front, so I broke in through a window in your conservatory. The police didn't search the back of the house or they would never have left."

"I see." He looked suddenly old and shrunken in his tailored navy suit. "What are you going to do about it?"

"I'm going to have to let the FBI and the SEC know about Corpus Christi's involvement. I don't plan to tell them about tonight's ambush, if that's any consolation." Nor could I bring myself to tell him about Agnes's note. If she'd been killed because of her investigation into the Ajax takeover, then in some way or other, her mother bore responsibility for her death. Dr. Paciorek didn't need to hear that tonight.

He stared bitterly at the desk top for a long time. When he looked up, he was almost surprised to see me sitting there.

Wherever he'd been was a long way away. "Thanks, Victoria. You've been more generous than I had a right to expect."

I finished my own brandy, embarrassed. "Don't thank me. However this ends, it's going to be bad for you and your children. While I'm really most interested in Xavier O'Faolin, your wife is heavily involved in Corpus Christi. Their money is being used in an attempt to take over Ajax insurance. When the facts come out, she's going to be right up front on the firing line."

"But wouldn't it be possible to show she was just O'Faolin's dupe?" He smiled bitterly. "Which she has been, since she first met him in Panama."

I looked at him with genuine pity. "Dr. Paciorek, let me tell you the situation as I understand it. The Banco Ambrosiano is missing over a billion dollars, which disappeared into unknown Panamanian companies. Based on a letter from a Panamanian named Figueredo to Archbishop O'Faolin, it looks as though O'Faolin knows where that money is. He's in sort of a bind. As long as he doesn't use it, no one will know where it is. Once he starts to move it, the game is up.

"O'Faolin's no dummy. If he can get some large financial institution, like an insurance company, under his control, he can launder the money and use it however he wants. Michael Sindona tried that on behalf of the mob with the Franklin National Bank, only he was stupid enough to strip the bank's assets. So he's languishing now in a federal prison.

"Corpus Christi in Chicago has a huge endowment, thanks to Mrs. Paciorek. O'Faolin is a member and recruited your wife. Very well. Let them put together a dummy corporation, call it Wood-Sage, and use that to acquire Ajax stock. Once the connection comes out between Corpus Christi and the Ajax takeover—and it will; the SEC is investigating like crazy—your wife's involvement will be front-page news. Especially here in Chicago."

"But that's not criminal," the doctor pointed out.

I frowned unhappily. At last I said, "Look. I didn't want to tell you this. Particularly not tonight, when you've had such a shock. But there's Agnes's death, you see."

"Yes?" His voice was harsh.

"She was looking into the takeover for one of the Ajax

officers. . . . She found out about the Corpus Christi involvement. She was killed that night while waiting to meet with someone to discuss it."

His white, stricken face was like an open wound in the room. I could think of nothing to say to ease that pain. At last he looked up and gave a ghastly smile. "Yes. I can see. Even if Xavier is the main culprit, Catherine can't avoid her own responsibility for her daughter's death. No wonder she's been so . . ." His voice trailed off.

I got up. "I wish I could think of some comfort for you. I can't. But if you want my help, please call me. My answering service takes messages twenty-four hours a day." I put my card on the desk in front of him and left.

I was bone-weary and stiff. I'd have gladly lain down in front of the family-room fire and passed out, but I willed my aching body down the front stairs to the street. Going by road, it was only a five-minute walk to my car instead of the half hour it had taken me cross-country.

My watch said three when I moved the stiff Toyota back onto the tollway. I found a motel at the first southbound exit, checked in, and fell asleep without bothering to undress.

XXIV

Baiting the Trap

IT WAS PAST noon when I woke again. Every muscle ached. I'd remembered to put the Smith & Wesson aside before going to sleep, but not the holster. My left side was sore from where the leather had pressed into my breast all night. My clothes stank. I'd fought Walter Novick in this shirt, put in a heavy stint of cross-country hiking, and slept in it. The smell bore acute witness to these activities.

I longed for a bath, but not if it meant redonning my repellent apparel. I picked up the Toyota and maneuvered its clumsy steering down the expressway to the Bellerophon. Mrs. Climzak gave me a darkling glance from behind the counter but forebore any criticism, so I gathered no one had tried burglarizing my apartment in the night.

It was only after a long soak in the stained porcelain tub that

205

I realized how hungry I was. Dry, reclothed, I stiffly descended the four flights of stairs.

What would the don's reaction be to losing Novick? Would he be gunning for me, or would he realize Novick wasn't salvageable and cut his losses? Only the Shadow knew. Just in case Pasquale was pissed, I braved Mrs. Climzak's breathy protests and went past the front desk to explore the Bellerophon's nether regions. The lobby's back entrance led to a hallway where her apartment was situated. Her mules flopping, she scampered behind me like an angry hen. "Miss Warshawski! Miss Warshawski! What are you doing back here? Get out. Get out before I call my husband. Before I call the police!"

Her apartment door opened and the fabled Mr. Climzak appeared, in a T-shirt and baggy trousers. A day's growth of beard helped hide his drink-reddened cheeks. He didn't look as though he could throw me out, but he might be alert enough to call the police.

"Just looking for the back door," I told him brightly, continuing down the passage.

As I undid the dead bolt, Mrs. Climzak hissed, "This is the last straw. You will have to find other lodgings."

I looked at her before going outside. "I hope so, Mrs. Climzak. I certainly hope so."

No hail of machine-gun bullets strafed me in the alley. Nor were any suspicious-looking cars hovering on the street. I found a Polish restaurant and ate heartily, if not healthily, of cabbage soup, chicken, dumplings, and apple tart.

I felt decidedly more human. Over a second cup of coffee, an idea began glimmering at the back of my brain. Preposterous. It would need Murray's cooperation. And Uncle Stefan's.

Illinois Bell, poverty-stricken by the AT&T dismemberment, had raised the price of pay phone calls to a quarter. After fishing for change, I reached Murray at the desk of the *Herald-Star*. If I gave him a big, huge story would he sit on it until it came to an end?

"Ain't you dead yet, Warshawski? What am I supposed to do in exchange for this big huge story?"

"Run a couple of lines on the front page of the evening and morning editions."

"I'm not the editor—I don't control what goes on the front page. Or even page sixty-two of the middle section."

"Murray! I'm shocked. You told me you were an important newspaperman. Can it be you lied? Can it be I have to go to the *Tribune* and talk to Lipinski?"

Grumbling, he agreed to meet me at the Golden Glow around five P.M. The schoolroom clock over the counter said two-thirty. Time to check things out with Uncle Stefan.

Another quarter to my answering service reminded me I hadn't told Phyllis I wouldn't be back to her place last night. Or Roger that I'd miss his board meeting. And Bobby wanted to see me to talk about Walter Novick. "Not your jurisdiction," I muttered.

"What was that?" the operator said.

"Nothing. Any other calls?"

Dr. Paciorek wanted to talk to me. He'd left his paging number at the hospital for me. Frowning, I put another quarter in the machine. Twenty-five cents gets you three tries. Clicked from operator to operator at the hospital, I finally connected with Dr. Paciorek.

"Victoria! I was afraid you wouldn't get my message." His normally controlled voice was rough and human. "Could you come back to the house tonight? I know it's a lot to ask. O'Faolin's coming out—I'm going to settle this matter."

I rubbed my eyes with my free hand. Would this upset my other plans? Dr. Paciorek breathed anxiously in my ear while I considered. Maybe I could put a little advance pressure on the archbishop. "I guess so. Can't make it before eight, though."

"Fine. Fine. Thanks very much, Victoria."

"Don't thank me for anything, Dr. Paciorek. This story is not going to have a happy ending."

A long silence, then "I realize that" and he hung up.

Jim Streeter met me at Uncle Stefan's door. "The doctors say the old man can be released tomorrow. He's been trying to reach his niece. I guess she's planning on taking him home with her. What do you want us to do?"

Of course he would be going home with Lotty, I thought in irritation. "I'd better talk to him."

Uncle Stefan was delighted to see me, delighted to be going

207

home. "And why are you frowning, my little niece? Aren't you pleased for me?"

"Oh, certainly. Yes, I'm very pleased. How are you feeling?"

"Fine. Chipper. Yes, chipper." He beamed proudly at producing this colloquial word. "Every day I go for physical therapy and every day I am stronger, walk farther. All I need now is chocolate."

I grinned and sat on the bed. "I have a favor to ask of you. Please say no if you don't want to do it, because there's some danger involved. Not a lot, but some."

He cocked a lively eye at me and demanded details.

"Instead of going to Lotty's, would you come home with me? I need you to pretend you're dead for twenty-four hours, then arise from the grave with a flourish."

"Lotty will be *wutend*." He beamed.

"No doubt, if that means what I think it does. Console yourself with the thought that it's me she wants to murder."

He patted my hand comfortingly. "Lotty is a headstrong girl. Don't worry about her."

"You didn't see a second man in your apartment the day you were stabbed, did you?"

He shook his head. "Just the—the thug."

"Would you be willing to say that you saw him? He was there, you see. Just hovering outside until your thug had stabbed you."

"If you say he was there, my dear niece, I believe you."

XXV

Knight takes Bishop

MURRAY GRUDGINGLY AGREED to run the story. "I'll have to tell Gil the whole tale," he warned me. Gil was the front page editor.

I explained the entire situation to him—Ajax, the Banco Ambrosiano, Corpus Christi.

Murray finished his beer and signaled to the waitress for another. Sal was busy behind the bar with commuting drinkers. "You know, it's probably O'Faolin who backed away the FBI from the case."

I nodded. "That's what I think. Between Mrs. Paciorek and him, there's enough money and power to strangle a dozen investigations. I'd like to get Derek out to the priory with me tomorrow, but he doesn't listen to me at the best of times. Neither does Bobby. And today wasn't the best of times."

I'd spent a frustrating afternoon on the phone. I'd had a long talk with Bobby, in which he read me the riot act for not fingering Novick earlier. He refused to listen to my story. Refused to send men out to the priory to question the archbishop or Pelly. And was aghast at the accusation against Mrs. Paciorek. Bobby was a salt-of-the-earth Catholic; he wasn't taking on a prince of the Church. Nor yet a princess.

Derek Hatfield was even less cooperative. A suggestion that he at least block O'Faolin's departure for forty-eight hours was met with frosty contempt. As so often happened in my encounters with Derek, I ended the discussion with a rude remark. That is, I made a rude remark and he hung up. Same thing, really.

A conversation with Freeman Carter, my lawyer, was more fruitful. He was just as skeptical as Bobby and Derek, but at least he worked for me and promised to get some names—in exchange for a hundred and a quarter an hour.

"I'll be at the priory," Murray promised.

"No disrespect, but I'd like a dozen men with guns."

"Just remember, Miss Warshawski: The pen is mightier than the pencil," Murray said portentously.

I laughed reluctantly.

"We'll tape it," Murray promised. "And I'll have someone there with a camera."

"It'll have to do. . . . And you'll take Uncle Stefan home with you?"

Murray grimaced. "Only if you pay for the funeral when Lotty finds out what I've done." He'd met Lotty enough times to know what her temper was like.

I looked at my watch and excused myself. It was close to six, the time I was to call back Freeman at his club before he left for a dinner meeting.

Sal let me use the phone in the cube she calls an office, a windowless room directly behind the bar with one-way glass overlooking the floor. Freeman was brisk, but brief. He gave me two names, Mrs. Paciorek's attorney and her broker. And yes, the broker had handled a twelve-million-dollar transaction for Corpus Christi to buy Ajax shares.

I whistled to myself as Freeman hung up. Worth a hundred twenty-five dollars. I looked at my watch again. Time for one more call, this time to Ferrant, still at his Ajax office.

He sounded more tired than ever. "I talked to the board today and tried urging them to find my permanent replacement. They need someone managing the insurance operations, or those will go to hell and there won't be anything left to take over. All my energy is going into meetings with legal eagles and financial wizards and I don't have time to do the only thing I do well—broker insurance deals."

"Roger, I think I may have a way out of the problem for you. I don't want to tell you what it is, because you'd have to tell your partner and your board. It may not work, but if a lot of people know about it, it definitely won't work."

Roger turned this over. When he spoke again, his voice had more energy than I'd heard for some time. "Yes. You're right. So I won't press you . . . Could I see you tonight? Dinner maybe?"

"A very late dinner—say ten o'clock?"

That suited his schedule; he would be closeted with eagles and wizards for several hours yet. "Can I tell them we may have a break coming our way?"

"As long as you don't tell them who you heard it from."

When I got back to the table, Murray had left a brief note torn from his steno notebook informing me he was off to talk to Gil to try to make the last edition.

The one advantage the rented Toyota had over my little Omega was that its heater worked. January was sliding into February without any noticeable change in the weather. The thermometer had dropped below freezing New Year's Eve and hadn't climbed above it since. As I slid out of the underground garage and turned onto Lake Shore Drive, the car was already warm enough that I could take off my coat.

Exiting at Half Day Road, I wondered how safe it was to drive right up to the Pacioreks' front door. What if Dr. Paciorek agreed with O'Faolin that I should be bumped off? It might save his wife's reputation. What if O'Faolin knocked him out with a crucifix and shot me?

The doctor met me at the door, his face grave and pinched. He looked as though he hadn't slept since I left him the night before. "Catherine and Xavier are in the family room. They don't know you're here—I didn't think Xavier would stay if he knew you were coming."

"Probably not." I followed him down the familiar hallway into the familiar, hot living room.

Mrs. Paciorek sat, as usual, by the fire. O'Faolin had pulled a straight-backed chair up to the couch on which she sat. As Dr. Paciorek and I came in, they looked toward the door and let out simultaneous gasps.

O'Faolin was on his feet and coming toward the door. Paciorek put out an arm, strong through years of sawing people open, and propelled him back into the room.

"We need to talk." His voice had recovered its firmness. "You and Catherine haven't been saying anything to the point; I thought Victoria could help us out."

O'Faolin gave me a look that made my stomach jump. Hatred and destruction. I tried to force down my own fury at the sight of him—the man who tried to get me blinded, who burned my apartment. Now was not the time to try to strangle him, but the urge was strong.

"Good evening, Archbishop. Good evening, Mrs. Paciorek." I was pleased to hear my voice come out without a quaver. "Let's talk about Ajax and Corpus Christi and Agnes."

O'Faolin had himself back under control. "Topics about which I know very little, Miss Warshawski."

The accentless voice was supercilious. "Xavier, I hope you have a confessor with a lot of pull."

He narrowed his eyes slightly, whether at my use of his first name or at the accusation I couldn't know.

"How dare you talk to the archbishop like that?" Mrs. Paciorek spat out.

"You know me, Catherine: brave enough to try anything. It all comes with practice, really."

Dr. Paciorek held up his hands pleadingly. "Now that you've all insulted each other, could we get down to some real conversation? Victoria, you talked last night about the link between Corpus Christi and Ajax. What evidence do you have?"

I fished in my purse for the greasy photocopy of Raúl Díaz Figueredo's letter to O'Faolin. "I guess what I really have is O'Faolin's involvement in the Ajax takeover. You read Spanish, don't you?"

The doctor nodded silently and I handed the photocopy across to him. He read it carefully, several times, then showed it to O'Faolin.

"So it *was* you!" he hissed.

I shrugged. "I don't know what was me, but I do know this letter shows you being advised that Ajax was the best, if not easiest takeover target. You've got a billion dollars in Banco Ambrosiano assets sitting in Panama banks. You can't use them—if you withdraw the money and start spending it, the Bank of Italy is going to come down on you like lions on an early Christian.

"So you remembered Michael Sindona and the Franklin National Bank and realized what you needed was a U.S. financial institution to launder money through. And an insurance company is better than a bank in lots of ways because you can play all these games with loss reserves and your life-company assets and nobody will really be able to tell. Figueredo got someone to check out the available stock companies. My guess is Ajax looked good because it's in Chicago. The money boys are myopic when something happens outside New York City—it'll take them longer to notice what's going on. With me so far?"

Catherine had gone quite pale. Her mouth was set in a thin line. O'Faolin, however, was at ease, smiling contemptuously. "It's a beautiful theory. But if a friend of mine points out that Ajax is a good takeover target, that is not illegal. And if I am taking it over, that, too, is not illegal, although where I would get such money is a good question. But so far as I know, I am not taking it over."

He sank back in his chair, legs stretched out, ankles crossed.

"Alas for the venality of the human condition," I tried a contemptuous smile myself, but suavity is not my long suit. "My attorney, Freeman Carter, spoke with yours this afternoon, Mrs. Paciorek. Freeman belongs to the same club as

212

Fuller Gibson and Fuller didn't mind telling him who handles the brokerage business for the Paciorek Trust. And then it wasn't too difficult getting verification of the note Agnes left for me: Corpus Christi used twelve million to buy Ajax shares in the name of the Wood-Sage Corporation."

No one said anything for a minute. Mrs. Paciorek made a strangled little noise and fainted, falling over on the couch. Paciorek went to her side while O'Faolin got up and strolled toward the door. I stood in the doorway, blocking his path. He was half a foot taller than I and maybe forty pounds heavier, but I was twenty years younger.

He tried to shove me aside with his left arm. Since his weight was forward on that side, I grabbed the arm and pulled, sending him sprawling on his face into the hall. This small piece of violence unleashed the fury I'd been holding barely in check. Panting slightly, I waited for him to climb to his feet.

He got up, backing warily away from me. I laughed slightly. "Not scared are you, Xavier?" I curled my right fingers at the second joint, and came in with my left elbow to his diaphragm. He landed an inexpert blow on my shoulder, while I used my crooked fingers to push at his eyes. Holding the back of his head with my left hand I pushed up with the right while he shoved at me and kicked. Not a fighter.

"I might blind you. I might kill you. If you fight, you up the pressure."

I felt an arm on my left shoulder, pulling, and shrugged it away, but it pulled more insistently. I came away, gasping for air, red rage swirling through my head. "Let go of me! Let go of me!"

"Victoria!" It was Dr. Paciorek. I felt a stinging on my face, realized he'd slapped me, and came slowly back to the marble hallway.

"He tried to blind me," I panted. "He tried to burn me to death. He probably killed Agnes. You should have let me kill him."

O'Faolin was white except for his eyes—the skin around them was scarlet from the pressure of my fingers. He straightened his clerical collar. "She's mad, Thomas. Call the police."

Paciorek let go of my arm and I leaned against the wall. As reality returned, I remembered the other part of my plan.

"Oh, yes. Stefan Herschel died tonight. That's another crime that this prince of peace is responsible for."

Paciorek frowned. "Who is Stefan Herschel?"

"He was an old man, a master engraver, who tried to interest Xavier here in buying a forged stock certificate. Xavier stole the certificate, but not before his buddy Walter Novick had stabbed the man. Walter is the man who was lying shot on your lawn last night. He gets around."

"Is this true?" Paciorek demanded.

"This woman is a lunatic, Thomas. How can you believe what she says? The old man is dead, apparently, so how can you verify your story? All of this is hearsay, anyway: an old man dead; Corpus Christi buying Ajax shares; Figueredo writing about Ajax's investment potential—how does that implicate me in a crime?"

Paciorek was pale. "Whether you are implicated or not, Catherine is. Thanks to you, it's her money that funds Corpus Christi here in Chicago. And it's that money that's being used to buy Ajax stock. And now, maybe because she was looking into that, my oldest daughter is dead. O'Faolin, I hold you responsible. You got Catherine involved in all this."

"For years you have insisted I was Catherine's evil genius, her Rasputin." O'Faolin was haughty. "So it is no surprise to me that you blame me now."

He turned on his heel and left. Neither Paciorek nor I moved to stop him. Paciorek looked wearier than ever. "How much of that is true?"

"How much of what?" I said irritably. "Is Corpus Christi behind Wood-Sage? Yes, that's true. And Wood-Sage behind the Ajax takeover bid? Yes, they filed Friday with the SEC. And Agnes killed because of looking into it? Never will be proved. Probable."

"I need a drink," he muttered. "Months go by and I have one glass of wine. Here I am drinking two days in a row." He led me through the labyrinth to his study.

"How's Catherine?"

"Catherine?" The name seemed to surprise him. "Oh, Catherine. She's all right. Just shock. She doesn't need me, in any event." He looked in his liquor cupboard. "We finished

214

the brandy last night, didn't we? I have some whiskey. You drink Chivas?"

"You have Black Label?"

He pawed through the little cupboard. No Black Label. I accepted a Chivas and sat in the leather armchair.

"What about the old man? The engraver?"

I shrugged. "He's dead. That makes O'Faolin an accessory, if Novick can make the identification stick. Trouble is, it won't be in time. He'll be on that plane to Rome tomorrow at ten. As long as he never comes back to Chicago, he'll be home free."

"And the Ajax takeover?" He finished the whiskey in a gulp and poured another. He offered the bottle to me, but I shook my head—I didn't want to be drunk for the drive back to Chicago.

"I think I can stop that."

"How?"

I shook my head. "It's a small piece of SEC law. So small that Xavier probably never noticed it."

"I see." He finished his second drink and poured himself a third. There wasn't any point in watching him get drunk. At the door I turned for a moment to look at him. He was staring into the bottom of the glass, but he sensed my departure. Without looking up, he said, "You say Agnes's death will never be proved. But how sure are you?"

"There's no evidence," I said helplessly.

He put the glass down with a snap. "Don't. When someone has a fatal heart condition, I tell them. I tell them these things are never certain and that gutsy people and lucky people beat the odds. But without a scan I know what's happening. As one professional to another, how sure are you about Agnes's death?"

I met his brown eyes and saw with a twinge that tears swam in them. "As one professional to another—very certain."

"I see. That's all I wanted to know. Thank you for coming up tonight, Victoria."

I didn't like to leave him in this state. He ignored my outstretched arm, picked up a journal lying on a corner of the desk, and studied it intently. I didn't tell him it was upside down.

215

XXVI

Loading the Gun

ROGER MET ME at Grillon's, an old Chicago tradition where waiters leave you alone instead of popping up every five minutes to ask if everything is to your satisfaction. They rolled a huge joint of beef up to the table and cut off rare slices for us. Stilton, flown in from Melton Mowbray just for the restaurant, went well with a '64 port. Despite my worries and the ugly scene I'd been through with O'Faolin, I felt good.

Roger was bouyant. "You've given me something to look forward to, V.I. I told the board that I had a private-inquiry agent looking into the matter and that he thought he had a way out. They were most keen, but since I didn't have any information, I couldn't give them any."

I smiled tiredly and clasped his hand. It was midnight when we finished the port and the waiter brought our check. Roger asked hesitantly if he could come home with me. I shook my head regretfully.

"Not that I wouldn't like it—the company would be most welcome. But it's not much of a place and right now what's there is a shambles. Someone was pawing through it looking for a document and I just don't feel like sharing the mess."

"Is that the way an American girl tells someone to go to hell?"

I leaned across the table and kissed him. "When I tell you to go to hell, you won't have any doubts at all that that's what you heard. . . . I guess what I'm telling you is that I'm homeless and don't like it. I feel disoriented and I need to be alone with it."

He nodded soberly. "People on my staff are always telling me, 'I can deal with that.' I guess that's an Americanism. Anyway, I can deal with that."

When he offered to drive me, I gratefully accepted, abandoning the Toyota in the underground garage. If it wasn't still there in the morning, no big loss.

It was after one-thirty when he deposited me in front of the

Bellerophon. Courteously waiting until I was safely inside, he waved and drove off.

Mrs. Climzak had sat up for me. As soon as I came in the door she came huffing over, her face resembling an angry peony.

"You're going to have to leave, Miss Warshawski, or whatever your name really is."

"I want to, Mrs. Climzak. I don't like the Bellerophon any better than it likes me. But we'll both have to stick it out until the end of the week."

"This isn't funny!" She stamped her foot. I was afraid some of the petals might start falling off. "You have disrupted your apartment. You have strange men in at all hours of the night."

"Not disrupted, Mrs. Climzak. You mean there's been an irruption in the apartment. I don't think you disrupt apartments, only meetings."

"Don't try to change the subject. Now, tonight, two men burst in and almost frightened my husband to death."

"What did they do—show him a job application?"

"You get out of here by eight tomorrow morning. And take those men with you."

"What men?" I started to say, then realized what she was talking about. My heart began beating faster. I wished I hadn't drunk so much at dinner, but the Smith & Wesson gently pushing into my side brought some comfort. "They're still in the apartment? You didn't call the police?"

"Why should I?" she said in thin triumph. "I figured they were *your* problem, not mine."

"Thanks, Mrs. Climzak. Don't call the mayor's office for your good-citizen medal—they'll call you."

Pushing my way past her I went behind the lobby desk, picked up the phone and dialed my room. She was squawking and pulling at my arm but I ignored her—I'd beaten up an archbishop today. An old lady wasn't going to trouble me any.

After fifteen rings, a gravelly voice I knew well answered. "Ernesto. It's V. I. Warshawski. You going to shoot me if I come up to my room?"

"Where are you, Warshawski? We've been waiting here since eight o'clock."

"Sorry. I got carried away by religion."

He asked again where I was and told me to wait for him in the lobby. When I'd hung up, Mrs. Climzak was shrieking that she was going to get her husband to call the cops if I touched that phone again.

I leaned over and kissed her. "Would you really? There are a couple of gangsters waiting to cart me off. If you call the cops, you might be in time to rescue me."

She gazed at me in horror and dashed off to the nether regions. Ernesto, looking the picture of a corporate executive, came through the stairwell door, a seedy, thin man in an ill-fitting chauffeur's uniform at his heels.

Surely, if they meant to shoot me, they would have hidden outside and not broadcast their faces to the world like this. Surely. Yet my hands didn't believe me. They started sweating and I was afraid they might be trembling so I stuck them into my pockets.

"Your room's a mess, Warshawski."

"If I'd known you were coming, I would've cleaned up."

He ignored the sarcasm. "Someone's been searching it. Sloppy job. You know that?"

I told him I knew it and followed him into the cold night. The limousine was parked around the corner. Ernesto and I sat in the backseat, me not blindfolded this time. I lay against the comfortable upholstery, but couldn't sleep. This has to work, I told myself. Has to. This can't be a summons to shoot me in revenge for wounding Walter Novick. For that they'd just gun me down on the street.

Jumbled with these thoughts was O'Faolin's contemptuous face as he left me tonight, Paciorek's despair. And somewhere in the city, a furious Lotty, hearing that Uncle Stefan was going home with Murray, was going to play the tethered goat for me.

On North Avenue we turned into the parking lot of an enormous restaurant. No wonder they hadn't blindfolded me—nothing secret about this place. A huge neon sign with a champagne glass bubbling over perched on top of the marquee. Underneath it, flashing lights proclaimed this as Torfino's Restaurant, Italian food and wine.

When the limousine pulled up in front of the entrance, a doorman sprang from nowhere to open the car for Ernesto and me. The driver took off, whispering hoarsely the first sound I'd heard from him. "Call when you're ready."

I followed Ernesto through the restaurant, empty of customers, to a hallway behind the kitchen. Spare linoleum and green, grease-spattered walls gave it a common institutional look. A bored young man stood guard at a closed door. He moved to one side as Ernesto approached. Behind the door lay a private office where the don sat talking on a phone, gently smoking a large cigar. He nodded at Ernesto and waved a hand at me, signaling me to come in.

Like the don's library, this office was decorated in red. Here the effect was cheap. The curtains were rayon, the seat covers vinyl, the desk a mere box on four legs.

Pasquale hung up and asked Ernesto what had taken him so long. In Italian Ernesto explained my long absence. "Further, someone else is interested in Signorina Warshawski. Her room has been carelessly searched."

"And who would that be, Miss Warshawski?" Pasquale asked with grave courtesy.

I blinked a few times, trying to readjust myself to the imaginary world of honor. "I thought you might know, Don Pasquale. I assumed it was done by your henchman, Walter Novick, at the request of Mrs. Paciorek."

The don looked at his cigar, measuring the ash, then turned to Ernesto. "Do we know a Walter Novick, Ernesto?"

Ernesto gave a disdainful shrug. "He has run a few errands for you, Don. He is the type who likes to grab at the coattails of the powerful."

Pasquale nodded regally. "I regret that Novick gave the appearance of being under my protection. As Ernesto said, he had illusions above his abilities. These illusions led him to use my name in a compromising way." Again he examined the ash. Still not ripe. "This Novick is acquainted with many petty criminals. A man like that frequently engages in foolish or dangerous exploits with such criminals in order to impress a man such as myself." He gave a world-weary shrug. I knew, and he knew that such exploits were the acts of the childish, but—what would you? The ash now proved ready for a gentle tapping.

219

"Among these criminals were some forgers. Novick conceived an act of staggering folly: to engage these forgers to make fake stock certificates and put them in the safe of a religious house."

He paused to invite my comment on this staggering folly. "How, Don, did these forgers know for which companies and in which denominations to make the fakes?"

Pasquale hunched a shoulder impatiently. "Priests are guileless men. They talk indiscreetly. Someone no doubt overheard them. Such things have happened before."

"You would have no objection to my bringing this tale to Derek Hatfield?"

He smiled blandly. "None whatsoever. Although it is merely hearsay—I can see no benefit to my talking to Hatfield myself."

"And you wouldn't know the names of these forgers, would you?"

"Regrettably, no, my dear Miss Warshawski."

"And you wouldn't know why these forgers used the priory, would you?"

"One presumes, Miss Warshawski, because it was easy for them. It is not of great interest to me."

I could feel sweat prickling on the palms of my hands. My mouth was dry. This was my chance; I just hoped Pasquale, student of human terror that he was, couldn't detect my nervousness. "Unfortunately, Don, you may have to take an interest."

Pasquale didn't change position, nor did he alter his look of polite attention. But his expression somehow froze and the eyes glittered in a way that made cold sweat break out on my forehead. His voice, when he spoke, chilled my marrow. "Is that a threat, Miss Warshawski?"

Out of the corner of one eye, I could see Ernesto, who'd been slouching in a vinyl chair, come to attention. "Not a threat, Don Pasquale. Just for your information. Novick's in the hospital, and he's going to talk. And Archbishop O'Faolin's going to say it was all your idea about the forgeries, and attacking me, and all that stuff. He isn't going to know anything about it."

Pasquale had relaxed slightly. I was breathing more easily.

Ernesto sank back in his chair and started looking at his pocket diary.

"As you may know, Don, the SEC will not allow anyone with known Mafia connections to own an insurance company or a bank. So O'Faolin is going to back away from Novick as fast as he can. He'll leave on a ten o'clock flight tomorrow night and let you handle the situation as best you can."

The don nodded with a return of his grave courtesy. "As always, your comments are fascinating, Miss Warshawski. If I knew this O'Faolin"—he spread his hands deprecatingly. "Meanwhile, I am desolated by the discomfort Walter Novick has brought into your life." He looked at Ernesto; a red-leather checkbook materialized. The don wrote in it. "Would twenty-five thousand cover the loss to your apartment?"

I swallowed a few times. Twenty-five thousand would get me a co-op, replace my mother's piano, or enable me to spend the rest of the winter in the Caribbean. What did I want with such things, however? "Your generosity is fabled, Don Pasquale. Yet I have done nothing to deserve it."

He persisted, politely. Keeping my eyes on a poor reproduction of Garibaldi over the pressed-wood desk, I steadfastly resisted. Pasquale finally gave me a measuring look and told Ernesto to see that I got home safely.

XXVII

Luck of the Archbishop

AT FOUR-THIRTY IN early February the sky is already turning dark. Inside the Chapel of Our Lady of the Rosary, the candles created warming circles of light. Behind an ornately carved wooden screen, separating the friars' choir stalls from the secular mob, the room was dim. I could barely make out Uncle Stefan's features, but knew he was there from the comforting clasp of his hand. Murray was at my left. Beyond him was Cordelia Hull, one of his staff photographers.

As Father Carroll began to chant the introit in his high clear tenor, my depression deepened. I shouldn't be here. After making a complete fool of myself in as many ways as possible,

I should have retired to the Bellerophon and pulled the covers over my head for a month.

The day had started badly. Lotty, enraged at the four-paragraph story in the *Herald-Star* announcing her uncle's sudden relapse and death, was not mollified by his decision to go home with Murray. According to Murray, the argument had been brief. Uncle Stefan chuckling and calling Lotty a hotheaded girl did not amuse her and she had switched to German to give vent to her fury. Uncle Stefan told her she was interfering where it was none of her business whereat she tore off in her green Datsun to find me. I didn't have the advantage of knowing Lotty as a headstrong little girl willfully riding her pony up the castle steps at Kleinsee. Besides, her accusations were too close to my nerve centers. Egotistical. So single-minded I would sacrifice Uncle Stefan trying to solve a problem that had the FBI and the SEC baffled.

"But, Lotty. I put my own body on the line, too. That arson at my apartment—"

She contemptuously swept away my protest. Hadn't the police asked for full information? Hadn't I withheld it in my usual arrogant way? And now I wanted someone to weep because I was suffering the consequences?

When I tried to suggest to Uncle Stefan—and Murray—that we drop the project and retire quietly, Murray had been angry in his turn: not after all he'd been through to sell Gil on the project. If I was too lily-livered all of a sudden to follow through on this, he wasn't. He'd take Uncle Stefan to the priory himself and I could go sulk in my tent and enjoy it alone.

Uncle Stefan took me to one side. "Really, Victoria. By now you should know better than to pay the least heed to Lotty when she is in such a tantrum. If you are letting her overset you it is only because you are very tired." He patted my hand and insisted that Murray go to a bakery and buy some chocolate cake. "And none of that Sara Lee or Davidson cake. I mean a real bakery, young man. There must be one in your area."

So Murray returned with a hazelnut chocolate cake and whipped cream. Uncle Stefan cut me a large slice, poured cream over it, and stood watching me eat it with anxious benevolence. "So, *Nichtchen*, now you are feeling better, right?"

I wasn't, not really. Somehow I couldn't re-create the terror I'd felt earlier dealing with O'Faolin. All I could think of was Father Carroll's probable reaction to my antics in his chapel. But at three-thirty I'd followed Uncle Stefan into the backseat of Murray's Pontiac Fiero.

We reached the chapel early and were able to get seats in the front row behind the wooden screen. I was assuming that Rosa, hard at work on priory finances, would attend the service, but I didn't want to run the risk of her recognizing me, even in the gloomy half light, by turning around and peering.

Around us people joined in the service, knowing which chants permitted group singing, which ones were solo perform-ances. The four of us sat quietly.

When the offertory announced the beginning of the mass, my heart started beating faster. Shame, fear, anticipation all crowded together. Next to me Uncle Stefan continued to breathe calmly while my palms turned wet and my breath came in short, gasping chunks.

Through the rood screen I could see the priests forming a large semicircle around the altar. Pelly and O'Faolin stood side by side, Pelly small, intent, O'Faolin tall and self-assured, the chief executive officer at an office picnic. O'Faolin wore a black cassock instead of the white Dominican robe. He was not part of the order.

We let the congregation file past us to receive communion. When Rosa's ramrod back and cast-iron hair marched by, I gently nudged Uncle Stefan. We stood up together and joined the procession.

Some half dozen priests were passing out wafers. At the altar the procession split as people quietly went to the man with the fewest communicants in front of him. Uncle Stefan and I moved behind Rosa to Archbishop O'Faolin.

The archbishop wasn't looking at people's faces. He had performed this ritual so many times that his mind was far from the benevolent superiority of his face. Rosa turned to go back to her seat. She saw me blocking her path and gave an audible gasp. It brought O'Faolin abruptly to the present. His startled gaze went from me to Uncle Stefan. The engraver grabbed my sleeve and said loudly.

"Victoria! This man helped to stab me."

The archbishop dropped the ciborium. "You!" he hissed. His eyes glittered. "You're dead. So help me God, you're dead."

A camera flashed. Cordelia Hull on the job. Murray, grinning, held up his microphone. "Any more comments for posterity, Archbishop?"

By now the mass had come to a complete halt. One of the more level-headed young brothers had leaped to retrieve the spilled communion wafers from the floor before they were stepped on. The few remaining communicants stood gaping. Carroll was at my side.

"What is the meaning of this, Miss Warshawski? This is a church, not a gladiator's arena. Clear these newspaper people so we can finish the mass. Then I'd like to see you in my office."

"Certainly, Prior." My face felt red but I spoke calmly. "I'd appreciate it if you'd bring Father Pelly along, too. And Rosa will be there." My aunt, rooted at my side, now tried to make for the door. I held her thin wiry arm in a grasp tight enough to make her wince. "We're going to talk, Rosa. So don't try to leave."

O'Faolin started justifying himself to Carroll. "She's mad, Prior. She's dug up some old man to hurl accusations at me. She thinks I tried to kill her and she's been persecuting me ever since I came out to the priory."

"That's a lie," Uncle Stefan piped up. "Whether this man is an archbishop I couldn't say. But that he stole my stocks and watched a hoodlum try to kill me, that I know. Listen to him now!"

The prior held up his arms. "Enough!" I hadn't known the gentle voice could carry so much authority. "We're here to worship the Lord. These accusations make a mockery of the Lord's Supper. Archbishop, you will have your turn to speak. Later."

He called the congregation to order, and gave a pithy homily on how the devil could be at our side to tempt us even at the very gates of heaven, and had everyone join in a group confession. Still holding on to Rosa, I moved away from the center of the chapel to one side. As the congregation prayed, I watched O'Faolin head toward the exit behind the altar. Pelly, standing near him, looked wretched. If he left now with O'Faolin, he made a public statement of complicity. If he stayed behind, the archbishop would never forgive him. His choices flitted across his intense, mobile face with the clarity of a stock quotation on an electronic ticker. At length, his cheeks flushed with misery, he joined his brothers in the final prayers and filed silently with them from the chapel.

As soon as Carroll was out of sight, the congregation burst into loud commentary. Above the clatter I listened for a different sound. It didn't come.

Rosa started muttering invectives at me in a loud undertone.

"Not here, Auntie dear. Save it for the prior's study." With Stefan and Murray on my heels, I guided my aunt firmly through the gaping, chattering crowd to the hallway door. Cordelia stayed behind to get a few group photos.

Pelly was sitting with Carroll and Jablonski. Rosa started to say something when she saw him, but he shook his head and she shut up. Power in the word. If we were all still alive at the end of the session, I might try to hire him as her keeper.

As soon as we were seated, Carroll demanded to know who Murray and Uncle Stefan were. He told Murray that he could stay only on condition that none of the conversation was either recorded or reported. Murray shrugged. "Then there isn't much point in my staying."

Carroll was adamant. Murray acquiesced.

"I tried to get Xavier to join us but he is getting ready to go to the airport and refuses to say anything. I want an orderly explanation from the rest of you. Starting with Miss Warshawski."

I took a deep breath. Rosa said, "Don't listen to her, Father. She is nothing but a spite-filled—"

"You will have your turn, Mrs. Vignelli." Carroll spoke with such cold authority that Rosa surprised herself by shutting up.

"This tale has its roots some thirty-five years ago in Panama," I told Carroll. "At that time, Xavier O'Faolin was a priest working in the Barrio. He was a member of Corpus Christi and a man of deep ambition. Catherine Savage, a young idealistic woman with a vast fortune, joined Corpus Christi under his persuasion and turned most of her money into a trust for the use of Corpus Christi.

"She met and married Thomas Paciorek, a young doctor in the service. She spent four more years in Panama and developed a lasting interest in a seminary where Dominicans could continue the work she and O'Faolin had undertaken among the poor."

As I got well into my story, I finally started relaxing. My voice came out without a tremor and my breathing returned to normal. I kept a wary eye on Rosa.

"Toward the end of her stint in Panama, a young man came to the Priory of San Tomás who shared her passion and her idealism. Not to spin out the obvious, it was Augustine Pelly. He, too, joined Corpus Christi. He, too, fell under Xavier O'Faolin's influence. When O'Faolin's ambition and acuity got him a coveted promotion to Rome, Pelly followed and served as his secretary for several years—not a typical venue for a Dominican friar.

"When he rejoined his brothers, this time in Chicago, he met Mrs. Vignelli, another ardent, if very angry, soul. She, too, joined Corpus Christi. It gave some meaning to an otherwise bitter life."

Rosa made an angry gesture. "And if it is bitter, whose fault is that?"

"We'll get to that in a moment," I said coldly. "The next important incident in this tale took place about three years ago when Roberto Calvi, prompted by his own internal devils, set up some Panamanian subsidiaries for the Banco Ambrosiano, using over a billion dollars in bank assets. When he died, that money had completely disappeared. We probably will never know what he meant to use it for. But we do know where much of it is now."

As I sketched the transactions between Figueredo and O'Faolin and the effort to take over Ajax, I continued to strain for sounds in the background. I stole a look at my watch. Six o'clock. Surely . . .

"That brings me to the forgeries, Prior. That they played a role in the takeover, I feel certain. For it was to stop my investigation that O'Faolin dug up a petty hoodlum named

226

Walter Novick. He got him to throw acid at me and to burn my apartment building down. Indeed, it was sheer luck that kept seven people from being murdered by his mania to stop my investigation into the forgeries.

"What puzzles me is Rosa's role and that played by her son, Albert. I can only think that Rosa didn't know the forgeries had been put in the safe by Corpus Christi until *after* she called me in to investigate. Suddenly, and with uncharacteristic humility, she tried to get me out of the case. She wouldn't discuss it. She mouthed pieties. Yet initially she was so fearful of an FBI frame-up that she forced me to listen to repeated insults in order to clear her blameless character."

Rosa could contain herself no longer. "Insults! Why should I ask you for help? What have I not suffered at the hands of that whore who called herself your mother!"

"Rosa." This was Pelly. "Rosa. Calm yourself. You do the Church no favor with these accusations."

Rosa was beyond his influence. The demon that had rocked her sanity two weeks ago was too close to her now. "I took her in. Oh, how I was betrayed. Sweet Gabriella. Beautiful Gabriella. Talented Gabriella." Her face contorted in an angry mimicry. "Oh, yes. The darling of the family. Do you know what your precious Gabriella did? Did she ever have the courage to tell you? Not she, filthy whore.

"She came to me. I took her in from the goodness of my heart. I was forty and my belly was swollen with child. What did I want with a baby? I hated men. Hated their foul hands touching me in the night. I, who kept myself pure and childless, destroyed by the lusts of your uncle. Carrying my shame for all the world to see.

"Did she pity me? Not she! While I worked my fingers to the bone for her, she seduced my husband. If I would divorce him, he would take my child. He would support me. Only let him live with his sweet, talented Gabriella."

Spit was flecking her lips. We all sat, unable to think of anything that might stop the flow.

"So I threw her into the street. Who would not have? I made her promise to disappear and leave no word. Yes, she had that much shame. And what did Carl do? He shot himself.

227

Shot himself because of a whore from the streets. Left me alone with Albert. That whore, that shameless one!"

She was screaming louder and louder, repeating herself now. I stumbled into the hallway to find a washroom. As I staggered along, catching the bile in my hands, I felt Carroll's arm around me, guiding me to a tiny dark room with a sink. I couldn't talk, couldn't think. Heaving, gasping for air, choking up images of Gabriella. Her beautiful, haunted face. How could she think my father and I would not forgive her?

Carroll wiped my face with cold towels. Gradually the terrible shuddering stopped. Leading me to a small room, he sat me on a sofa. He disappeared for a few minutes, then returned with a cup of green tea. I gulped it gratefully.

"I need to finish this conversation," he said. "I need to find out why Augustine did what he did. For it must have been he who put the forged certificates in the safe. Your aunt is fundamentally a pitiable creature. Can you be strong enough to keep that in mind and help me end this story as fast as possible?"

"Oh, yes." My voice was hoarse from gagging. "Yes." My weariness amazed me. If I could forget this day . . . And the sooner it ended the sooner it would go away. I dragged myself up again, shook off Carroll's supportive arm. Followed him back into the study.

Pelly, Murray, and Stefan were still there. From the prior's closed inner office Rosa's screams came in a mind-shattering stream.

Uncle Stefan, pale and shaking, rushed to my side and began murmuring various soothing things at me in German I thought I heard the word chocolate and smiled in spite of myself.

Murray said to Carroll, "Jablonski is in there with her. He's called for an ambulance."

"Just as well." Carroll moved the rest of us back to the small room where he'd given me tea. Pelly could scarcely walk. His normally sunburned face was pale and his lips kept moving meaninglessly. Rosa's demented outburst had shaken the remains of his self-confidence. The story he told Carroll confirmed my analysis.

They needed money to acquire Ajax. Mrs. Paciorek was supplying as much as she could, but it wasn't enough. Besides, they didn't want to get the SEC involved too early by having all the purchases come from one source.

Pelly knew about the five million in blue chip shares in the priory safe. He wrote to O'Faolin, saying he would be glad to use them, but didn't want to arouse suspicions by their disappearing. Several months later, the forgeries arrived in the mail. Who created them he didn't know, but presumably it was done under O'Faolin's direction. Pelly substituted them for the real ones in the safe. After all, the shares hadn't been used in a decade or more. The chances were good that the Ajax purchase would long since have become history when the deception was discovered.

Unfortunately, he was out of town when the chapter voted to sell the shares so they could build a new roof. When he returned from his annual retreat in Panama, it was to find the priory in an uproar and Rosa fired from her position as treasurer. He called Rosa and told her to dismiss me, that Corpus Christi knew all about the forgeries and would protect her.

"Xavier came to Chicago a few days later," he muttered miserably, unable to look at either me or Carroll. "He—he took over things at once. He was most annoyed with me for letting so much publicity escape over the forgeries, especially because he said the amount was trivial compared to what we needed. He was annoyed, too, that—that Warshawski here was still poking around in the situation. He told me he'd take over, that he would see—see that she stopped. I just assumed she was a Catholic—Warshawski, you know—that she would be persuaded by an archbishop. I didn't know about the acid. Or the arson. Not until much later, anyway."

"The FBI investigation," I croaked hoarsely. "How did O'Faolin put the brakes on that?"

Pelly smiled wretchedly. "He and Jerome Farber were good friends. And Mrs. Paciorek, of course. Among them, they have a lot of influence in Chicago."

No one spoke. Beyond the heavy silence, we could hear the sirens of Rosa's ambulance.

Carroll's face, strained and grief-stricken, rebuked any comment. "Augustine. We'll talk later. Go to your room now and

229

meditate. You will have to talk to the FBI. After that, I don't know."

As Pelly wrapped himself in what dignity he could, I heard the sound I had been waiting for. A dull roar, an explosion muffled by distance and stone walls.

Murray looked at me sharply. "What was that?"

He and Carroll got to their feet and looked uncertainly at the door. I stayed where I was. A few minutes later, a young brother, red-haired and panting, hurled himself into the room. The front of his white habit was streaked with ash.

"Prior!" he gasped. "Prior! I'm sorry to interrupt. But you'd better come. Down at the gates. Quickly!"

Murray followed the prior from the room. A story he could use. I didn't know what had happened to Cordelia Hull and her camera, but no doubt she was close at hand.

Uncle Stefan looked at me doubtfully. "Should we go, Victoria?"

I shook my head. "Not unless you have a taste for bomb sites. Someone just set off a radio bomb in O'Faolin's car." I hoped to God he was on his own, that no brother was with him. Yes, Archbishop. No one is lucky forever.

XXVIII

The Myth of Iphigenia

FERRANT LEFT FOR England the day of the first real thaw. He had stayed long enough to install a proper vice-president of special risks at Ajax. Long enough to help me furnish my new apartment.

His check for stopping the takeover was the largest fee I'd ever collected. It easily paid for a Steinway grand to replace Gabriella's old upright. It didn't cover the cost of a co-op. But a few days after O'Faolin's death, an envelope containing twenty-five crisp thousand-dollar bills arrived in my office mail. No note, no return address. It seemed churlish to try to trace it. Anyway, I'd always wanted to own my own home. Roger helped me find a co-op on Racine near Lincoln, in a clean, quiet little building with four other units and a well-cared-for lobby.

For nearly a week after the bombing I spent most of my time in the Federal Building. Talking to the FBI, talking to the SEC. When I wasn't there, I was with Mallory. His pride was badly wounded. He wanted to assuage it by getting my license revoked, but my lawyer easily put a stop to that. What hurt Bobby the most was a letter he got from Dr. Paciorek. A suicide note, really, pouring out guilt and grief over the doctor's wife and daughter. They found Catherine's body in front of the family room fire. His was in the study. Murray told me more about it than I wanted to know.

After that, I didn't have anything to do except sleep and eat and furnish the new place. I didn't like to think too much. About Rosa, or my mother, or the ugliness I'd found in myself that night with Walter Novick in the snow. Roger helped keep the thoughts at bay. At least during the day. He couldn't do much about my dreams.

After dropping him at the airport, I felt empty and lonely. And scared. Roger had kept some demons away. Now I'd have to deal with them. Maybe I'd do it some place else, though. Take Uncle Stefan up on his offer to go to the Bahamas for a week. Or fly to Arizona and watch the Cubs go through spring training.

I sat in front of the apartment for a while, playing with the keys in the ignition. Across the street the door of a dark green Datsun opened. The car seemed familiar, with its creased fender and scratched paint. Lotty crossed the street and stood in front of the Omega, looking unlike herself, looking for once as small as a five-foot-tall person should. I climbed out of the Omega and locked the door.

"May we talk, Vic?"

I nodded without speaking and led her into the building. She didn't say anything else until we were inside my apartment. I hung her coat on a hook in the small entryway and ushered her into the living room where a comfortable chaos was already starting to build on the new furniture.

"Stefan told me Roger was leaving today. I wanted to wait for him to go before I sought you out. . . . I have a lot to say to you. A lot to unsay, also. Can you—will you"—her clever, ugly face contorted in a surprising spasm. She steadied herself and started again. "You have been the daughter I never had,

231

V.I. As well as one of the best friends a woman could ever desire. And I abused you. I want your forgiveness. I want to— not to go back to where we were. We can't. I want to continue our friendship from here . . . Let me explain—not justify— explain. . . . I've never talked about my family and the war. It's too close to the bone.

"My parents shipped my brother, Hugo, and me to London in 1938. They were to follow but never made it out of Vienna. Hugo and I spent the whole war wondering, waiting. Later we learned they had died in Buchenwald in 1941. My grandmother, all my uncles and cousins. Of that whole large happy family at Kleinsee only Hugo and I remained.

"Stefan—Stefan is a lovable rogue. If he were as hateful as your aunt, though, I would still need to protect him. He and Hugo and I are all that remain of that idyllic time. When he was stabbed—I went mad, a little. I couldn't admit that he chose his fate. I couldn't admit that he had a right to do so. I blamed you. And it was very wrong of me."

My throat was tight and the first few times I tried speaking the words came out in a whispered choke. "Lotty. Lotty, I've been through hell and beyond this winter. I have been so alone. Do you know the torment I have been through? Agnes died because I involved her in my machinations. Dr. Paciorek. Did you see what happened? He killed his wife and shot himself. And all because I chose to be narrow-minded, pig-headed, bullying my way down a road the FBI and the SEC couldn't travel."

Lotty flinched. "Vic. Don't torment me by throwing my angry words back at me. I've been in that hell this winter, too. But mine was worse. I created misery for my dearest friend. Stefan—Stefan told me about the scene at the priory. About Rosa and Gabriella. Oh, my dear. How much I knew you needed me, and how I tortured myself for knowing I had only myself to thank that I couldn't go to you."

"Do you know what my middle name is, Lotty?" I burst out. "Do you know the myth of Iphigenia? How Agamemnon sacrificed her to get a fair wind to sail for Troy? Since that terrible day at the priory, I can't stop dreaming about it. Only in my dreams it's Gabriella. She keeps laying me on the pyre and setting the torch to it and weeping for me. Oh, Lotty!

Why didn't she tell me? Why did she make me give her that terrible promise? Why did she do it?"

And suddenly the grief for Gabriella, the grief for myself overwhelmed me and I started to weep. The tears of many years of silence would not stop. Lotty was at my side holding me. "Yes, my darling, yes, cry, yes, that's right. They named you well, Victoria Iphigenia. For don't you know that in Greek legend Iphigenia is also Artemis the huntress?"

FOR THE BEST IN PAPERBACKS, LOOK FOR THE

In every corner of the world, on every subject under the sun, Penguin represents quality and variety – the very best in publishing today.

For complete information about books available from Penguin – including Puffins, Penguin Classics and Arkana – and how to order them, write to us at the appropriate address below. Please note that for copyright reasons the selection of books varies from country to country.

In the United Kingdom: Please write to *Dept E.P., Penguin Books Ltd, Harmondsworth, Middlesex, UB7 0DA.*

If you have any difficulty in obtaining a title, please send your order with the correct money, plus ten per cent for postage and packaging, to *PO Box No 11, West Drayton, Middlesex*

In the United States: Please write to *Dept BA, Penguin, 299 Murray Hill Parkway, East Rutherford, New Jersey 07073*

In Canada: Please write to *Penguin Books Canada Ltd, 2801 John Street, Markham, Ontario L3R 1B4*

In Australia: Please write to the *Marketing Department, Penguin Books Australia Ltd, P.O. Box 257, Ringwood, Victoria 3134*

In New Zealand: Please write to the *Marketing Department, Penguin Books (NZ) Ltd, Private Bag, Takapuna, Auckland 9*

In India: Please write to *Penguin Overseas Ltd, 706 Eros Apartments, 56 Nehru Place, New Delhi, 110019*

In the Netherlands: Please write to *Penguin Books Netherlands B.V., Postbus 195, NL–1380AD Weesp*

In West Germany: Please write to *Penguin Books Ltd, Friedrichstrasse 10–12, D–6000 Frankfurt/Main 1*

In Spain: Please write to *Alhambra Longman S.A., Fernandez de la Hoz 9, E–28010 Madrid*

In Italy: Please write to *Penguin Italia s.r.l., Via Como 4, I-20096 Pioltello (Milano)*

In France: Please write to *Penguin Books Ltd, 39 Rue de Montmorency, F-75003 Paris*

In Japan: Please write to *Longman Penguin Japan Co Ltd, Yamaguchi Building, 2–12–9 Kanda Jimbocho, Chiyoda-Ku, Tokyo 101*

CRIME AND MYSTERY IN PENGUIN

The Blunderer Patricia Highsmith

Walter Stackhouse wishes his wife was dead. His wish comes true when Clara's body is found at the bottom of a cliff. But there are uncanny similarities between her death and that of a woman called Helen Kimmel – murdered by her husband... 'Almost unputdownable' – *Observer*

Farewell, My Lovely Raymond Chandler

Moose Malloy was a big man but not more than six feet five inches tall and not wider than a beer truck. He looked about as inconspicuous as a tarantula on a slice of angel food. Marlowe's greatest case, Chandler's greatest book.

Death on Site Janet Neel

Why does experienced climber Alan Fraser – employed by the powerful Vernon family on their vast building sites – fall from the Highland rock face? Back on the site in London, suppressed emotions explode and there is another fall. But this time it's murder. 'A splendid follow-up' (*The Times*) to the prizewinning *Death's Bright Angel*.

Crimson Joy Robert B. Parker

Just because all the victims are black women doesn't necessarily make the killer racist or sexist. Just because he sends Quirk a letter saying he's a cop doesn't mean it's true. *Crimson Joy* pits Spenser against a psychopath.

Toxic Shock Sara Paretsky

Vic Warshawski was not always Chicago's slickest Private Investigator. She used to play nurse-maid to Caroline Djiak, and now Caroline is employing Vic to find out who her father was. But on the seedy South Side something a lot more serious than a paternity suit is being concealed. 'Paretsky is as much of a pro as her private eye' – *Listener*

CRIME AND MYSTERY IN PENGUIN

The Chief Inspector's Daughter Sheila Radley

The Chief Inspector's daughter finds her employer murdered – and introduces Quantrill to an esoteric world of romantic novels and oriental art. 'In Sheila Radley we have one to rival ... Ruth Rendell' – Susan Hill

Bitter Medicine Sara Paretsky

Consuelo is sixteen, heavily pregnant and married to Fabiano – an unemployed gangster. The last thing she needs is a negligent doctor. 'Paretsky's writing is as attention-grabbing as a .38, her books all assured, gripping and convincing' – *Time Out*

Halo Parade Bill James

You-know-who has been dealing in you-know-what, and Harpur will give anything to bring him to justice. 'Crackling dialogue and seamy people ... wickedly satisfying' – *Sunday Times*. 'James is in the first rank of crime writers' – *Irish Independent*

Killer's Choice Ed McBain

Who killed Annie Boone? Employer, lover, ex-husband, girlfriend? A tense, terrifying and tautly written novel from the author of *The Mugger*, *The Pusher*, *Lady Killer* and a dozen other first class thrillers.

Lonely Hearts John Harvey

A serial killer is on the loose in Nottingham – preying on women who seek companionship, and even love, through the pages of their local paper. 'Beautifully downbeat ... superbly well-finished ... his characterization is excellent ... Resnick is a detective it would be good to meet again' – *The Times*

CRIME AND MYSTERY IN PENGUIN

Call for the Dead   John Le Carré

The classic work of espionage which introduced the world to George Smiley. 'Brilliant … highly intelligent, realistic. Constant suspense. Excellent writing' – *Observer*

Sheep's Clothing   Celia Dale

Alone in their bedsits, with their treasures and hidden savings, old ladies are easy prey. Especially when faced with two nice women who say they're from the social services … 'I can't think of anyone whose stories of suspense I appreciate more' – Ruth Rendell. 'Don't miss it' – *Guardian*

Glitz   Elmore Leonard

Underneath the boardwalk a lot of insects creep. But the creepiest of all was Teddy. Devoted to his parrot-loving mother, Teddy was a rapist-killer. And Teddy had a personal grudge … 'After finishing *Glitz* I went out to the bookstore and bought everything else of Elmore Leonard I could find' – Stephen King

This Way Out   Sheila Radley

Derek Cartwright had always considered himself a decent, honourable man. The thought of doing away with his mother-in-law would never have entered his head if he had not begun to suffer from bad dreams – and if he had not met Hugh Packer.

Count the Days   Lin Summerfield

To the villagers of Upper Grisham, eleven-year-old Margie had been the girl who had everything: flaxen hair, a shiny bike, party dresses – loving parents, too. But days turn to weeks and weeks to months before anyone finds out what has become of Margie… 'Considerable menace and subtlety, carrying a cruel kick' – *Sunday Times*